Sister of Night

KADALYNN HERBOLD

LIGHTLOCK PUBLISHING

To my extended Tribe, thank you so very much for being my family
and my support

To my Mr. H, I love you so much. I am so honored and am so thankful
you have been in my life longer than you have not been a part of it.

To everyone else: Breathe, Love, Be a Tree, Always a Final Girl

When Love came down to present me with sympathy, I rebuked her and showed no regret. When Mercy came down to grant me asylum within Heaven, I pitied her and left her side. When Vengeance came down to arm me with the greatest power, I finally knew life and death were one.

-Samantha "Sammy" Schreber

Chapter One

"You belong here," a voice whispered in Khira's ear. The voice seemed far away, yet familiar. Khira Chamberlin sat on a soft gray cushion which laid on a white wicker bench. She found herself facing an ivory painted wooded vanity. She gazed into the mirror; her purple eyes shining beyond her umber bangs as the streaks of cornflower hue that normally peaked through her shoulder- length hair disappeared. Her hands lay in her lap, and she could feel someone behind her brushing her tresses. How did she know that voice? Only one woman occurred to her.

"You belong here, you know this," Khira's mother, Eve, told her in an authoritarian voice. "You should come and stay here with me. I need you and you have always desired to hear that. You do not know how much I have missed you." While the words themselves intended to be heartfelt, her mother presented them in a cold demeanor.

As Khira began to tear up, a male voice chimed in the discussion. "Do not believe her." Khira turned to face this new person. A sandy blonde-haired man stood in the doorway. "Do not believe her," he repeated his statement, however his lips did not move.

While his steel gray eyes proved a little disconcerting, his demeanor comforted Khira and left her feeling protected. His crinkled forehead displayed sincere concern for Khira and a sly smile, sneaking past subtle facial hair, put her at ease. She could trust this tall stranger, even if she did not understand why.

She turned back towards the mirror. Her mother's eyes morphed from a chestnut color to a shade which reflected Khira's own lilac eyes. Her mother's dark blonde hair faded into an ivory mane mixed with lighter pure silver highlights. This woman's face matched her mother's but did not hold the same presence.

Khira's attention got pulled back to the strange man who had now entered the room. He took giant strides towards her; while the room was small to cross, his treks towards her mimicked a great heroic journey, with the award being the privilege to sit next to her. Her face turned towards him; her mother's imposter copied Khira's movement for a brief second before turning back to face Khira with a disapproving demeanor. The man's presence overshadowed the influence of her mother's doppelganger.

"You called me here. I can guide you as you need, but only at your will." He pushed some of her hair behind her ears and then cupped the palms of his hands against her shoulders, giving her a slight squeeze. He pulled her up from the bench and into a close embrace. He kissed her on her forehead before kissing her eyes closed and then married his lips against her assuring Khira that this man could easily be her soul mate.

He stepped away and headed back towards the door. The stranger turned and reached out for her to follow him. Trust pushed her to shadow him.

Khira took in her surroundings. While the room had felt like hers, the decorations felt old and distant; nothing in the room reflected her personality. The man squeezed her hand in assurance. The bottom of her feet sunk into a plush rose-colored carpet. She tried to take a step, but the floor seemed to take hold of her toes, as her feet descended in further. Determined, she strained to free her feet. She struggled but her willpower became victorious. Khira followed the man to the room's doorway.

"If you leave, the lions will get you. If you leave, the lions will bleed you out" her mother's revenant voice called out. Khira turned back towards the mirror, only to find an empty frame surrounded by broken glass. Khira's worried eyes returned to search for her knight, but he had stepped out into the hallway. "The lions will eat you if you go out there," echoed the ghastly voice as the warning faded away.

"Do not believe her. Follow me to escape her grasp. Your quest awaits," the man called to her as he reappeared, moving back towards her. He picked her up and carried her towards the door as if newlyweds crossing the threshold. The hallway had been replaced by a coastal shoreline, with a full moon reflected in the black waters. As he approached, the waters parted, leaving exposed ground beneath his feet. She looked down and saw a trail of blood from his steps. Did he carry her over glass, not sand? "Close your eyes, my love," he whispered to her.

The waves of the ocean grew louder and louder, engulfing her fear. They called to her, forming an ancient language. She held onto the stranger's neck and dug her face into his shoulder. With her vision blocked, her hearing became more focused. The incantations turned into a name. *"DDDaaaa...,"* played in her ear. Lights played hide and seek against her closed eyes. She felt her eyes move back and forth behind her lids. *"David."* The name was solid against her brain. *"David."* The ocean called out louder and louder. *"David, I mean it!"* Khira opened her eyes.

****

Khira yawned. She still could not comprehend the ruckus outside of her room. Her surroundings surprised her, but she did not know if the dream or her routine hangover caused her uncertainty. She did not remember arriving home, let alone traveling up to her bedroom. She curled her toes. Sure enough, the black flea market army boots still trapped her feet. She debated taking off the boots and going back to sleep. Her toes decided to curl again, on their own accord, not waiting for her decision.

Khira pulled her black duvet back along with silver silk sheets, exposing the fact that she had not taken anything off from her night of partying. She sighed. She should have tired of this lifestyle by now, yet what else would she do to pass the nights in the quiet Texas town of Thirlestane? Play Uno with her cousin? No, thank you. It was fortunate that Austin was nearby. Responsibility could come later in life.

Putting one foot behind the other, she pulled against her heel, pushing the boot halfway off. She repeated this action for the other foot. Khira imagined a bull's-eye on the back of her bedroom door. She closed her eyes before flicking one foot with determined precision. Thump. She flicked the other foot. She felt a thud on her bed. A swing and a miss.

She opened her eyes to see that one boot had indeed landed on the bed and the other boot had landed on her desk: neither anywhere near the door. *Bahness!* Khira turned over and buried her face in her pillow, silencing a desperate huff.

Her brain turned back towards dreamland. However, before her thoughts could drift back to sleep, she found herself circling around the concept of dreams. She had just woken from a dream yet could not grasp at any remaining plot pieces; the more she tried to remember, the further away her dream slipped away from her. She wanted to knock her brain around, put it in a chokehold, and force it to remember. As if her thoughts came to fruition, she heard knocking outside her room.

She turned her head from the pillow. Did she really hear knocking or were her brain's defenses on overdrive? Khira pursed her lips at the quandary. She waited to see if the door to her thoughts would open or if her sanity would prove a victor and let her know that she imagined this bizarre scenario.

She took a beat with her breath. Silence. *So, I am going crazy.* As soon as Khira finished the thought, another knock came from the hallway. However, the knock was not at her bedroom door, so why should she care what her cousin, Paige, did with her time? Now, Khira almost felt as crazy as Paige. God forbid that her paternal genes touched her in the head. Why could she not turn back and fall asleep instead of continuing this debate?

****

Paige had gotten up early to finish the many errands on her mental countdown of goals for the day. Straight out of bed, she pulled on a pair of pink velour shorts, yanked a white camisole over her head, and slipped into some oversized glittered unicorn slippers. She looked ready for a sorority scene in Legally Blonde.

Lists ran through her mind non-stop as she gathered her day clothes, dropped them off in the bathroom, started the shower, and headed downstairs to start the coffee. She always preferred to let the steam of the shower give way a little before entering the baptism of water. The warm thought of steeping under the waterfall triggered a pause to her hectic mind. She snagged a hair band from the bathroom. As she padded downstairs, she continued replaying her list as she pulled up her long, dark blond hair up into a messy bun on top of her head.

As she entered the kitchen, Paige gave the room a quick glance. She walked over to the coffee maker and bent down to the cabinets underneath. She pulled an airlock container of coffee beans. She finished putting the beans into the grinder. Once she approved of the fine consistency of the grounds, she poured them into the pot and started the coffee. She headed back to the haven upstairs.

She placed her hand on the bathroom door handle. A little jiggle gave enough to reveal that someone had locked the door shut. Paige glanced over her shoulder back towards Khira's bedroom. She snuck over there and pressed her ear to the door. She listened for the symphony of Khira's deep breathing through the closed door. "Deep breathing" translated to Paige's polite idea of a woman's snoring. Silence. Hmmm. She could knock, but she feared the wrath of her cousin.

Before she decided on any action, she heard singing from the bathroom. Khira never showed any signs of happiness, so only one other person, David, could be blamed. Paige returned to the bathroom door and rapped a gentle knock. "David? David, please open the door." She knocked a little louder. "David? David, I mean it!"

"David, if you don't unlock this door, then I'll go *Constantine* all over your ass. Just tempt me!" Paige yelled through the door. She could race back downstairs to get a key, but the thought of seeing David in full morning glory made her gag a little.

The shower noise dimmed and a husky, effeminate voice spoke. "Lover, please! You need me around to help improve your ugly ass face for your ugly ass "OnlyFans" website. You could always use the master bathroom in the swanky master bedroom you use for those ugly ass subscribers of yours, but no! You'd rather break my concentration this morning! Shame on you! Now back to your regularly scheduled program...'Your sweet nature, dahling...'" David sang the rest of his response while the sound of the water played a staccato backup.

Paige turned towards her bedroom. She glanced once more at her cousin's bedroom door. She hoped her fight with David didn't bother Khira too much. A thump came from the room, followed by a second. Paige scurried into her bedroom before her cousin could emerge and yell at her.

****

Surprised with the resulting quietness outside her bedroom door, Khira debated once more whether or not to exit her haven. Aromas of Blue Hawaiian coffee slithered its way up to the second floor. The coffee gods intervened and sung inspiration to her, offering her a chance to extend a bit of humanity for the day. Khira sat up in bed like Frankenstein's monster coming to life. Saliva formed in her mouth, beckoning her to go downstairs to the treasure in a coffee cup that awaited her.

She moved out of her bed in a zombie-like state. As she crossed her bedroom towards the door, she caught her reflection in the mirror that hung above her dresser. The words *you belong here* stung her head, making her aware of the headache brewing from the previous night's binge drinking. She paused at her reflection. She raised an armpit and before even testing her ripeness, decided that she should change clothes before heading downstairs. Khira hoped to not run into her cousin downstairs; she didn't think she could handle another morning of judgmental glances from Paige. She stripped down to her panties and walked over to her closet.

She had taken the doors down years ago. This morning she regretted that decision as there were piles of clothes strewn about like landmines. She knelt and leaned in to reach the closest pair of jeans. Khira lost her balance as she pulled them out. One leg smacked her in the face. At least no odor from the navy stonewashed denim struck her. She leaned back and pulled her panties off. She laid down and looked behind at the dresser. She could go to the dresser and pull a fresh pair of underwear or go commando. Her lazy self soon decided on the latter and kicked both legs into the pair of low-rise jeans at once. Halfway done with putting on today's human costume. Now to find the perfect tee.

Khira walked back towards her reflection in the mirror. *Do I belong here?* That question was stuck on auto-play in her mind. She dismissed the self-doubt as she reached for the middle drawer. She had forgotten what shirt was on top, but at once decided fate had placed it there in her sleep. She pulled the black t-shirt over her dark brown tresses and shot her arms through the short sleeves. She bent over and shook her head and laughed.

Knowing her blue tresses weren't going anywhere, the scene from *Scott Pilgrim Vs. The World* that showed an "evil ex" slapping the blue out of a character's hair ran through her head. She returned to the upright position at a pace that wouldn't make her too dizzy. She read the backward red letters on her shirt aloud. "I'm not okay. I promise." *Preach*, she thought. Even in silence, the song by My Chemical Romance became Khira's earworm.

Humming the tune under her breath, Khira walked over to her bedroom door; her mind hit the pause button to the song as she pressed her hand against the wood and turned the knob with her other hand. She hoped that the click from the door's latch would not capture Paige's attention, if her cousin still roamed the hallway. She made her escape after first peeking out. The sound of water pings against a shower curtain and steam escaping under the bathroom door told Khira that her cousin was otherwise occupied. Not one to waste a good getaway, Khira headed downstairs.

****

While her cousin seemed to always bother her, Khira did appreciate the coffee that Paige always made first thing in the morning. Khira opened a cabinet to get one of the many random coffee mugs she and her cousin had collected over the years. She thought she heard a roar when she went to reach for a lion-shaped mug. She put it back. She reached for a different mug from one of the local coffee shops. She poured some honey into the mug before taking out a carton of soy milk from the fridge. She stirred the sticky contents and once satisfied, she poured in the coffee. She sat down at the kitchen table and sipped her elixir of life.

Khira looked up from her mug to notice Paige enter the room. *Dammit! Escape plan didn't work,* she thought. She knew even without saying a word that Paige could sense the disdain in her cousin. She set the coffee aside and turned to her cell phone for distraction until she could find a way out of this exchange.

Paige waited a couple of minutes before trying to break Khira's silent treatment. "Good Morning, Khira." Nothing broke her cousin's wall. Paige remained determined, even if she had to speak for the both of them. "So, Paige, do you have plans for today, hmm? Fly the Concorde to Köln? Jet ski to that private island you own? Oh, I know....take in an audience with the Pope," Paige spoke, trying to get a reaction from Khira. Paige walked over to the cabinet and pulled a Marvin the Martian coffee mug out. She went to the coffee maker and poured the liquid elixir through the alien's head. She sat across from Khira and decided on a second attempt for a conversation.

"The same thing we do every night Pinky - try to take over the world, one dick and cunt at a time!" Paige's smile melted into a frown as her cartoon reference along with her adult-themed website combined into one ugly baby that did nothing to destroy Khira's foul mood. She tried not to fear her bitch of a roommate/cousin, but she failed. The world already scared Paige, and she usually hid that fear behind witty banter. Khira hardly ever participated. Maybe Paige could get a bite with a change of subject. "Now, Miss Chamberlin, what on Earth wakes you up at this hour? Do you plan to put in some hours for me or do you plan to escape with that heaven-sent elixir and hide away in your cave of doom?"

Before Khira had a chance to respond, David yelped with perfect acoustics, causing his cry to echo down from above, and distracting Paige for a moment. Paige turned back towards the staircase as she heard David yell, "Damn! Prettiest queen out there!"followed by a slapping sound, which Paige deduced as David slapping his ass. David turned his attention back to his song.

Ignoring a singing David, Paige turned her focus back on Khira. "What did I ask? Oh, yes. Are you going to 'cum' to the dark side for my subscribers or do you plan to flee, leaving me high and dry? I've always told you that you could 'work' off your rent anytime." Paige attempted to gain more strength within her voice as she spoke. Paige was both proud and ashamed of her line of work, managing her own adult porn website. She gave a mental laugh as she thought maybe her mom had foreseen this employment by naming her Elizabeth Paige Kimmel; she wondered if her mom realized that she had given her daughter a play on Bettie Page's name. Her train of thought trailed off; broken by sounds escaping from her cousin.

Without looking up, Khira mumbled something unintelligible before clearing her voice to make her next response stand firm against Paige's attempts at humor. "You know I will never grace your dominion. I could never compare to your 'talents,'" Khira felt disgusted by the image of her naked cousin jacking off for strangers across the web, "and wouldn't want you to lose any upstanding customers." *How upstanding could they really be?* "If you want to know my plans, you could put in a GPS app on my phone. But oh yes, you could never break my password. So in the meantime, I plan to run by the library for a few hours before heading off to downtown Austin to check out that new exhibit of cow dung at the museum."

Paige knew that Khira lied most of the time. She gave her cousin a saddened expression, expressing her hurt in a physical manner. Unfazed by her cousin's attempt at manipulation of puppy dog eyes, Khira continued, "Look. I don't get involved in your business and you don't get the privilege to get all up in mine. That's our agreement." Khira glanced up at the clock. She even surprised herself that she had left her haven before noon. "However, one cup of coffee does not do this body good. I need a whole IV. I'll see you when I see you, cousin." She swallowed the last drop of coffee and got up.

Khira thought about apologizing for the bitchy attempt of conversation followed by grief, a result of her depression, but decided actions spoke louder. She paused next to Paige, leaned down and gave Paige a soft peck on the forehead. She left the room with all due speed before Paige could turn a frown to a surprised smile and make her more uncomfortable.

Khira did not know how to interact with anyone, let alone her family. Her brain lacked this socializing chip. This absence exiled her from the rest of society. Fate shortchanged her in that department by taking her parents during an influential time before she even knew them.

She never had the opportunity to learn patience from her brother or even form a sibling rivalry. She lost her toddler brother in the same car crash as her parents. She considered their deaths the reason she could never hold onto a relationship with a guy for more than the required minimum of thirty minutes of intercourse. She cared more for Paige than her cousin could ever realize, but Khira did not know how to express that herself.

Khira passed David's female persona, not even acknowledging how fierce she looked. As much as Khira ignored David, the latter disregarded her roommate's rude behavior. Most of David's friends had called her "Cyn," short for Cynthia Latex since her typical get-up consisted of a long, silky dark blond wig.

Today Cyn's wig was jeweled with a faux fur peachy broad hair band to match a long tight peach sweater, accented with a large black pleather belt to show all her man-built curves. Tight black capri pants coated her legs. High black boots completed the ensemble. She felt as confident as Meghan McCain in this look. Cyn felt despair radiating from Paige though, so she hustled over to hug Paige, who could not even form words. "I still say it's a wonder that we allow that bitch to grace our presence, Paigeyboo. I guess we keep hoping we can rub off on her in a good way, right?" Paige fought back tears. The outside world scared her. Now, she had to overcome a rising fear of her own home.

Chapter Two

With earbuds in place blasting a soundtrack of her life, Khira became a carriage horse with blinders, focused on the destination she had in mind; a place that felt more like her one true home these days. Her thoughts carried her back to her mother. Khira had gotten along with the woman for the most part, but never developed a strong mother/daughter bond. Even within her thoughts, Khira often lingered on Eve, her Christian name, or classified as the biological mother and nothing more beyond that scope of an emotional attachment.

Eve Chamberlain kept by her husband's side, leaving her daughter at arm's length, only providing attention to Khira when she deemed ta new lesson was necessary. With as much strength that her mother's lilac eyes held, her body often seemed too fragile to sustain her own soul. Khira reflected on this relationship and concluded that an over-wrought stress of paranoia must have caused her mother's distress. It was a wonder that Paige wasn't related to the maternal side of Khira's family since her cousin was more like Eve than Khira would care to admit.

"Fall Back Down" by Rancid had just left Khira's ears as Depeche Mode's eerie instrumental piece, "Memphisto" crept in to take its place. Her thoughts of Eve started to visit her at a more frequent pace these days. She sensed an increasing paranoia of her own, weary of surroundings and strangers passing by.

She felt as if she were participating in a hidden camera game of Hunter vs. Prey. Everyone pretended not to notice her, instead they looked straight through her without expression or emotion as the strangers walked past her. She imagined their faces changing into ghouls after she passed. She was becoming more and more her mother's daughter.

Khira turned south at the intersection of Central Drive and Mockingbird Lane in downtown Thirlestane. Her destination was just a block further. As she waited for the green man to tell her she could cross the street, her thoughts turned to that last night with Eve. Her mother sat, sinking claws into her head. That night, Eve felt she had one last lesson to bestow upon her daughter. She somehow knew she did not have much time left. "Khira, can you come into my bedroom for a second?"

Eve's soft purple eyes drowned in crimson sea from crying while trying to stay concentrated on the ground as her daughter entered the room. Khira ignored this dramatic scene and sat down beside her mother, hands folded into her lap, bowing her own head down, causing her long pigtails to slide down her shoulders. Anyone else looking in could mistake the scene as her mother worshipping with a silent prayer.

"Khira, my dear daughter, I love you so much even though you may doubt me. Please remember this," Eve's almond shaped eyes took a different demeanor before starting again. "People will let you down. I will let you down. This is rule of nature, even beyond the human heart. This life is a touched one, fragile at most. I would give my life for you," she stated as she put her hand on Khira's shoulder, "but I cannot always protect you. You must look out for yourself first and foremost. Keep friends at a distance, so that you cannot hurt them. Keep your enemies close in order to glean their secrets." Eve took her hand off of Khira's shoulder and instead placed it under her daughter's chin, turning the teen's face towards her. "Look at me. Trust no one! Never trust your heart. Don't even rely on what I have taught you! Only trust your instincts!" Eve removed her hand and brought both hands up in an attempt to hide the tears escaping the captive lavender eyes. Khira believed her mother was drunk at the time and left to avoid any further unwarranted drama. Only later would she start understanding her mother's words.

Either the light was taking forever, or her thoughts of that night caused her to miss permission to cross. With no cars nearby, Khira took a chance by crossing against the light. She felt a shadow and just kept thinking it was the suspicion and threw away the thought of any stalker nearby.

Khira stopped short of the door to the bookstore where she felt safe. She paused taking out one headphone to see if she could hear any halting of foot falls as her own had ceased. A young man passed her, entering the craft store next door. She glanced at the name of the store embroidered on the glass pane. The sign read The Historian's Hideaway. There were times she felt the better name would be Khira's Cave.

Her pulse eased a little as she pulled on the handle to the building. Once inside, she returned the ear bud to the proper place, as Panic!

at the Disco's acoustic version of "This is Gospel" soothed her. She stopped by the fiction section to see if Alex Kimmell's "The Key to Everything" was where she had left it. Luckily, her hidden treasure awaited her.

After she grabbed the book, she walked towards her spot in the back corner between the knitting books and travel section, where no one roamed. She sat on the floor and pulled out a sketchbook, a couple of colored pencils, a bottle of *Fuze*, and a small pillow. So caught up in her comfort ritual, she did not notice that the young man from the craft store stepped into the bookstore. He headed into the Goth section, where they stashed all the Vampire porn.

****

Khira's stomach interrupted Nothing,Nowhere's song "Blood" right when Kenny Hoopla started his verse. She looked up from her sketches that she had started after finishing "The Key to Everything." She dropped a piece of kohl to the floor as she picked up her phone. Khira checked it, and per usual, no one had bothered her the entire three hours she had been there. She often came here during the week while everyone else worked mundane occupations. She could not remember how she discovered the bookstore, much less the quiet spot between the aisles that provided an escape.

Her stomach growled again. She needed food before deciding how to continue her mission of avoiding being at home with Paige. She gathered her things, placing them back into the black hole of her bag. She stretched and her stomach protested once more. Time to grab grub.

Khira looked down again at her phone and switched the song to an anthem from Yungblud. She threw the strap of her bag over her shoulder, mimicking a hipster hobo. She imagined that she did not look too feminine in this pose, but she never quite cared how she projected herself, or so she claimed.

She started to walk towards the entrance of the bookstore. She kept her head down hoping that action would act as an invisibility cloak. She grinned thinking that she just needed to walk past a Harry Potter clearance stand for that to come true.

Her smirk and downtrodden head caused her to be distracted enough to run into a young man who had just left the Gothic Literature section. Khira lost her balance; out of instinct, she shot her right arm back to catch herself. "Bastard," she said, louder than she intended due to the pounding music escaping the headphones.

She pulled the cords, tugging against her ears. She looked up at the man who had collided into her. He looked familiar although she thought his own mother wouldn't have recognized him looking so gaunt. He had glittered powder decorating his skin, however no amount of powder could cover the dark circles hovering below his grey eyes. His fair skin and dyed black hair made his emo features more predominant. *Damn stupid Twilight,* she thought as she tried not to stare at this vamp wannabe.

The *boy* squatted down in attempts to help Khira with her fallen belongings. Khira kept slapping at the boy's hands as she hurried to stuff her possessions back into her messenger sack. He was violated her privacy, dammit! Once she felt she had gotten everything in order, she made a quick break for the exit.

After Khira left, the boy got up, holding Khira's sketch book in his hand. He walked back through the Gothic Literature section and arrived at an office. After a couple of raps, the door swung open. A tall man with a honey-colored fade and a clean-cut goatee stepped out, looking around for the person who had disturbed his day. The pale boy handed the book off to the man, who was a complete contrast in his heather gray Fioravanti suit. With a slight bow, the vampire wannabe went back to the *Twilight* book tween section as if a sentinel at his post.

After closing the door, Zachary Duvall, the owner of The Historian's Hideaway, returned to his chair behind a great wooden desk. He placed the book on his desk and turned around back to the security monitors. He brought up one of his hands, rubbing against symmetrical facial stubble. Manipulating the joystick that controlled the outside cameras, his cerulean eyes followed Khira as far as he could.

****

David had felt comfortable enough to let Paige set with her thoughts. It helped her to recognize her depression, and process her emotions, before moving on to living real life. Granted, nothing helped her agoraphobia.

In the middle of this dark episode, she replayed that fated day in her head; the date when her entire world crumbled. First, she had decided on a whim to go down to a local coffee shop that many of her friends on campus had raved about. On the way there, she got mugged by a scrawny kid who had held a knife to her throat. The kid took off with her stuff, but not without leaving shallow cuts along her long pale neck.

Paige held her hand to her neck and walked down to the shop in order to call the cops. They took her report there and even bought her a cup of coffee with a breakfast muffin to calm her down. She laughed to herself that a police officer would think that sugar and caffeine could calm a college student down. The staff was nice enough to offer bandages her for cuts after cops left. She stayed at the coffee shop a bit wondering about her life.

The waiters took pity on her and switched out the coffee the police had provided with a free large "Whole Lotta Love" Latte. They left her alone in a back booth for her to collect her thoughts, only coming by to see if there was anyone, they could call for her. Paige was too ashamed to let any of her friends or family members know what she had just gone through. When she felt she overstayed her welcome, she thought maybe fresh air would benefit her.

She walked the north campus of Austin Community College, in hopes of finding a park nearby. Just past the campus while attempting to take a short cut between some stray crossroads, Paige was then attacked by a man in a mask. He shoved her to the ground, pinning her with his knees up on her thighs. She hit her head against the concrete, making her dazed.

He had already penetrated her when she began to struggle, allowing her to slip out of his grasp. She felt like the vexed heroine in a horror movie who kept making wrong choices. As she ran across streets towards a nearby clinic, she was clipped by a speeding car. The car took off after the hit and run, leaving honest bystanders with the responsibility to take her to a hospital.

The same cops from before visited her at St. David's hospital to take a statement of these new crimes. After they left, Paige decided right then and there that she would give up on the outside world. She thought to herself that she had enough going in her life that she could maintain living in Thirlestane, within the limits of her house without ever having to leave.

If she could not take the remaining college courses online, she would quit school all together. If she needed food, Paige could order pizza, Chinese and even groceries from the internet; send email, text and IM's to communicate. She would not even have to open her front door. Thirelstane being so close to Austin allowed her to fulfill nearly every desire in an online capacity. "Fuck you," she whispered through quivering lips and past tears as she sunk into the hospital bed. She caught a glimpse of a figure standing in the doorway of the hospital room.

David came in through the open door, stating that he had overhead the officers. His sad eyes comforted her. She sobbed louder as he came closer towards her. David's aura felt more of protection than of threat giving Paige the only sense of security during that day. After unloading all the horrific events into this newfound friend's ears, Paige invited him to live with her and Khira. She felt that with what she had been through, Khira would have no say in this new living arrangement. Hell, why even tell her bitch of a cousin that they would get a new roommate. Still no amount of comfort from her home gave strength enough to stray. A buzz from the doorbell interrupted her thoughts.

Paige debated whether or not to answer the door as another buzz came through. Anxiety rushed at her, while panic set in further like a leech with each step that Paige took towards the front door. She reached the door, but the fear still remained as she knew she might have to open up, revealing the outside world.

"Who is it?" she asked, thinking how that always signed the death certificate in bad horror flicks.

"I have a package and need a signature."

Paige clicked a button on the side of the hallway below a dark screen. Lines flickered a bit before showing a man in a pair of khaki pants and a white short sleeved button dress shirt, holding a large manila envelope. Satisfied that the boogeyman wasn't pretending to deliver a knife instead, Paige took a deep breath, held it in while she mentally repeated a mantra "Breathe, love, be a tree, survivor" a couple of times before opening the door. She focused on the electronic clipboard instead of looking at the man. Her hand shook the plastic pen as she provided a signature. The delivery man handed her the envelope addressed to "K. Chamberlin." A shadow danced off the envelope as the guy must have tipped his hat. With her eyes glued to the ground, she felt him leaving. She thought she heard him whistle a tune as he walked away. If she was not mistaken, the tune was "She Talks to Angels," not that it mattered.

Paige held the package in one hand, turned and closed the door with her back. Pride took her for a moment as she needed the taste of victory for her small accomplishment of getting past the agoraphobia in answering the door. Then she remembered the door remained unlocked. A fury of fearful simulated possibilities attacked her mind. She dropped the envelope, turned in a haste and fastened the lock. So much for getting through the panic.

"Is everything alright," David's husky voice called down. Of course, he would appear after she needed his assistance.

She picked up the envelope from the ground. "Just a goody for Khira, boo," Paige responded. Anything dealing with Khira would raise enough curiosity for David to come down from his sanctuary. Paige went to the kitchen to make a closer inspection of the package. The envelope stared back at her from the table. She flipped it over. The back of this package had been sealed with an ebony wax seal emblazoned with the head of a bird. She struggled for a moment whether to wait for Khira or to take a small peek.

It arrived via messenger, not USPS, so would it unlawful for her to open it? She even held the small package up to her ear, listening for an imaginary bomb. With no ticking sounds coming from the envelope, she shook it. The contents only made a soft shuffling sound. She imagined Khira walking in on her while opening it. The wrath she would receive if that happened. She scooted her chair back and stared at the package. Paige could not help it as her curiosity got the better of her.

She went over to the junk drawer at the edge of the countertop nearby to retrieve a letter opener. Paige slid the sleek silver opener under the seal, making sure to scrape any signs that wax was ever on the sleeve. She opened the top flap and held the envelope at an angle; three leather bound books fell from the package. The first book was a sapphire book held a cover stamped with an intertwined image of a waning moon with a waxing moon, like an image Paige had seen for the zodiac sign for Gemini. The second book was an emerald and had a stamped gold tribal image of a Lion. The last book was chestnut in color and was plain looking except for a stamped image of a leaf at the upper right-hand corner of the cover. After flipping through the blank pages of the brown book, Paige tossed it to the side.

Next, she opened the green book. The first page was marked with the name Liam Wallace inked in an elegant style. Inside this book were recipes, "magical" spells, and children's rhymes. A couple of pages had sketches of twin girls. She could not find much sense or logic to the order within the pages. Maybe Khira was hiding a different life from her or could there be a different K. Chamberlin waiting for these books that seemed to have come from some asylum. Paige remembered the name Liam Wallace from some Mel Gibson movie, but that character could not have owned any books like these.

Paige brought the cobalt book closer. She examined it more than the others, because this one seemed to have a historical feel. A soft welcoming aroma came from the old pages like potpourri the loomed antique stores. Old books were the best. This musky smell gave a comforting warmth, like the smell of chicken noodle soup.

She inspected the worn and weathered surface, massaging the crevices within the leather with the tips of her fingers. They always contained the secrets of the universe within them. For a moment, Paige wondered if this book could be as dangerous as the book in the

"Neverending Story." Undaunted, she opened the cover to see what appeared to be a plain white page. *Again, another blank book? What a gyp.* However, something caught her eye. A name written in small letters in the lower left-hand corner, close to the seam, emerged. In dark red letters, the name "Lorelai" appeared to her. Paige gathered the books and the envelope. She rushed upstairs towards her room and passed David, determined to keep this secret treasure to herself.

****

An old man sat behind a large wooden desk. This antique desk had been hand-carved centuries ago. On the Northeast corner of this desk, a large Raven, with outstretched wings, had been carved into the wood, while an engraved Lion sat watching guard at the Northwest corner. In the center of the desk, a sun and moon were embossed with a single closed rosebud in the middle of them. One stained-glass lamp remained lit upon the desk, casting shadows of blues, greens, reds and a soft yellow across the room. Just enough light unveiled an abundance of clutter. If there had been any organization to the stacks and piles of paper on his desk, it was lost upon itself. The man appeared to be in his late eighties, with long silver flecks protruding from bushy eyebrows. His hands shook a little more with each page he lifted from his desk. "Ah, yes," he said aloud, as if it was natural that he came upon this piece of paper. He coughed aloud, as if preparing to speak to a crowd, albeit one in his own mind. After a silent pause, he repeated, "Ah, yes," before reading the report before him.

To the head of Brânswood:

The Auryn has been received, but the wrong ears are listening. Morla holds it within her possession at this moment. I vow the Auryn will be delivered to the Childlike Empress. I trust that the speech was delivered from your door to this protected residence. While this mission's path is unknown I can only follow the instincts taught to me by the Nothing's

Queen and implement the ideology that I assume you hold dear to your moons.-Squirrel

"Ah, yes." The man took the letter and folded the paper into an origami dahlia, flattened it and pushed it into an envelope. He licked and sealed the envelope, smacking the gum from the flap between his lips. He then rose from his chair. Feeling along the wall, he came to a bookcase. He counted three shelves from the bottom and counted five books from the left. He opened the cornflower blue leather-bound book found there and stuffed the envelope within the tome before shelving it. He turned his back and as he returned to his chair, the sound of the book sliding out rung in the darkness. "Ah, yes," answered the man before picking up the next letter.

Chapter Three

I still eat, if only air, while I divert my parents' attention with conversation. I still bleed, but it seeps from my eyes as tears instead of providing the lifeforce within me. I still feel, but my soul is slipping away into a darkness instead of embracing this new existence. I still live, but today is the first day of the death bestowed like a crown of ever-growing maggots, instead of the gift that Lilian claims she has given me. Lilian tells me that I must retrain myself for this new world. I wish to confess our sin and shame to our parents, for I do not have the same faith in what is to come as my sister does.

Lilian loves me, but this has been a curse, a selfish deed. She has changed so much, even with her beliefs. She claims God smiled upon us to lead the others like us down this remarkable path. I cannot share her philosophies, even wondering if there are others like us, save the man who sickened Lilian.

This is a sickness, but I am not Job and cannot bear these boils bestowed upon me and praise God begging, "Yes! Give me more!" I have heard the myths and stories, but we do not even have a Teacher to tell us what is true and what is false. We have only Liam, a blasphemous leader, whose words we must accept as truth. We must leave our lives and our fates now to a stranger. Lilian is so eager to abide by his every wish; while I feel trapped between reality and fairy tales, I have no hope of escaping. This is a noose tighten around my neck by a charlatan I have no trust for.

I can no longer pray to a God who has betrayed me. Why should He hear the cries of one who is no longer His child? Have I betrayed Him by continuing in this lie? I lay my cold, white hand upon my heart and imagine the strong heartbeat that was there but a few days ago.

I feel so hollow and alone. I may go mad if left in this state. Lying to my parents leaves my heart in despair, but betraying my one true dearest friend, my sister, tears my heart to pieces. I fear her now. I fear that she looks through the mask that I have put on. May she read my thoughts and rid me of this curse. Let her marry her stranger and live his ways so that I may rest in peace...

****

Paige closed the book with regrets for prying in this diary meant for Khira. Lorelai's misfortune made Paige forget her own fears for a moment. The horrors that Lorelai may have faced made the memories that locked her into this mental cage seem minuscule in comparison.

She looked over to her desk, where her monitor stood dark. She had not turned on the web camera when she brought the books into her room. She wanted privacy, away from David, away from everyone. She sensed he hovered outside her door for a bit. When Paige needed control from her mental demons, she had found an inner power as a mistress in a virtual world under her rule. She needed that strength to push down the severity of the agoraphobia. The depression and anxiety fed on the self-esteem issues she carried around.

Paige was technically "obese" by the popular body mass index; "big-boned' according to her mother; and full-figured by the media's perspective. At first, she never gave much thought to her weight. She had grown up with idols like Marilyn Monroe and Mae West. She had an old soul and believed these are what true women looked like.

Her thoughts did not begin to turn against her self-image until her mom started putting her on diets and forcing Paige to exercise with her. While towards the end of elementary school, she kept her mother's actions a secret from her classmates. She was too nice to everyone to be bullied as a child so she would not to give them any ammunition. Besides, she was already being bullied at home. Although everyone's friend, she felt alone.

Again, she was in solitary, locked behind her bedroom door. Her cousin kept Paige at arm's length. David proved a nice distraction at times. Yet, Paige could not help but wonder why he was so nice to her, why it had been so easy for him to move in with them. She paused. Khira's mistrust must be contagious.

Paige retreated from her bed and walked over to her computer. She did not even bother to guilt herself into putting in a session for her expectant virtual fans. She moved her mouse to get the PC out of sleep mode to shut off the machine. She walked over to her bedroom door and placed her ear against the wood. She listened for any sign indicating that Khira had gotten home. The house was silent. The only signal that someone else could possibly be in the house was David's sighing and humming outside Paige's bedroom door. She unlocked her door and strutted back to the bed, picking up Lorelai's journal.

"What have you been doing in here?"

"Nothing," she whispered, opening the book back to her spot.

"Oh, what's that?" David asked as he approached Paige like a curious cat and perched over her.

"Nothing," she responded louder this time.

"Doesn't look like nothing. Doesn't look like it belongs to you either, boo." David sneered. Paige shot him a glance that spoke leave me alone. David knew it well. "Please forgive me, hon." Then he whispered a single word "cysgu." Once the spell left his lips, Paige fell into a deep sleep.

****

Khira stopped to grab a bite from a local coffee bar before heading home. She tried to balance her messenger bag, iced latte, and the bag that held a dinner container as she fumbled for the doorknob. As soon as her fingers touched metal, everything collapsed to the ground and sprawled across the sidewalk at her feet. "FUCKING CHRIST!" escaped her lips as she opened the door. Her hand covered her mouth as if to rewind the words that may have announced her entrance to her cousin. The house remained still.

She picked up the crushed container from the bag, her dinner still somewhat intact. She left the mostly empty cup of coffee on the sidewalk. The liquid had kept away from the rest of the items, leaving behind a small stream heading to the street. She gathered everything else up and juggled the remaining items while attempting to unlock the front door.

She dropped everything but the dinner container onto the floor in the foyer and closed the door. When turned back around, she noticed that her sketchbook was not among the many things she picked up. *Crap!* Khira retraced her steps, trying to recall where she could have misplaced her prize. She remembered the crash at the bookstore.

She pulled her phone to check the time the store would open the next day, as it was already most likely closed. She would have to call tomorrow. She felt violated that something precious to her was out of her possession; however, there was nothing she could do about it for the time being.

She kicked her messenger bag close to a small table in the foyer and stepped into the kitchen to retrieve a fork. With utensil and dinner in hand, she headed up to her sanctum with hopes of avoiding Paige along the route. When Khira reached her bedroom door, she was sort of surprised that she did not need to duck or dodge her cousin. It almost offended her that Paige did not at least poke her head out to check on her. Maybe Paige was "*working*." She gagged.

She made mental plans to leave for the night at once. She scarfed down her dinner and shoved the misshapen container in a trash can. She walked into her closet, expecting the clothes to tell her tonight's destination. She plotted onto the floor, looking at the different articles, each a different persona. One outfit could whisk her to a museum. Another would grant her passage into a foreign horror movie. Her eyes stopped at the role she most wanted to tackle for the evening.

She got dressed. She gave herself a small cat eye with matte black liner, gave her lashes a quick sweep with mascara and applied gloss to her nude lips. It took a bit longer to wrangle her hair into the style needed. She was ready to take on the stage of the real world.

Khira left her room, closing the door behind her with soft precision. Downstairs matched the volume of the second floor, preserving the tomblike silence. She tiptoed to her cousin's door, expecting to hear moanings or clicking other than than a keyboard. The soundless nature made Khira question if she should check to see if her cousin was still alive in there. A quick sniff declared no decomposing body lay within the room. She rapped against the door. "Yeah?" Paige inquired. The sign that her cousin was unharmed signaled Khira to leave before giving Paige another opportunity to question the night's life choice.

****

Zachary kept watch on his assignment from afar. He had learned Khira's name by looking through her mail. He managed to narrow down his target, since the latest intel did not match the roommate that made money as a cam girl. A quick glance through the content there showed Paige Montgomery could have been a relative but was nowhere near the description provided by the previous scouts.

The former failed incidents had come as a surprise to Zachary, but then again, Lilian had sent off minions rather than someone higher in rank or even the professionals of the Independent Sector. By fortune's grace, Khira often visited the bookstore he owned. After scrolling back through countless of security footage, Zachary surmised he could have killed Khira months ago.

On this night, he had followed her to a club in the warehouse district of nearby Austin. The music played loud enough to make a deaf man dance. Although Zachary did not prefer this noise, he had to fit into the background. A small smirk dressed his mouth as his thoughts wandered back into his familiar patterns; the thought of torturing his victim for hours enticed him.

Khira Chamberlin danced away, wearing a short plaid skirt, tight black buttoned blouse, and chunky-heeled thigh-high boots. She created her own tempo to the music, paying no heed to those around her. As the music continued, he listened to the lyrics of the song. The electronic Goth music taunted how pretty one became when she cried. Had the DJ invaded his thoughts? Zachary could imagine the girl hogtied while he took turns with different knives causing such small torturous cuts; what fun. The gods must have planned this. In between the torture scenes playing in his mind, his thoughts wandered to whether or not her blood could turn.

He wished that Lilian would soon escalate his role from voyeur to executioner. He took great pleasure in slaughtering the Untouched and could have been in charge of the Independent Sector by now. He did wonder for a short time, why exactly Lilian had given this task to him instead of their sister Sector. He preferred her decision to take the role on himself. Kill Orders never said he could *not* have fun before he completed the job.

Zachary never had a choice in his status as Untouched. His human parents had birthed him a vampire. As an only child to a lower middle-class family, his parents dragged him from one doctor to the next, all with several misdiagnoses. They had always wanted children, but their path to parenting proved a hard one on them. They had given up and his mother decided she would surround herself with children by working at a local children's nursery.

Lo and behold, a month later, she got pregnant with Zachary. Although no complications existed with the pregnancy, once born, the doctors knew he exhibited "special" tendencies. Both of his parents carried genetic markers for the disease and passed it down to him, a rarity in his time. He had a lack of appetite, yet maintained an excessive thirst with nothing seeming to help. His eyes, sensitive to the sun, forced him inside most days, yet his vitamin "D" numbers were through the roof. His bones and muscles remained strong even as his diet failed him, labeling him malnourished. He presented challenge after challenge to doctors. Once he took up to 32 pills daily, not including his iron supplements.

He considered Lilian the biggest blessing when she found him in middle school. At such an impressionable age, she became his mentor, his new mother. Lilian taught him for the first time in his life, he had nothing wrong with him; quite the contrary. She explained to him that he went even beyond Adam as a direct son of God, not a mundane human muddied by a family tree.

Touched, she had called him. As a pure born, Zachary could withstand the sun's light longer than most before becoming weakened or gaining an onset of advanced aging. Still, he wore heavy sunglasses to protect his slate eyes. His aging all together slowed after going through puberty since he stayed indoors most of the time. Lilian had given him a purpose. However, some days he wondered who benefitted more from that purpose; him or her.

Memories faded like the smoke from the room. The music pulsated back into his ears, reminding him of his current mission. Zachary kept his gaze on her, still contemplating how he would end her if given the chance. Could he at least get some satisfaction before having to kill her? Maybe get in a little sexual gratification? She gyrated her hips, as if to confirm his desires.

Yes, he needed to violate her. He had dreamt about nestling his mouth into her chest before penetrating her from the moment he set eyes saw her on the security footage. He wanted to sink his extended canines, which were now hidden, but itching to pierce into her thigh with her legs up on his shoulders. Lost in this fantasy he created, Khira kept dancing oblivious to Zachary's scheme.

Shit, what am I? The typical cliché Vampire falling in love (or lust, more honestly) with the mortal in one of those insipid Vampire shows that always screwed up the mythology? Lilian better not figure out his new weakness. Zachary knew she would exploit it as much as possible. He thought it possible to take the Southern Sector from her. Reed Harris would be his only other obstacle. The time just wasn't right for a coup. For now, he had to focus on the subject at hand.

Khira noticed the handsome man keeping tabs on her. Maybe she would cop a free drink tonight after all. She was "Mary Katherine" tonight; "Catholic schoolgirl in trouble motif" with her crimson lip-stick, fishnet stockings, plaid skirt and tight black silk blouse that enhanced her natural 36Ds. She portrayed Miss Perfect, the people pleaser, who was more than willing to go down on some chump before jumping onto his hard dick, bouncing up and down with her braided pigtails flying, as if featured in an "R" rated version of Britney Spears' video for "Oops, I did it again." Mary Katherine served as her mask.

Playing these different roles always bettered her life, hands down. She had been creating other egos to portray since high school. She kept this part a secret from her deceased father's family, who would over-react or deem her crazy. Khira adopted her mother's mantra "People will only let you down" early on after her parents' passing. She did not trust her aunt or her cousin, the only family willing to take the orphan in.

Khira's aunt had appointed her Paige's guard. With the threat of homelessness, she pretended to look out for her cousin. Khira was imprisoned by duty until her aunt passed away the day after Paige's eighteenth birthday. Khira had another month before she would be of legal age. However, even when she became an adult, she had no other place to go. Once Paige developed agoraphobia, life became a cell block, as if a vacuum, sucking the life out of Khira. She no longer wanted to dwell on her life so she pushed those thoughts away so that she could remain Mary Katherine for the time being.

Khira pulled a nearby girl into a grinding session on the dance floor. So pathetic two girls dancing together could guarantee about five drinks for each. The dancing progressed until the girl's girlfriend came into the picture, trying to get into the drink action. The poor, virtuous sheepish girl hesitated about whom she should dance with; her girlfriend or this intriguing new soul who chose her.

Khira didn't need a drink that much. Screw the girls. Forget Mary Katherine's innocence. Khira went up to the stranger, grabbed his waist, and planted a kiss. She pulled his head down and to the side, bringing his ears towards her lips, "You place. Now. No names; no relationship; no other parties. You are *mine* tonight." She left him there while she headed to the parking lot. He high-tailed out of the club, telling his buddy to cover his tab.

Khira's boldness surprised Zachary as he watched her take off with some poor frat kid that would have no idea what to do with her. Not only did it intrigue him, but it also excited him even more. Khira charmed him somehow in a way Lilian never could. This stranger had power within her, so remarkable for an Untouched. Zachary wondered if Khira even knew that Vampires existedoutside of novels and cheesy B-movies. Why waste time on this quandary when he could get back to that daydream of torturing her. He vacillated on whether to pull her arms and legs off her body bit by bit like plucking them off an insect or jamming her into a spiked wall. Either way, he already decided that he'd have her before finishing her off.

****

The old man was on his hands and knees using what little light emanated from the desk lamp to guide his quest. He scrounged along the bottom section of the bookcase knowing that the prized book he needed should be the seventh one from the left. However the tome wasn't there. "Humph," and with that, he moved to the next bookshelf. Still on his hands and knees, he seemed to nose book after book trying to find the one fit for the most current message from Squirrel:

To the head of Brânswood:

The hour has passed. Morla has taken court with the Ivory Tower. Fortunately, the words of the Nothing's Queen remains silent. However, this couldn't have been the intention of the Southern Oracle. Shouldn't have Uyulala dictacted as much? My own eyes feel closed on what should guide my path. I know you cannot provide anymore direction. While I will attempt to lure Morla away from such pressing matters, my watch over the Auryn and the Childlike Empress will be ever faithful. -Squirrel

The old man had taken such care to file the latest of faulty decisions. He wondered why Ruby had kept such secrets away from him; he was weary of the Phoenix. Still, any mishaps needed to be filed away.

As he crawled around, his fingernails seemed to dig into the wooden floor beneath him. When one of his hands seemed stuck, he would bring it up to his mouth and bite off the nails. The book was still unfound. He headed over to the bookcase closest to the door of his office, which seemed to be encased in shadows. Again he searched for the warranted book and again, his hands dug into the floor, his nails having grown back already.

"Max, can you hear me? Max?" A female voice came from the sun/moon emblem.

"Humph," he replied. Max looked over his shoulder at the desk and then turned back towards the bookcase. He found the book he was looking for. He placed a folded origami bear in between the pages and then put the book into his mouth. Continuing on his hands and knees, he took the book back to its rightful place. A whisp whithered within the room, noting to Max another new message awaited him

"Max, I know that you do not like to be interrupted, but this is important. Max?" The voice continued, but he just kept ignoring the noise. He placed the book back into the correct bookshelf and stood up.

Before making his way back to the desk, he paused as the annoying interrupting voice pierced through the air once more. "Max, Ruby says that the change will be coming sooner than expected and you need to be prepared. Max?" The old man kicked at the desk to stifle the voice.

Max went ahead with business, trying to push the outside disturbance away from his sanctuary. The most recent missive nested at the top of a stack of papers. It appeared to be from Dragonfly. Max examined the message. It seemed distorted and had not been encrypted. He made out a sentence here and there.

"Hrmmm," he grunted in concern. He focused his eyes, and words became clearer. Finally, a look into Lilian's dealings, he thought. The information would be useful in figuring out what the vampires were up, even with the possibility of diving into procedures within their hidden labs. He hadn't realized that Dragonfly was assigned to Thirlestane Manor. Through the dealings he had seen earlier, the agent's tasks had seemed much more mundane. Something was amiss.

After folding the latest message into the shape of a heart, the old man got back down onto his knees and searched for a new book. His body ached. Between the popping of his joints, he could still hear a scurry within his walls. He paused to see if the interruption still remained outside his door. There appeared to be a silence at last. After he found the larger book, he got up to his feet and continued the path to his desk. However, his peace was broken yet again by a muffled voice.

"Max, you know that Ruby has never been wrong." Max kept ignoring the voice while he sat the book down on the desk and took his seat. He shook his hands and looked down at them. The once rugged nails now looked like they had been manicured. His shaky hand brought forth a piece of paper that had lain on top of one of the many stacks upon his desk. He brought it close to his eyes. "Max, I know you can hear me. If need be, I'll send Ruby to you," the voice continued in a more agitated tone. He set the piece of paper back down upon his desk. Max picked up the heavy book. "Max, I just spoke to Ruby and..." He slammed the book against the lip of his desk, three times. The action made the whole room echo.

Once silence filled the room again, the old man picked up the letter. "Ah yes," escaped him. Max continued his duty.

****

Khira had overestimated this club beau of hers. Ah, the risk of facing the mystery dead on. It was not fair that he came before she even had a chance to breathe. Maybe if she could stop playing these games, she would be able to find someone to satisfy her. She knew to fit society's standards; she would need to grow up and decide on one persona. She could live easier as a lesbian. The thought drifted into her head and lingered. Khira couldn't identify her sexuality, because again, she couldn't place herself in either column A or column B. She didn't fit in anywhere.

She sat up in bed, pushing away the sound of the water hitting tile in a cramped bathroom within a small studio apartment. Her thoughts drifted to wonderment, a brief interlude of imagining the poor boy heartbroken to return to an empty room with no note or explanation or even blame for the lousy lay.

She gathered her belongings, glancing to "shop" for another outfit. Instead of her own black silk blouse she had donned earlier, she layered a Depeche Mode 101 vintage concert t-shirt with a Rolling Stones novelty necktie. At least it seemed possible that the loser may have had a decent taste in music, but most likely he picked up the items, hoping to fit in with other poseurs. She knew she could not knock him, because she played the biggest poseur of all. She tucked her blouse under her arm and without looking back walked out.

Chapter Four

"Isn't this what you wanted?"

She dared not answer.

"This life, this power...isn't all of this the life you had strived for?"

She raised her head and stared back into the face, that counseled her.

"Why are not you happy?"

" I am happy," she whispered, without intonation or feeling, as if she could command herself to be joyous. However, no words could convince her reflection. She stood in her chambers before her golden dressing mirrors. Rich elaborate décor splayed behind her as the full-length glass took in her nude body.

Though the looking glass reflected everything throughout the room, all one could see in unison within their surfaces was her reflection. But despite her efforts, all she could see was her twin sister's image staring back at her. The hair, body, identical to the sister that betrayed and abandoned her. Yet her eyes showed her identity. Hers lacked the gentle demeanor that found home in her sister's soft, violet eyes.

"Did you command something of me, Mistress?" spoke a small voice below her.

Shaken from her reverie, Lilian turned towards the voice. A young man knelt at her feet. He was clad in a leather harness adorned with decorative studs and a golden collar with sketched ruins circling his neck. His lithe frame belied the endowment that hung between his legs. He held a brush and a small bottle of rare, expensive imported polish. She had forgotten about him as usual. Her pets did not warrant her notice. "What did you say?"

He seemed taken aback for a moment and looked up at her with a curious expression. He lips turned upward in an innocent smile. "I asked if you commanded me, beautiful one. I did not wish to stop my task, of course, but I live to service you, as you well know."

A small sound echoed from behind her. Turning, she saw two of her maids tittering as they prepared her outfit and accessories for the evening. Both flinched as they saw her querying eyes. In place of a harness, each young girl wore an interpretation of a "French Maid's" outfit. While the frilly black and white garment was similar, the outfit exposed the young girls' breast as well as their sex, which was shaved bare. Practical as well as servile, they performed her every need.

They along with others executed duties within her trust. They averted their eyes and continued working. Had one of them laughed at her? With all that she had seen and heard of late, how could she be sure of anything? She turned back to the boy, remember her status and responsibility. After a moment of hesitation, she spoke. "No Samuel, continue your work."

"It's *Sammy*, my Queen."

Lilian paused at that, her eyebrow arching in concern. The hint of a sneer touched her lips. Such insolence! This was not the first time this thrall had caused her irritation. If there were more time, she would discipline this *boy*, but the adoring looks in his eyes as well as his eagerness to please made her stay her hand. More important things had to be dealt with this night. Pushing her ire deep down, she painted a smile upon her face. "Indeed. Continue, *Sammy*."

She caressed her "pet" and turned back to the mirror. The image of her sister now dissipated. Only her true reflection remained. Her snowy white tresses draped over her pallid shoulders. Her ample breasts stood proud and firm, and her skin showed nary a mark upon it. Steely muscles, toned beneath her skin, showed her strength despite her fragile looking form. The soft trim of hair above her mound matched her color in a show of natural splendor. She was a beautiful young woman by all accounts. Anyone who saw her would not think her older than mid-twenties, but they would be wrong.

"Oops!" A cold, wet sensation upon her foot disturbed her appraisal. Looking down she could see the trail of expensive crimson polish running between her toes. Sammy had put aside the liquid and was trying to stem the tide of color upon her foot.

"Clumsy idiot!" she spat, kicking Samuel upon the chest, pushing him across the room.

"I am sorry, Mistress! Please, forgive me! I can make it up to you!" He stammered. Sammy tried to approach Lilian, but an outward thrust hand caused him to pause in mid-stride.

"Enough! You are done here." With a long-manicured finger, she gestured to the door. "Go to the Parlor Room and see that the members of the Conclave have arrived and are prepared for the verdict."

For a moment Sammy pouted, his eyes downcast in disappointment. Then, like the rising dawn, a smile spread across his face. He bowed and replied, "Of course, Mistress. Anything for you." Her pet headed towards the door, wiping the remnants of polish off his bare chest.

As he attempted to pass through the portal on his assigned task, a stately, older woman appeared from the other side. Her attire was modest compared to those around her. Her dress was elaborate, but plain with monotone shades of grey. Sammy ran headlong into her. He clutched at her to avoid falling, embracing her in a tight hug. Moments passed and he realized what he was doing. Backing away, he flashed his most cheerful smile up at the woman. "My apologies, Lady Eleanor. I did not see you there."

Lady Eleanor looked down her nose at the young man as if he was something she found under a rock. She looked down at her stained garment. Red nail polish was smeared across her dress akin to a kinder-gartener's art project.

"I....uh....please, allow me," Sammy stammered. A low growl emerged from Lady Eleanor's throat. Her eyes shot daggers at the troublesome pet. Taking his cue, Sammy hurried past her and contin-ued his errand.

With a resounding sigh, Lady Eleanor continued past and entered the chambers of Mistress Lilian. She approached Lilian. After a curt bow, she spoke. "Mistress, guests have assembled and await your au-dience."

Lilian turned, looking at her in surprise. "Here already? I had no idea where the time had gone." Indeed, she had not. In all her pensive thoughts, she was not aware of the late hour. It was as if time, too, had turned against her. "Return to the audience chamber and await my arrival. I will present myself shortly."

With a stiff nod, Lady Eleanor backed out of Lilian's chambers and left the Mistress to continue dressing. Turning her attention back to her maids, Lilian snapped her fingers. They both stood at attention. "You," she said pointed at the maid to her left, a raven-haired lass. "Assemble my regalia." Turning to the other girl, a flaxen-haired beauty, she continued. "You, prepare the cascade." Both girls nodded in perfect unison as if but one unit before separating to their assigned tasks.

The first girl moved to the far side of the room where she touched a panel upon the wall. The wall proceeded to open and revealed a vast cavern of sectioned rooms containing a copious amount of clothing, shoes and other decorative adornments. Delving within the expansive wardrobe, the maid went to the back wall and pressed a combination of keys upon another panel. Unlocking the system, a series of drawers opened. She pulled out a large flat container and in doing so, a wisp of vapor trailed behind. The container carried a slight rime of frost upon it. After inspecting the box, the maid, closed the frigid drawers. She took the container back into the dressing room.

Meanwhile, her counterpart had gone across the room and entered the baths. Lilian followed the girl and entered the dressing chamber that preceded the baths proper. The room was circular with a raised pedestal in the center. Striding upon the dais, Lilian stood poised. The maid stood at a far wall and pressed a few buttons upon a panel. Above Lilian, an elaborate showerhead lowered from a hidden recess and began to spray. A soft mist descended upon her in a steamy cascade. The moist droplets clung to her skin in a glistening array. Her hands moved up and down her body, rubbing the liquid into her skin. The soft touch of her hands sliding along her exposed skin caused it to tingle while her nipples hardened.

As much as she wanted to indulge in a moment's pleasure, the matters of state beckoned her. After a few moments, the shower ceased. Her maid brought in a soft towel. Lilian looked down her body as her servant dried her. Her body took on a silky luster and her skin felt viscid from the oils embedded in the mist. Perfect. Now to dress and show all those who have come to her what real power she can display.

****

Striding down the hallways of her domain, she appeared as a crimson wraith, decked in a red silken cloak. Her eyes could not yet be seen as she had planned. None should see her splendor until the time of her choosing. Even so, her eyes noticed everything. Although she approached solo, she was far from alone. From time to time, a servant passed her on their way to their duties or as more elaborate décor appeared. There were more of her playthings ready to serve at her pleasure. From one place to another, pets dressed up the wall as living statues. Poised, polished and most of all natural, they painted a scene which reflected the decadent desires she attributed.

"Are you happy?"

She paused before the stairway, which lead down to the main hall. There it was again, her sister's words. No matter what she did or where she went, she could not escape those words. She glanced at the living sculptures that poised in their naked splendor. She wondered if they could hear her sister's voice like she did. It seemed to hiss at her louder than usual. Lilian pondered the words while awaiting news of the Conclave.

She was happy, wasn't she? She always assumed so, but the more she thought about it, the more she could hear the doubt riddled in the question. Why wasn't she happy? There were issues that could not be avoided. She aged little that was true; however, time was catching up to her. She was not like fine wine. She was more like a beautiful masterpiece needing restoration. She was still as beautiful as the day she turned, yet...

Lilian could already hear the conversations of her guests carry from downstairs, even though she was still quite a distance away. If she had her way, she would have preferred that they would vanish. However, she had a reputation and responsibilities to maintain. She glanced back and forth down the hallways. Where was that boy? Samuel seemed to be delayed. He had become yet another tool just chipping away at her patience. After a few more minutes of waiting, he appeared from the opposite end of the hallway nearest to the stairs. He took his time before getting into position next to her and kneeled.

"You are late," Lilian whispered. Her words were so quiet it was a wonder that they were spoken at all. She did not wait for an excuse from this underling. She regretted taking Reed's advice on endowing such a duty upon this creature. Not only did Sammy appear nothing more than a geeky "man-boy", but she was beginning to believe Sammy was unworthy. Task after task, he failed to please her. "Are they waiting in the Parlor room as I requested?" she whispered again to Sammy.

"Yes, my mistress. They await your decision of the Crucible."

"Very well, I will render my verdict after my announcement to the Coven." Lilian began to step forward to continue down to her guests but was obstructed by the boy. He gazed up at her in loving adoration. "Can we let them wait just a little longer? I would rather please you than have you dirty yourself in the politics that they have cast upon you. I could make you happy on this glorious occas..."

With a flutter of crimson silk, Lilian's hand struck out, slicing the air in a grandiose gesture. Sammy was taken aback. He was used to his Mistress' discipline, but this display was unlike any he had ever seen. So grand, so beautiful! Her power struck him like a wave, and he could not help but love her more for it. The moment passed. She was once again standing before him, her cloak closing upon her like a slumbering rose. Sammy's eyes drank in the sight of her, and he was about to rejoice when his sight fell upon her bloodied hand. The tips of her fingers were setting droplets of life upon the floor. The boy was at a loss of words.

He was about to comment when he found he could not find his voice. Looking again he could see that a spray of red had spattered the wall of the hallway. Glancing down, he saw that the same redness was running down his chest. He moved to wipe it away when everything began to go dark. Just as he passed into the beyond, he gazed once more unto his reason for being as his last thought escaped him, *"It won't come off."* His head lolled back and the vicious tear now evident upon his throat gaped open as his body collapsed upon the hallway floor and his head tore from the body. It rolled nearby setting back down, leaving Sammy gazing up unto his Mistress as he always had done before. The smell of fresh blood was intoxicating. She raised her hand to her lips and licked at the blood thereon. With her other hand, she snapped her fingers twice.

One of the female pets against the wall stepped up to Lilian's side, while a young boy came to drag the body away. Lilian took an appraising look at the young girl. The girl wore nothing but a collar with a small bell. This redheaded creature was petite in size although her breasts were quite ample. She was young to be sure, but the fiery nest of hair above her sex belied her appearance. The soft, natural tattooing of wine stains on her face looked like faded tiger stripes. "And what is your name, my new pet?" Lilian asked. The girl tilted her head and gazed back as if deciding how to respond. The young boy looked up to see whom Lilian was speaking to.

"Oh, that one doesn't talk, my Mistress," the boy stated. He was young and seemed to have problems with the mechanics of getting a good hold of Sammy's limp body. Blood from Sammy's body pooled at Lilian's feet. "I believe her name is Kitty. If you would like, I could have another pet," he now looked at her, lost for words, "who is more adequate for any needs you may have." Kitty gave the young boy a sneer before looking back to Lilian with a sweet smile.

"No. I think Kitty will be willing to prove herself." Lilian did not return Kitty's smile. She looked over to the boy, "Dispose of that body." The boy did as his Mistress commanded. Lilian could not let her guests wait much longer. "Come, Kitty." Kitty began to trail after Lilian but turned back to take the golden collar from about Sammy's now severed head. She flashed the boy a show of her tongue as she ran back after her Mistress as the new favorite Pet.

****

The assembled guests mingled about the grand chamber. As with most party guests, there was the random assortment of personalities. Some seemed pleased to be there. Others felt angry and resentful to be summoned like servants. Those bored of the waiting game lingered towards the exits. When one was invited to a gathering by Mistress Lilian, one attended, or else. After a few minutes, the attitude of the crowd began to change. The cacophony of voices waned. There was a powerful vibe in the air and the scent of that which they all knew so well, blood. It was not just blood, but Blood and *Power*. All eyes turned towards the landing of the grand staircase. The red-garbed figure looked down upon the assembled masses. It was time.

Dropping the silken cloak from her shoulders, the Mistress Lilian exposed herself to her coven and displayed her strength. Kitty went down to pick up the cloak. Out of nowhere, the young boy appeared to sweep in. He took it before she even had a chance to touch it.

Lilian began her descent down the staircase. Her hand hovered over the golden banister rail although she would not need the support. Her straight white hair covered her back and began to sway while her long lean legs commanded the steps beneath her feet. She stopped mid-way and waited for the eyes of the room to be commanded onto her body. Displayed over her elegant naked form were jewels positioned all around her body. They were crafted to adhere to her body and link to themselves by a magnetic frame around each jewel.

Yet, the sparkle and shine of the jewels would not be the hook to reel in her guests. It would be the sweet fragrance they produced. These were not precious rubies or garnets adorning her body. They were vials of blood. Each jewel contained the essence from her latest victims to the most treasured of her past conquests. The aroma of blood permeated the hall, demanding for her guests to take notice.

She continued down the staircase and then stopped short of the landing. Lilian spread her arms to welcome her guests. Her voice carried to every corner of the hall without aid or amplification. "Thank you for joining me on this special occasion in which we remember the fallen brethren that have helped us pave our path towards our future. Enjoy yourself tonight as one may never know what the next moon shall offer us."

The applause and recognition of the crowd was as grand as could be expected. The Mistress who commanded the loyalty of so many expected as much, even if some felt it was not deserved. She allowed those brave enough to approach her and bask in her splendor, fawning over her commanding presence. Such false platitudes sickened her. "*Are you happy?*" echoed in her ear, Happiness was not an option on this night of the Crucible. Duty demanded she make her presence known. Once the guests turned back to rejoin the festivities, her smile faded from her lips like a raindrop sliding down a pane of glass. Now that one duty was complete, she had another to attend to.

Chapter Five

The "Parlor" was a gaming room although this room did not have a single board game or deck of cards. Rather, this room served as a dungeon, decorated complete with chains, holding captive neither enemies nor vassals, but those who dared to prove themselves worthy of the trust of The Touched, some not by choice. Bodies of tortured men and women known as *Familiars* were hung upon crosses, most with pans and sheeting underneath them as not to waste any of their precious blood. A rack of tools such as various knives, picks, cuffs, and braces were organized on a silver doctor's tray wrapped in clear plastic near each cross.

At this time, no one attended the bodies. Their whimpering cries of suffering went unnoticed. Just beyond this macabre gallery hid a passage to an inner sanctum beyond. Within that chamber, there was a small group of nine people assembled near an elaborate golden

Elizabethan throne. They were assembled on each side of the throne, seated in smaller, but still quite embellished, chairs of their own. The chairs formed a circular enclosure around the center of the room, as if only a round table was missing between the attendees.

Most of these guests had come to oversee the final ruling of the Crucible to determine if a certain prospective candidate was determined worthy enough to join the ranks of the *Touched*. On either side of the throne were Lilian's two lieutenants; to the left sat Zachary Duvall and, on the right, Reed Harris, a silver-tongued and charismatic man. Zachary had been by Lilian's side much longer than Reed. While Zachary was a true born Touched, Reed had been sired during a Crucible of his own. His charm and striking pale skin, contrasting his dark eyes and hair, had gotten him far within the Southern Sector. He had first been assigned to the Panhandle Sector before requesting to be transferred. Reed was ambitious and at times, it would get the best of him.

Five of the other seven people were respected coven leaders from around the United States. Some had come to the event alone while others brought only one pet with them to bear witness.

One of the oldest was Christian Adams of the Panhandle Sector. His dusky features seemed to blend with the shadows of the chamber while his mocha rich eyes watched the others with a wry humor. Although Reed was no longer under his tutelage, Christian maintained a close relationship with Lilian's lieutenant. Christian wore custom tailored Cubavera shirts. On this occasion, his shirt was a deep purple that made him appear as if a black Hispanic prince.

Across from Christian sat Soleil Johansson of the Western Sector. Soleil was a young petite woman; her green eyes surveyed the room. Her short spiky strawberry-blonde hair and "bohemian" style dress seemed out of place in this dark arena. It was said she won her title as

Western Leader because no one else wanted the position. Her pet, who sat on the floor near her feet, was a woman who wore a loose knitted halter top with no bra and a rainbow broom skirt. The halter barely covered the majority of the pet's breasts. The rest of her body bore henna tattoos, while her hair consisted of trails of cerise dreadlocks. It was common knowledge that those of the West were more hedonistic and free-spirited than most *Touched*. Both Soleil and her pet reflected that notion.

Wes Michaels of the Eastern Sector, on the other hand, was the complete opposite. His calm demeanor and well-groomed reflected the strong discipline he held over his coven. He wore an apple green collarless shirt with caramel slacks. His shoes and belt blended with his pants. His olive complexion stood out against his shirt. His head was slick with no hair among it except for his black bushy eyebrows. The negotiator and peacemaker of the clans, he served as a counterbalance to some of the more aggressive vampire lords such as Zaida Allsong of the Northern Sector.

Zaida was a newcomer and had been turned only a couple of decades. She presented herself much as a popular conceived notion of modern vampires. Dark leathers and long magenta hair gave her an urban street feel that bolstered her antagonistic tendencies. Her pet was entrapped within a prison of vinyl and leather, hiding whatever sex the person had been designated at birth. This pet moved much like a dog in heat, an obvious display of frustration and rage. She stared across the room at Cecelia Marquez of the Independent Sector.

Mistress Marquez held a power close to Lilian with the use of her exotic looks, however she was more of a rival to Zaida, but one would never think so from her apparent disdain towards the Northern Sector Mistress. Cecelia held her purebred status above those who had been turned. The members of her sect were employed as assassins by other covens. Rumor had it that the quiet, Geisha-like pet of hers was the deadliest weapon in her arsenal, although hardly anyone had seen this pet of hers and lived afterwards. These leaders awaited the arrival of Mistress Lilian with anticipation.

Lilian approached the outer realm of the Parlor from a hidden side entrance, a security measure as not to ever have her back turned to those within. Her paranoia made her sure more than one of them would take advantage of her if she ever got so careless. She emerged from a camouflage concealment in the wall behind the throne and appeared before the elite members before her. Kitty trailed behind her, now wearing the favored golden collar. An ornamental chain linked her to her Mistress and Lilian had no qualms about heaving her pet along behind her. The young redheaded girl was almost at a stampeding pace in order just to keep up to Lilian's speed. Lilian came to an abrupt stop but hesitated before sitting. She waited as the seven vampires stood and bowed before her in respect. Lilian could now take her place on the throne.

This jury had come to Lilian as an arbiter. It was common knowledge that Lilian ran the complete Southern Alliance of Covens since she had located to Crow's End, Texas back in the early 1900's. Lilian came into so much power in both the local Touched and Untouched communities in the area with the money she brought along with her then Governor, Liam Wallace. The Southern Sector was the first one to organize and track local Touched persons. By the 1930's, the small town of Crow's End faded away and gave way to a more modern city, Thirlestane. Some areas of the upper-class town still clutched onto the Crow's End moniker such as the town library and local cemetery, for the sake of sentiment. She remembered her sister Lorelai hiding in the library day after day before finding a sanctuary of her own. Soon, others across the states began to organize themselves through the help of

Lilian and her local allies. She could have taken her position anywhere. Still, just being there in the town of Thirlestane with her, Lilian held more confidence. Now with all her power, she had a decision to make.

As Lilian sat, Kitty knelt at her feet. She snapped her fingers and, the young errand boy appeared. The boy approached Lilian and whispered in her ear. As he awaited an answer, she nodded. He dashed out for brief seconds before leading in another young man, this one looking to be close to his late teens, up from the gallery entrance. The teenager stepped forward, moving between the leaders of the Northern and Eastern Sectors, before standing within an engraved circle upon the floor. His chest swollen with pride and confidence. He opened his mouth to speak the reverent words like those who had stood there before him. Lilian raised her hand at him before any words left his mouth. Her hand was still stained with Samuel's blood and made for a most demanding gesture. With this, the young man closed his mouth and knelt within the circle.

"Tobias, you have remained in our coven, first as a familiar, and then trained as a pet. You came before this court with a request to be turned. Although your actions have done nothing but enrich this establishment, it has never been our decision. We have tasted your blood and you cannot be turned." Tobias sank as her words penetrated his heart deeper than fangs at his throat. Lilian continued, "We wish nothing more than if it could be otherwise, but it is the will of those who created us and not the decision of the Conclave."

The boy's eyes cast down to the floor and his disappointment was as thick in the air as the sweetest blood. Lilian took note of his sorrow, and she could not help but sympathize. She must be feeling her age. She could hear the whispered murmurs of the assembled jury. Some also felt sorrow that this worthy child could not join their ancient ranks, while others delighted in his failure. Many of those who failed the Crucible were often destined for a cruel fate. No one, who knows the workings of Lilian's inner sanctum and were not of the chosen, left her domain alive. Then, despite expectation, Lilian continued. "Fear not, Tobias, for we will reward you." His head perked up and his eyes shone with excitement. The whispered murmurs grew louder. "We cannot embrace you, but we have decided to bestow the rank of 'Decoy' upon you. You may not have our blood within your veins, but you bear a Touched heart. You are to relocate and report to Christian Adams for the remainder of your contract" Her words prompted forth the Panhandle Master to rise from his seat next to Reed and join this new decoy. Tobias bowed his head and smiled. He turned to his new master and bowed before him as well. Christian slapped him and then hugged him. One could only assume this to be Christian's custom. Lilian then announced, "Now let us celebrate this honor and feast as if tomorrow will never come!"

Lilian rose waiting for the exodus from all those in her attendance, save for Kitty and Zachary. The women left first as Wes followed in a short cadence. Christian pushed Tobias out of the room in a playful manner before Reed walked up to him and led him through the doorway, swinging his left arm around Christian's shoulders. It was an odd gesture, Lilian thought, since she had never seen such an obvious display of affection from Reed. Christian was the more affectionate one of the two when they were with company. They may not realize that Lilian knew of their escapades, but she did. She didn't see much harm from it. She couldn't give too much thought to it, as she had other things to attend to.

****

"Master, I am in need of a favor," Reed stated as if setting up a chessboard. He had waited until Tobias was out of earshot before beginning his first move. Christian turned to regard his cherished companion. In all the long years he had associated with this man, from his early years of servitude to the more recent status as an officer in Lilian's inner circle, Reed had rarely asked anything of him. His curiosity piqued thus allowing his friend to continue.

"I need some assistance. An opportunity has presented itself that could benefit both of us in the long run," Reed paused. He so often enjoyed these mind games that he and Christian played. He continued, "I would be willing to share the rewards of this venture with you if you still trust in my allegiance to you. I ask you this only once and you know that I'm prepared to be with you, by your side, should you need assistance with anything you desire." Reed whispered into his past lover's ear. "Anything," he repeated.

Christian regarded Reed's words and their potential meaning. Whatever plans he had concocted did little to move his interest. He had no time for such games. There was more important work to be done. Still, he cared much for his favorite former companion even if they came at odds. He thought of all possible outcomes before responding. "You know not to ask of me anything that I may not give and what I *can* give is yours, should you *earn* it. You should have learned this by now, *Lieutenant*." Christian added the last remark as to remind Reed of his place. He still enjoyed manipulating his former pet. What he hadn't realized though was that Reed had surpassed him in the art of subterfuge years ago. The raven haired "pupil" had already learned how to maneuver his chess pieces where he most suited them.

"Very well, Master. I will ask no more of this." Reed gave a slight bow. This seemed to please his former mentor. Though he did not expect his request to be warranted such a careful thought, he knew he had to keep up the pretense. They continued their pace back to the festivities with Reed trailing behind. He snuck a quick glance back to see Lilian speaking with that scurrying sewer rat, Zachary. If only his Touched blood was stronger, perhaps he could discern what they were saying. Glancing back over to Christian, he decided to change the subject and his lover's mind.

Focusing his gaze upon young Tobias, who was ahead of the pair basking in the acclaim by the other vampires around him, Reed turned back to Christian and asked, "Is there any way I can then 'test out' your latest stud? He does show promise and that body begs to be put through its paces." Reed then stopped and grabbed Christian's hand. He bent over and kissed it. Reed raised his eyes to look direction into Christian's and gave a small smile, showing off his tapering fangs. He found such small tokens of respect offered much leverage to get where he wanted to be within his former master's graces. He knew what it took to broker his former master's favor. He hoped it would be enough to allow him to enact his secret plans.

Christian looked down at Reed and gave a wry smile. His former pet was persistent this night. A part of him wanted to give into Reed's request, but he knew he could not give him the satisfaction. He was the one who was selected to receive his new ward and to not initiate him was to show weakness. Besides, Christian felt there was no area that Reed exceeded him. "I see no reason for you to get the first test drive. My experience far outweighs your meager talents, my young man." Christian was getting a little testy, but it stirred excitement in him. His fangs, too, became erect. He hoped soon they would not be the only things searching for something to sink into.

"You misunderstand, my Lord." Reed lingered on the word "Lord" to feed into Christian's hunger to dominate him. Reed was not as weak or dumb as he wanted Christian to believe. "First of all, I do not wish to take him tonight for his first night should always be broken in by his new Master. There are new rules to learn...up close," Reed leaned into Christian's ear, closing in almost to whisper. Instead, he paused and gave Christian a slight lingering kiss on the cheek. "To learn how a decoy should act; how a decoy should blend in; how a decoy gathers intel; but most importantly, how to truly please his Master"

Reed's hand moved in to rest upon Christian's back. "He needs to learn this so that he can be convincing enough to fool the Untouched. He needs to learn from the best, as he's not going to learn it here under Lilian's guard. Why do you think I persuaded her to give him to you? I saw the potential in him that you could unlock, my Lord." Reed paused drowning him in compliments to allow Christian to grasp the importance of his words. "I would just like to make sure he is worthy enough. My task would be able to test what a quick learner he is under you. I wouldn't want him to fail you."

Christian turned to face his young protégé; his tall stature ensured his eyes would loom above Reed. "It is *my* judgment that decides if he succeeds or fails as a decoy, as he is deemed fit to be one by your Mistress. Yet somehow, you've taken it upon yourself to try and usurp my position in this coven. Do you think you can use that to maneuver your fangs into a governor's set? I have seen your balls myself and they are not that big. If you request this of me again, I will personally take it up with your Mistress. Is that understood?" Christian's anger started to bubble over into causing a scene. Already a few of the guests had turned to investigate the raised voices.

"Again, you misunderstand, my Lord," Reed replied in a dread whisper. He moved closer and grabbed Christian's crotch and squeezed. "You have no more business with my Mistress. She gives you an audience when *I* tell her to. If you so much as whisper any indication of treason about me towards her, I will bring your whole house down. You see, I have learned much from you, *Master.*" Reed released his grasp. The lieutenant took a moment to brush himself to appear more a gentleman. "I *ask* this favor of you. Do not make me demand it."

"I see, my love." Christian replied hesitating a little. He grazed Reed's arm with his hand before using it to claw into him. "I will concede, but I will expect payment for your request." Christian left Reed at his place. Reed gave a bow for a last parting gesture. He turned to the awaiting crowd and smiled to any still looking. He wondered how long he would have to wait until all these guests bowed to him instead.

****

Lilian tugged at Kitty's chain hard once before inquiring from Zachary the status of the quest she had sent him on. "Have you a progress report on your assignment?"

Zachary took pause and looked down at the newest pet. Lilian had never seen harm that having a pet present may entail when discussing Sector strategies. However, Zachary did. Secret meetings and whispers in shadowed hallways were his stock in trade. Once he saw the tattooing on the face, he realized that this must have been the "Kitty" he had heard about. She was the mute pet. Her handicap put him more at ease. Lilian noticed his obvious, though subtle, discomfort and just nodded at him to begin his report.

"Yes, my Mistress. Surveillance proves that she knows nothing of our society. She continues her visits to the store, but I have not made any formal contact. I await your orders on how to proceed. Am I clear in my understanding that I am to terminate her?" Zachary asked. It had been many years since an assassination had been contracted through this coven. This had to be a special request, although the request seemed to be coming straight from Lilian.

"Yes, you are to terminate the child. No need for any other contact other than the kill."

He nodded. "Understood. I did not want to proceed without an advisement from you, Mistress. I felt that any communication with the target would be unnecessary should that be the task at hand." Seeing the look of anger and disappointment in her eyes, he added, "I'll take care of everything right away. I promise not to fail you."

"Do not promise, just kill her! Do not bother soiling your hands with torture. For as much as I know you enjoy it, such an act is a luxury we cannot afford. Swift and clean is all that I require." she commanded.

"Yes, my Mistress." He paused to see if she had any reply. When enough silence confirmed permission to leave, he took her hand and kissed it, signing the contract on his mission. He moved back towards the main door of the parlor but stayed behind just out of sight. He stood by and watched her leave the Parlor by her secret path.

Zachary took out his cell phone and pulled his pictures. He did not know why he did not want to show the woman's picture to Lilian as proof that he had found the young woman, or even mention that he had Khira's sketchbook. There was something about this untouched human that designated her as special. Maybe Lilian's strong desire to having her executed just marked this uniqueness in her, but he doubted it. His curiosity of Lilian's strong desire for this girl's death was going to be a problem.

Chapter Six

Lilian watched her guests in boredom. Many of them she had sired herself and though each had her favor at one time or another, they now were deemed trash rather than worthy members of her coven. They did not understand the need to govern themselves so that their power may grow in excess. Most wanted power without having to do the work. They could not understand the maneuvers that allowed vampires to move into the positions that would soon answer all problems.

The endgame would reveal the answers for everything. Striking humans too soon could be a downfall for their kind, their culture, and their custom of living. However, these days it seemed their custom was living off her money. She often laughed when she heard the term "old money" because it was her money that was invested in Thirlestane. She never had to want for anything.

Her mansion was a mixture of the castle the town was named after and the Hugh Hefner mansion, what with as many scantily clad people roaming the property. She never missed her mortal coil when she had all this. The one she missed most was the thing she would never have, her sister, Lorelai. Many of the other Coven Leaders assumed she left the position of Governor open due to a longing for Liam Wallace, the only Touched to assume the position for the Southern Sector. However, she kept the position open to allow her lieutenants to be more competitive.

Lilian tugged at Kitty before dropping the chain all together. Still with no words, Kitty bowed before her dominatrix. "Very good, my child. Fetch me my cloak. You and I shall share some alone time tonight. I believe you have earned it." Kitty nodded before taking her leave.

As she left her mistress' side, the young boy approached and encircled Kitty in a dance-like movement blocking the pet's journey to her Mistress' desire. Lilian caught notice of this but wanted to test her pet's response. Kitty was focused on her mission and moved to avoid the boy and complete her task. The boy spun and twirled around Kitty, always seeming to obstruct her no matter where she turned. Kitty's eyes narrowed and with a hiss swiped at the boy. The boy smiled and twirled away every time she reached.

Once Lilian's distant approval was met, she snapped her fingers. The boy stopped in an instant. He pouted and then rushed to Lilian's side. Kitty continued on her way. "People do not always see your playful side, Matthew, but you will earn more respect by not playing with the pets. One day, you may be able to do as you please. You could even earn a pet of your own. Try to make steps towards progress before I have to tear your head off and toss you to be Sammie's lover in death." All of these words left Lilian's mouth before she even turned to face the child. "As much as you play in my heart, know this," she turned to look into his eyes. "I will have no remorse ending you in a heartbeat. You would be missed, but you have seen how easily those around me can be replaced."

****

Kitty went to the cloakroom where all the guest's coats were put away. She knew that the Mistress' cloak was kept here in a special closet. Finding the room, she opened the closet door but as she reached for the cloak, her arm was grabbed, and she was pulled inside. She gasped, but no scream emerged from her throat. She knew better.

Reed came up from behind her, pulling his body into hers. "You have proven yourself useful with your quickness. I knew you would please the Mistress, my dear Kitty." He could feel her heart beating against him, and her skin felt warm to the touch.

Though his grasp was not intended for anything sensual, but rather so that he could have her full attention and whisper his intent, he found he could not hold in his desire to pet her himself. Her back pressed into his chest and his hand hovered over her stomach, moving inch by inch up towards her breasts. She moaned even before he got right under them. He took his free hand and cupped her mouth, which almost betrayed her. His other hand squeezed her left nipple. She squirmed for a second then settled back into her perspective role as Reed's pet.

He took his hand off her mouth but not off her nipple. It pulsated between his fingers much like he knew he would make her lips pulsate later. She moved her hands onto him searching for a way to please him. Tempted, he knew better than to indulge himself. "No Kitty, you haven't much time before you are to return to her. I just wanted to tell you myself how pleased I am with you. Once my plan plays out, you will be rewarded beyond anything she can offer you. Remember this." He released his grasp on her and fled from the shrouded closet. Kitty paused to slow her heart and catch her breath. She felt a little wet already. She took the nearest coat and used the liner to clean herself. Once she felt that her body could not betray her to Lilian, she grabbed her mistress' cloak and went to return to her side.

****

The moonlight shone upon the flowers and trees, creating a beautiful scene. Lilian enjoyed taking midnight walks through her garden. The smell of jasmine and moonflowers perfumed the brisk air. Although covered with her cloak, the chill of the autumn Texas night was still able to decorate Lilian's skin with goose bumps. It was good to experience these sensations again or at least Lilian felt good enough to allow herself to enjoy them. Kitty bounced with each tread behind her. Lilian thought now was the time to test Kitty's loyalty. Even if this young, new pet should succeed, Lilian did not know if she would allow herself to trust her. Instead, she would allow the brief luxury of being in the moment. Small steps.

Lilian led her pet to a bench in a clearing. Kitty sat on the ground while Lilian took her place on the bench above her. "Tonight, I will tell you a story. This story is your gift and your gift alone. You are not allowed to share it with anyone. Do you understand?" Again, no words escaped Kitty. She looked up at Lilian with bright expressive eyes, nodded, and looked back down. The cold stung the pet's skin, and she began to shiver but still, she made no complaint. "Sit with me. I will share my cloak. I will give you a world to escape to, at least for a little while." Kitty stood up and sat next to Lilian, allowing her legs to drape over her mistress's lap, as Lilian wrapped Kitty in the warmth of her cloak. The pet could feel Lilian's body heat next to hers as one of Lilian's arms wrapped around Kitty's shoulders.

"Once, long ago, there were two beautiful little girls. These girls were identical twin sisters. They were so identical; in fact, they were almost as one person. These girls were as close as anyone could be with another person. They had a secret language all their own that they shared with no one. They challenged their friends to keep up with them at charades and other mind games. These sisters loved no one more than they loved each other, and they promised to stay together forever." Kitty found herself envisioning these little girls. She imagined them in detail.

Lilian's words were so hypnotic. Her vampire's voice enhanced her fable and impressed her mind upon Kitty. "One fanciful night, at a ball that the girls attended on their 16th birthday, one of the sisters received an offering from the gods. This gift was bestowed upon her through a young, handsome man. This would be the only time a male came between the sisters. The gifted girl decided to share this offering with her twin. However, the present was never hers to share. Mysteriously like a dream, her twin vanished. The girl did not know what she had done wrong. Had she received a gift or had she been cursed? It was something that would weigh on the thoughts of that special little girl all the rest of her days."

Lilian broke her train of thought to test her companion. "What do you think, my pet?" Kitty, still faraway in her vision, let one tear drop from her eye and laid her head down upon Lilian's chest. There was a moment of silence for the end of what Kitty thought was Lilian's fairy tale. Lilian concluded with, "Whatever the gods touch upon us is a gift. We are the ones tested on how we use this offering, and we must treasure it, much as I treasure you. Now come, let us go back so that we can warm you up properly." Kitty knew this was just another reward. She was always a quick learner.

****

After the party had pretty much concluded, Zachary headed towards his manor office within the parlor. A few guests lingered here and there in the halls, but most had gone before the rising of the sun. Some of the pets had started the massive cleanup effort to restore the mansion to its former perfection. These were newer pets and were forced to serve the menial tasks before they could be assigned to more suitable roles.

Zachary noticed that one of the female pets had short, wavy, light brown hair that was reminiscent of Khira's, minus the blue streaks. Dark thoughts began to stir that rivaled the lust he carried for his target. The girl's body was unlike Khira's, but it would do. He walked over to her and told her that she was finished for the night. She nodded and set her work aside. Postponing plans to fulfill Lilian's assassination request, he instead pulled the young girl into a nearby bedroom just beyond his office.

She lingered in the doorway while he stood over by the bed. He motioned her to enter with a wave of his hand. "On your knees," he demanded of this pet. She obeyed. "You will look up at me when you take my pants off for me. Pull the zipper with your teeth, girl." Again, she followed his instructions to the tee.

After she removed his pants, he sat at the edge of the bed and closed his eyes, envisioning that Khira had replaced this pet. "Make me hard," he commanded through a slight whisper. The girl, sitting on her feet, took his sex into her hands and started stroking him. He felt himself get a little hard, but still not to the stage he wanted. The pet sensed this and pulled up onto her knees. She took his cock and placed it into the fold between her breasts. While bouncing up and down, the pet succeeded at bringing him to a full erection without knowing that images of Khira managed to do a better job than she could.

Zachary brushed her hair with his hands. He then grabbed at the tresses and used them to control her head while forcing himself into this pet's mouth. She seemed experienced. She did not seem to have a gag reflex. He wondered if Khira had the same kind of talent.

The thought trickled with another image of Khira with blood draping her body. Zachary felt a thirst for his target. He looked down and realized this girl before him could not suffice for Lilian's foe. Anger for both his Mistress and his target raged within. Zachary pulled the pet towards him and drilled down her throat. He lingered for a few seconds until he heard her suffocating as his cock blocked her from taking any air through her mouth or her nose. He pulled her off him. She looked up at him. "Beg for it," he demanded.

Before she could finish saying please, he pulled her closer to him. He rocked her head back and forth over his erection. She began to moan. The pet swallowed every bit of his cum, and then smiled up at him. His illusion vanished as he focused on her face. His reflection in a mirror on the wall caught his attention.

Disgusted by what he saw, disgusted with the fact that Lilian's request almost deemed him as nothing more than an errand boy, disgusted that it was not Khira before him, he picked up a nearby Waterford vase and threw it shattering both bodies of glass. The pet retreated to a corner, alarmed. Zachary became more upset by this and growled at her. She shook with fear. Zachary redressed and left the room unsatisfied, despite his spent lust. He closed the door to the bedroom and sat at his desk. Time to plan Khira's demise.

Chapter Seven

Khira put on her headphones, turned back at the house to give a mental "fuck you" salute. She had woken up from the same dream that she had had every night that week and it was started to strain on her already bitchy mood. She avoided her cousin on her exodus, but the thought of their strained relationship raised Khira's stress level. The previous night's escapade was shorter lived than the actual sex session. She required a different train of thought, an improved escape of this world. She needed new inspiration. On top of that she needed her sketchbook.

She pushed play on the music app on her phone and Suicidal Tendancies' "Feel like Shit....Déjà Vu" lyrics mirrored her distracted mind. Her thoughts could not escape the dream. She felt pulled by both the woman and the man. However, they both lost her with discussions of Lions. While the imagery of the sea and broken glass sand had been so vivid that she could smell copper from the traces of blood left behind in the footprints, her morbid mind preferred other horror themed reveries.

She made her way towards The Historian's Hideaway. Khira checked the time on her phone. While it was a decent time for any normal day, she began to wonder if the bookstore would be open on a Saturday. She attempted to support local businesses as much as possible, but weekend trips almost made that impossible to know if the shops would be open. She hit skip a couple of times on the player before deciding to rest upon "Funtime" by Iggy Pop.

As she crossed a nearby street on her way to the bookstore, Khira collided into a handsome stranger, who had turned the corner. "Don't you watch where you're going, you moron?" Khira sighed at the stranger.

"Sorry, I just make it a habit to make those around me uncomfortable in any manner possible and today I decided to start with you," he replied without missing a beat.

Khira took a judgmental glance in his direction. The sun was behind him so a cheesy halo effects casted around him. She could not look into his eyes. They were protected by Oakley aviator sunglasses. Did anyone wear those anymore? There was something familiar about him, but she could not quite place the reason why. "Maybe you should invest your time in learning how-to walk in order to break that nasty habit."

The stranger walked off without any more comments. She tilted her head, pausing as he was headed in the same direction she was going. She flipped him off, not caring if he noticed that it seemed she was following him.

Her earbuds had fallen out due to the collision. As she placed them in, The Pretty Reckless' "House on a Hill" began the last chorus.

While Khira knew the song, she never remembered having added the song to any playlist. She paused at the side of the building to get in proper music mode. The piano opening to Hey Violet's "Unholy" blasted out. Khira was back on track to retrieve her treasure.

Zachary's thoughts of torture again filled his head after having to deal with Khira's attitude from the collision. He assumed she was headed towards his bookstore for her sketchbook. He would have little time to regroup. *Soon*, he thought of getting the chance to torture her.

****

Soft blues and greys from monitor screens filled a dark room. What could have been conceived as one giant monitor, was in fact 10 monitors embedded within the wall behind a desk. A young raven beauty sat facing them. Her eyes were clouded over in a red haze. Her head moved back and forth, as if scanning each monitor.

One monitor was fixed showing a couple of men, dragging a large bag behind them. The men walked down a corridor and appeared to come to a large metal wall. There was a strip of black within the middle of the wall. One man, shirtless showing large tan muscles adorned by tribal tattoos, stepped aside the bag, and began to fumble within. A leg plopped out. It flayed with a small spasm before returning to a stop. The man pulled the rest of the body out of the bag. He looked up at the other man.

The other man was dressed in black t-shirt with illegible writing on the back. He remained looking at the wall, as if determining measurements. His head moved back and forth, scanning the wall.

The tan man pulled out another body, or at least pieces of another body. It appeared as if he called to his associate either for assistance or simply to move out of the way. The dressed man, removed the remaining pieces from the bag. The bag hadn't been filled just with body parts but also wooden pieces. The two men began dressing the wall.

The female voyeur focused on another monitor. A bystander could have mistaken the scene to a scene from any of the *Paranormal Activity* movies as the colors displayed were black and white and the shot focused on a nursery. An Asian couple were putting together a baby's crib. The woman had a slight bump to her abdomen but did not appear to be close to delivery. After a few minutes, the woman needed and sat in a nearby rocker, allowing the man to take charge of the rest of the assembly.

Once satisfied with the Asian family, the woman's returned to a monitor to the lower right-hand corner. A bedroom adorned with purple and cream accents was in view. A computer desk was set a few feet from a queen size bed. A plump woman sat Indian style on the comforter with a couple of books spread out. She had one book within her grasp, contently reading the contents. Lights within the room flickered with a crystalline aura. The lights popped back and forth, sometimes hovering so close to the young female on the bed. Yet, the watcher already knew what had been written within the books.

The voyeur's eyes swirled from the cloudy status back to a greenish hue. As the eyes focused back to the original color of the iris, the woman brought her right hand up to push her raven locks behind the blue headband guarding her ear. She snapped her fingers, and her office became lit with a soft yellow glow. She gave a brief sigh before spinning her chair around to face her desk. A stack of pastel-colored papers sat at the left-hand side of her desk.

With a twist of her wrist, one lavender piece wiggled its way from the stack, swept up and landed in the woman's hand. She reviewed it before setting it down and scribbling some symbols on top of it. A small, silver, rectangle pad began to buzz. She picked up the device.

After a quick glance, she centered herself for some extra strength. It had only been a couple of days since her last vision of her death by the claws of a werewolf. For now, all she could do was put a leash on Max.

She produced a greater sigh before muttering under her breath, "Some things must only be controlled by me." She stood up from her chair. As she walked towards the door of her office, Ruby hovered her hand near her headband and activated a device in her ear. "Lisa, please have Marcus, Ethan, Ben and Lawrence meet me outside of Max's office. Thank you."

"Right away, Miss Kharas," answered the voice on the other side.

She removed the device and set it down on a shelving unit near the door. As she closed the door behind her, a shuffling noise came from inside. She smiled knowing that the device had returned to her desk and that the papers had been disposed of by the little helpers of Brânswood.

****

The drapes were drawn in Lilian's bedroom; a golden duvet rested on top of a California king sized mattress and a hand crafted white knitted blanket was folded neatly at the foot of her bed. She sat at her vanity while Kitty brushed her hair with a bronze brush decorated with an etched tree dyed red with white bristles often getting lost within Lilian's ivory hair. Thoughts and fears began to swarm the matriarch. Her paranoia and anxiety bested the Mistress. "Leave me Kitty. Fetch me my breakfast, but take your time returning." Lilian kissed her pet's hand, while Kitty bowed.

Once the door closed behind her latest charge, Lilian withdrew two of her diaries and a quill from a hidden space; one, a current record of her deeds and the other, a journal that contained memories of her dear sister. Lorelai may have passed, but Lilian would continue to keep the twin sister she knew and loved alive. That would have to wait. First, she needed to collect her thoughts on Khira.

The decision to kill the human girl would make things easier for Lilian in the long run. If people knew of Khira's family secret, Lilian feared that her reign would come to its end. Lilian thought first that she should take care of the task herself but knew too many questions would arise as to why she was performing an assassin's task. The Independent Sector disappointed her before so Zachary would have to take care of it. She must believe her Lieutenant would not cause a second failure. She had to trust him although to be honest, she trusted no one, including herself. Even without meeting Khira, Lilian had learned that the girl could destroy the whole legacy.

Lilian took the quill and pricked her finger. Ever since she turned, she had kept her diaries in her own blood. She had new life and since her handwriting would not change, she needed something more dramatic to notate this experience. She recorded the date. Before she could transcribe her thoughts, she needed to leave a few drops of blood in the bowl before her finger would heal. Afterwards, she brought her finger to her mouth out of habit, a holdover from her human life. She then began her journal.

No gods or stars, nor any other mystical being will keep me away from the task at hand. I will regret not knowing her as my sister knew her. However, my heart no longer bears enough love or energy to shred the power that has consumed my soul. That power proves more of an elixir of life than the precious blood that I feed upon. Absolute power feeds my life-force. My sister can no longer protect her or this legacy. As Liam taught me long ago, I must take charge of my fate.

Khira, my dear, you have no choice in this matter. Your mother sealed your fate with your very existence. You walk upon a plane in which you do not belong, a ghost in this world. I will correct the mistake that your mother made in bringing you into this world. Just as I had no choice upon my fate to become one of the Touched, I cannot lose what I have built for myself with the help of those who granted me this Gift. I will not take anything for granted. Let this diary provide you your only legacy. My word will determine your life or death.

Lilian felt herself getting angry and losing any mental balance she held. She closed the book, her finger already healed. She would not take the blame in this matter. She gave Lorelai the Gift. How dare she turn her back on their love, their bond! Even the others of the Touched did not come close to the power they held as sisters or even beyond that, as twins. Zachary should have taken care of things by now and she would no longer have the stress weigh upon her brow. She planned for Kitty to take her mind off such things.

****

Once at The Historian's Hideaway, Khira made her way to the customer service desk at the front of the store. Khira looked around, almost expecting the Goth wannabe the day before to still be perusing the pages of the Vampire books. She told the woman at the desk, her dilemma and the customer service employee believed that the store may have the sketchbook on hand but would have to look for it. Khira turned from the desk and started to roam the store.

Soon she heard her name called and Khira returned to the desk. Her attitude presented itself when she snatched up her book and headed towards the exit where she bumped into the stranger from before.

"If I didn't know better, I'd swear you were stalking me, Miss. Is this your way of apologizing for the rude finger gestures? I'd say you still need to work on your technique," Zachary told Khira. She was able to get a better look at the man. His eyes were a grayish blue and even without the sun creating a halo, his hair remained golden. She was curious how he would have known about her flipping him off if his back had been towards her.

"I was already here. You're the new one to the party. By the way, your nametag stating, 'My name is Mr. Stalker.' is missing. Besides, in some countries, certain hand gestures can convey compliments." Khira began to enjoy this wordplay with the stranger.

"Let's say that it's the gods that are the stalkers, leading this meeting to be fated," he replied to her comment. "The name is Zachary Duvall. I'm actually the owner of this store." He shot his hand out for an introductory handshake.

She ignored the civilized gesture and started to leave, "Free will is the way to go these days. Fate is so overrated."

He decided to play one more move to try and stop her. "Well, we could always debate it over dinner. Let's say the Mexican joint at the corner of Main Street and 7th Avenue? What do you say, Miss...." He made the pause so that she could fill in the blank with her name. Zachary didn't need to know her name but wanted to play his cards just right in this farce.

Khira paused in her escape and surveyed Zachary to see if a free dinner would be worth it. He was good eye candy. Fuck it. What the hell? Not like she has anything else better to do, she concluded, "I'll meet you there later tonight at 8:30." She proceeded to leave.

"Do I get a name?" He asked again, hoping that his portrayal of a gentleman was perfect.

"Get through dinner first. Then maybe you will earn a name," she answered never looking back at him. He could not help smiling. Good, this *will* be a fun cat and mouse game.

Chapter Eight

Khira returned to the house almost expecting the state of quietness that she had left it in. However, noise from the kitchen meant that Paige was back in the real world or at least her small part of it. The clattering of plates and then their obvious breakage sung out followed by multiple curses from her cousin. Khira was surprised by how many of those words Paige knew considering that her cousin did not have a way to stay in contact with people outside the household besides her website. Although, Khira would not necessarily describe the perverts who subscribed to the site as *people*.

As she walked in, Khira saw her cousin trying to reach for a pot from the top shelf. "Ever thought about bringing a chair over to help out with that height problem?" Khira retorted.

Paige ignored the comment while the pot seemed to float a little closer to her fingers. Khira went and sat down to spend a little time, attempting to be humane to her cousin. Paige continued to pay Khira no heed as she began to fill the pot with water to cook some fettuccine noodles for her famous Montegomery Turkey Spinach Pasta plate for dinner. Paige already had some ground turkey and mushrooms sizzling in a nearby pan. Without turning to look at her cousin, she told Khira, "I see you picked up something from your exodus this morning."

"Not much of an excursion. Rather a rescue mission. My sketchbook was being held captive by a gorgeous local merchant," Khira replied. "You better plan on leftovers from tonight, roomie. Some of us still have a social life. In fact, I probably should go change into something a little more 'inspiring' for tonight." Khira headed upstairs to start getting ready for her date with Zachary.

After Paige got the water to start boiling, she went over to the junk drawer and peeked to see if Khira had returned downstairs. She removed the hidden journal from the drawer and sat at the kitchen table. Paige opened the notebook back to the tenth page and continued reading. She knew that once Khira left for her date, the secret stash could be hers a little while longer before returning them to the proper owner. What Khira didn't know wouldn't kill her.

****

When I was younger, I admit that I had reveries of falling in love. I am not jealous that my sister has found a perverse ideology of passion. That devil will not tread on the bond we created and evolved since the womb. Instead, he darkens her heart against the good I know remains within.

Now, I now feel like I must walk this world alone, emptied from a part of my heart since she has given hers to another. I will never bare a child. I will never hunger for anything other than that crimson life force.

I have come to hate this existence and wish to end it. My upbringing and my twin sway my hand from such a drastic measure.

Liam states that we must track our lineage. I believe this to be for his ego more than the organization of what he deems as the Touched. He assures us that we are not alone, but we only have his word as gospel. I was one to always question Father's teaching from the good book. I am not bound to accept that monster for his promises.

Liam has heard of a certain creature like us but different all the same, that has the reputation in the studies of genealogy. He hopes that this "man" will help in his quest to tie down a true bloodline. I do not know of the need. I do not see myself siring anyone. I would not wish this curse onto my enemies let alone anyone I would spend forever with. Lilian is so enamored by Liam, she would do as is told. I am an island here. My tears flood my world. As much as I have addressed my fears to my twin, she no longer hears my words.

I hope that my journey will lead to a true desired life to where I will once again be human. I no longer wish to be a mother. I no longer see myself standing beside a husband. I just wish to be in the arms of mortality once more.

****

As Khira closed her bedroom door, she found herself excited about tonight's date with *Zachary*, the owner of The Historian's Hideaway. She attempted to picture him as a Zac, but his presence in her mind demanded the formal name. She went over to her stereo on her dresser to put on some mood music to help determine what persona she would take on for the Cantina.

Between flipping through songs and her mind racing with different outfits she had worn in the past for dates, she could not help but feel like she did not need to hide behind a mask for Zachary. She closed her eyes and recalled his features. He was not typical of the men she would attract at the clubs or local spots. He felt more refined and confident.

She settled on the Scarlett Johannson's cover of Tom Waits' "Falling Down." The downhearted tune settled her mind as thoughts drifted between Zachary and her mother. While Khira could find some solace in arms of one-night stands and different personas, she found little peace in herself. She felt cursed to follow her mother's depression down a rabbit hole to no end. She had read somewhere that mental illnesses could be hereditary but did not want to inherit anything other than her mother's eyes and her father's smile.

Khira attempted to lighten the music up by switching it to a song from her Vampire Weekend folder. While the tune was upbeat, the words were still a little bit unnerving with seriousness. Ezra Koenig belted out religious undertones regarding unbelievers. Khira pushed the lyrics beyond her ears and focused on the upbeat tempo to get her attire date ready.

She grabbed a shirt and some scissors to create something more her style. She had chosen the rest of her wardrobe minus some shoes. After finding the perfect pair of thigh high Converse stylized heals at the bottom of her closet, Khira returned to her main room to find her stereo had betrayed her by switching back to a sad melody. She sat at her vanity while female voices crooned through a cover of Peter Gabriel and Kate Bush's duet, "Don't give up." Without a brisk tempo, Khira faced the lyrics head on. She let the words wash over her like a baptism while she set aside a pallet of eye shadows, she would adorn on her lids. She became hesitant to begin to don the cosmetic, as the words gripped her heart. Khira embraced the song in defiance, not wanting to cry like her mother always would.

After finishing applying water-proof mascara, she dressed her lips with a cerise stain. Either the music player had a glitch or the file she had downloaded had doubled the song because The Pierces began to sing the lyrics to "Don't Give Up" once more. *Ghost in the Machine,* Khira thought, feeling a closeness to her deceased mother despite the strained relationship. She hovered her hand over different perfumes on top of the counter. Khira recognized one of the bottles but did not recall ever buying the scent that was her mother's favorite. Maybe Paige had in passing struck on a hidden memory of Eve and gifted the cologne to Khira.

She brought the bottle up to her nose. Khira's memories dipped into a pool and brought the fight from that last night up to the surface. She could not dwell on the recollection for too long. She was a strong woman, stronger due to the past occurrences.

She gave some spritzes to the air and leaned into the aroma as the words, "You're not beaten yet," rang into the air. Khira flashed a seductive smile into her mirror. Zachary would not be able to resist her. The poor man had no clue what to expect from her tonight.

****

Kitty stepped into the parlor room. She was supposed to be in the kitchen but made the detour. She had an ulterior mission and needed to be quick. Making sure she was not seen, Kitty went up to one of the bodies hanging from the wall. The body hung limp on a St Andrew's cross, unconscious. She hoped she would be able to awaken him and that he would be lucid enough to understand her. She grasped him and held him close. After what seemed an eternity, he awoke.

"They have found her," Kitty started in a small whisper to the shadowed figure hanging in the parlor room. She coughed a little and found her voice again. It had been so long she could not remember when she spoke last. "Mistress is having her put to death," she gave pause, looking to see if anyone was around. "Would Brânswood not frown upon this interfering more than what was assigned? Max has not been in touch since I was brought in. He was not even there when Ruby gave me this assignment. She made no mention of you being here. Have we not become pawns ourselves?"

The figure did not say anything aloud but coughed. A body passed by in the doorway of the parlor. After a few seconds, she attempted to speak, but was cut short.

The man began in a whisper, "Yes, Brânswood has its own rules and reputations to live by. However, they are not as innocent as all Untouched should be. Our actions in this appointment we have been given will correct the mistakes of the evil deeds Brânswood has allowed to transpire as you taught me to believe." He tried to cough again, but this time his throat was too dry to produce any spit to help lubricate the sound. Instead, a drop of blood slipped from the corner of his mouth.

He took a deep breath, pausing as if collecting thoughts that seemed just beyond his grasp. He then continued. "The sense you have to question the Sanctuary makes you brave and not weak, as they would want you to be. Do not let *any* of your masters catch the scent of this. You have surpassed any hope that I could have had for our mission, my dear Kitty."

She could not help but smile, in a sad gesture, at her teacher. Flynn used to often compliment his students into submission, using honey rather than whipping words. "We will be the dark angels of this world, hiding in the shadows, dropping the veil so that the light of purity will shine into our world and desecrate the evil that lies before us..." Flynn's words faded to a whisper as he lost consciousness. Kitty's heart wanted to reach out to him. His sanity had begun to fade.

The torture was getting to him. He was older than she and did not own the endurance of her youth. She hoped that he would hold out and keep his secrets for a while longer. There was still much to do. She did not know how much more strength she could display towards her teacher. Kitty lowered her eyes and kissed his feet.

"I must get to the kitchen soon before they notice my delay. As much as I'm enjoying the punishments, it is better to get punished pleasing the Mistress rather than fester her anger. Take care, Teacher." She left the hung man there in his condemnation. He continued to mumble, as if she had not taken her leave after all. Kitty wiped a small tear from her face. She made for Lilian's secret side exit to leave without a trace.

****

Khira arrived at the restaurant. She had been able to avoid Paige when she left the house. Paige must have locked herself away with her pasta. Khira was thankful as not to feel any judgmental looks from her cousin on tonight's attire. She thought she looked normal or at least normal for her. She was wearing tight, low-rise black jeans. She had already taken the time to tailor down the Depeche Mode 101 shirt to fit her frame and to present a little midriff. She would still fit in at the local hole-in-the-wall Mexican cantina. She could sure use a margarita or even a Corona. With her hankering for Enchiladas Suizas, the whole thing sounded just about perfect.

She laughed to herself thinking back to when her mother tried to teach her how to cook. As much as Khira always wanted to please her mother with each lesson, cooking was never a subject she would pass. She took the car keys for the Camero her aunt had left for Paige and headed to the restaurant.

Arriving outside the entrance, she stopped, took a deep breath, and opened. The place was pretty much as she expected. Red, white and green colors were displayed everywhere in salute to its "authentic" Mexican heritage. A small ceramic fountain was by the door with shiny pennies sparkling from beneath the rippling water. Most of the furniture was made of Formica or covered in plastic and scratchy Mariachi music blazed out an old speaker somewhere. It reminded her of a place she went to down in South Texas once.

She decided to go sit by the bar and wait for Mr. New Guy there. This was not the first time that Khira decided on a whim, to go out for a free dinner with some stranger she met on the street. *You only have one life and if you have your guard up, why shouldn't you at least enjoy a free meal from time to time*, she thought to herself. As soon as she placed her order for a Corona, her guest walked in.

Zachary headed straight to her without pause. He took her beer bottle as soon as it hit the bar and brought it to his lips. She just gave him a puzzled look. He looked over to the bartender and ordered, in Spanish, a margarita on the rocks without salt, made with Patrón Tequila, Grand Marnier and an extra twist of lime. "You know you wanted a margarita instead," he whispered to her. He was right. Still, his arrogance was unneeded. She would have gotten mad at him, but she was more puzzled on how he knew how she ordered her margarita?

When her drink arrived, Zachary turned to the bartender and said something before pointing to the table he led her to. He pulled the chair out for her, but before he allowed her to sit down, he took a napkin from the middle of the table to wipe down her chair. Yes, it was that kind of place, where bottle rings were on the table and bits of nacho chips were left on the chairs. This gentlemanlike action more than made up for the beer.

A waiter brought a tray of water, chips and two different salsas, one green and one red. "Muchas gracias," Zachary replied. He turned to Khira, "I hope that is enough Spanish to impress you, because that's all I know." A grin helped her ease into a laugh. "Good, you can laugh." She was thankful that the waiter had returned to take their orders and interrupted any response she could have given. More laughs came when they ended up ordering the same items. *Seems like he may be related to that New Jersey psychic or something,* she thought.

"I do converse with people. I have been known to laugh on occasion. I just tend to prefer hiding out on my own. Which is why your bookstore is appropriately named," Khira responded once the waiter had left. "While I socialize, I tend to keep to myself due to the loss of my family. I was young when my parents and my brother died. Hiding in books or my sketches have always been associated with my grieving," she said sipping her margarita. She didn't know why she was providing him with so much insight to her life. It was one thing to not be truthful at a club, but you also did not want to be truthful to a total stranger you just met off the street! Rules meant you did not bring baggage to the first date.

"Try some of the green salsa," he recommended. He looked at her, seeming to sense her apprehension. "I didn't ask you anything and you didn't tell me anything. It will all be ok," he said with reassurance. She stared back at him confused. He just looked at her with his bluish grey eyes and smiled. She got that familiar feeling again. *Déjà vu,* they called it. Maybe she was just remembering his eyes from when they met in the bookstore.

"What do you do when you aren't clumsy enough to bump into helpless girls?" she asked in hopes of getting the focus back on him. Men often preferred talking about themselves on dates anyway.

"I don't know if I would call you helpless," Zachary stated with a smirk. "Well, as you know, I own the bookstore. You see, I don't work much. So, I let people with greater passion earn my money for me." She was resigned to blink in response. He saw he was losing her. He could see her curiosity of him not asking for her name again was what kept her interested. "That's my day job. My night job is whisking away women and boring them with idle small talk. But really, I don't consider either one my job. I eat, sleep, let others count my money and just have them let me know which charities are the ones half my money goes to. Occasionally, I go peek in on what society is doing, but that's to mock them later." That got a laugh out of her. Soon after their laughs subsided, dinner had arrived.

Chapter Nine

After breakfast with Kitty, Lilian glid down the halls of her domain heading towards the parlor room. Reed was already down there preparing a new Familiar. Matthew told her this young man, this latest Familiar, looked as if he had stepped out of a classical epic saga. It was rare for her to be impressed with a simple description, but at both Reed's and Matthew's insistences, she came down to the parlor to judge for herself. In truth, she was glad for the distraction. With the delay of status from Zachary, she could use a moment's respite. Watching the Familiars get trained usually granted a small pleasure.

She entered the chamber and passed through the circle of initiates bound and donned black hoods, waiting to be processed as Familiars. The Mistress' minions were already subjecting older Familiars to more endurance trials. One dark-skinned woman was bound sideways and suffered from numerous minute cuts all over her body. Her blood seeped out from her wounds like tears betraying eyes and pooled below her in a special collector. Just before she would pass out from the pain, another cut was given. Every minute she endured; nutrients were fed into her via intravenous needles. Further on, Lilian spied another girl, this one dark of hair and pale of skin, enduring the sexual demands of a Touched soldier and his pet. She was bent over a special frame with much of her body bound by a harness. Her nipples were clamped, and her mouth gave pleasure to the vampire's throbbing cock. His pet explored her back passage with a strapped-on phallus.

Someone else caught Lilian's eye, or a small tattoo on the chest of an older man stole Lilian's attention. He was bound upon a wooden cross in a ritualistic manner, his head was covered with black velvet sack and was collared in a way that restricted him to draw shallow breaths. On his chest was the tattoo of a Crow's talon. Lilian recognized the symbol but did not alert the soldier torturing the old coot. Already his master had aroused him and supped upon his erection. Small cuts upon the shaft added to its robust flavor. The Familiar quivered and strained for air. His torturer swallowed the man's dick and stroked his own member in rhythmic pulses. Lilian paused fascinated by the display. Her own flesh tingled, and her distress now seemed a distant memory. In a strangled gasp, the Familiar came, his hot bloody cum spraying into his master's mouth. Not a drop was wasted.

Licking his lips, the Vampire spotted Lilian. He bowed and spoke to her. "Majesty," he replied. Lilian nodded, satisfied that the taskmasters were performing their duties. Before she took her leave, Lilian leaned into the old man and whispered so that her words would only be heard by him. "You will never see the sanctuary again." A whimper came as the body shivered and then went limp. His torturer poked at the body, but the man was dead. The vampire nodded to a younger soldier to clear the cross as to start the process on one of the initiates waiting. Lilian moved towards Reed.

Finding him at the end of the chamber, she could see him engaged with his new plaything. From what she could see, his claims about the new Familiar were true. The slave's hair consisted of long blonde locks and his body was well toned and muscled. A few tattoos decorated his skin but they were tasteful and accentuated his form rather than detracted from it; none of the tribal messes from the Independent sectors or that ran rampant on so many of the familiars that they had picked up back in the 90s. Not one of the tattoos symbolized that he too was a spy. He was stripped and seemed to be unconscious. Reed was fastening metal shackles to the Familiar's wrists and ankles causing the slave to straddle and exhibit his thick cock.

Reed, ever the perfectionist, took his time and enjoyed the moment. Lilian took pleasure in watching both men and speculating at what was to come. "And who is our latest guest," she inquired, after approaching behind her Lieutenant Governor. Her voice startled Reed, but he was swift to recover. He had not noticed when Lilian came into the room.

"He is my tribute to you, my beloved queen. I have dubbed him, 'Malcolm', after one of my favorite television characters." he replied.

Lilian's expression grew curious. "Does this man resemble this 'Malcolm'?"

"Ah, no, my queen, he does not. His appearance resembles the 'Mighty Thor' from Marvel Comics more, in my opinion; however, he does have Malcolm's spirit. The character of Malcolm was a passionate adventurer and anti-hero. He often befell trouble in his quest for wealth and glory, much as this one did in his acquisition." Reed checked the ties and manacles and nodded his approval that they were secure. "I will torture him much as Malcolm was tortured. I think you will enjoy it, my liege," he said with a smile.

"Television, Reed? Comic books? Really, you must stop indulging in these modern mediums," she said with a smile of her own. She ran a finger down "Malcolm's" chest, outlining his muscles.

A small cough from Reed disturbed her pondering as he stepped between her and the Familiar. "If you'll permit me, I must prepare him for you, my Mistress," Reed prefaced before grasping the boy's neck. He applied pressure to the neck just under the ear with his thumb, as if taming a cat. The boy still seemed not to move. However, to Reed's trained senses, he could see that he was not unconscious. It seemed that "Malcolm" was playing dead in the hopes that maybe he was in a dream. So much the better, thought Reed. He so enjoyed live prey. Reed went to pinch one of Mal's testicles, but Lilian was quick to restrain his hand.

"No. Leave Malcolm to me. He needs no preparation for my touch. He needs a firm hand up front," she said grasping Malcolm's testicles and giving them a firm squeeze. The pained gasp from the man's lips verified his conscious state and dispelled his delusion of dreaming. "Fetch Kitty from the kitchens," she told Reed. "She would do well to remember where she had come from and where she could go back should she disappoint."

For a moment, Reed made to contradict her and pout in his displeasure but before his lower lip stuck out, he smiled instead. He made a quick bow and headed out of the room. He started to hum a song by a local group named Dare Dick and the Purple Thurples. Reed started to sing the lyrics to "Nothing Lights My Soul Like a Little Doctor Foster." Lilian heard the words from her Lieutenant Governor's mouth of "She was the type of girl Stan Lee envisioned in the darkest realms of his dreams, yet she was real to the touch," as he made his exit from the Parlor Room.

Once Reed was gone, Lilian went to work. She slapped the new Familiar hard across the face, "Your act does not convince me that you can make it through your new education, my dear." Malcolm looked into her eyes and did not reply. She clutched his jaw with one hand and held it within a firm grasp. "You are no longer of your own life. You are now living my life. You reside now in my home. You breathe my air when I allow it. I am your Mistress. I am your Goddess. You are now a part of me. I control you as I control the fingers that dig into your flesh. Once your education is complete, then you will be rewarded. If you perform well, you can become not only yourself again, but perhaps something greater. If all goes perfect, you will become your own god."

****

After dinner, Khira excused herself to go wash up. It was not a sanitary issue or even a biological reason, but a reason to give her time to play judge and jury. Had he earned her name or even earned the right to take her out again? She waited outside the door of the unisex bathroom. All classy Mexican restaurants had them. Why else would there be a line to get in? She entered when it was her turn and once alone went over to the sink and started washing her hands. She looked at the mirror.

Mirror Khira always gave the best advice. "So...what do you think?" she asked of her reflection. Her image was quiet and thoughtful, as usual. "You're right. There's something off about him." For the life of her, she could not imagine what that could be. He had said the right things and was so handsome. Yet, she felt déjà vu in that she had somehow already met this guy countless of times before, but without it being like, "Here we go again, another loser". Zachary was different. He knew things about her that she had forgotten about herself. Yes, she decided. He had earned her real name and not just a club name. Should he decide to take her out again, yes she would go. Nodding in satisfaction to her reflected doppelganger, who agreed with her, she dried her hands and headed to the door. When she opened it, she was surprised that Zachary was right there. "Did the salsa go straight through you as well?" she said with a smile and a laugh.

He did not reply, but instead pushed her back into the bathroom and stepped inside. With one swift motion, he locked the door just before rushing her, knocking her against a far wall. He loomed over her, his eyes almost glowing. He darted his left hand to serve as a guard over her mouth. His right hand grabbed her wrists with her palms out towards him. He pulled her closer to him to whisper into her ear and in doing so, felt her fingertips brush against his crotch. "This isn't my choice or yours, realize this. However, you are fated for this tonight. Accept it and the dream will float on to heaven along with your soul. I'm sorry, but I don't think there will be a second date, my sweet."

The more he planned what to do to her, the harder his sex became, and before he knew it his fangs were engaged. He continued holding onto her wrists but removed his left hand and suffocated Khira's moaning with his own mouth. The whole elaborate maneuver appeared more like a dance move, had anyone had the misfortune to happen upon them. He reached his left hand up under her shirt and grabbed her breast. She had not been wearing a bra nor had she needed one as her young supple chest perked up for him. His mouth hungered over hers and he could taste the sweet spice of her that came from more than just her meal. Her mouth moved in sync with his. If he had not known better, he could have sworn she was kissing him back.

As if reading his thoughts, she wrapped her leg around his and tried to trip him to the ground. This did not seem to be a defensive maneuver, but if she was not going to have a choice in the matter then she wanted to dominate the situation. He released his grip, as he slowed himself down as he fell against the floor, touching his back against upon the tile. Khira dropped to her knees, straddling Zachary. She pulled off her top exposing both breasts and erected nipples to him. She leaned over. With her right hand, she ran her fingers through his hair and proceeded to grab him by it and pull him up to suck on her nipples. Instead, he bit them. He had meant to be gentle with his bite, but his fangs betrayed him. How could he kill her now when she was the one torturing him? The agony intensified as he realized he was not inside her. Then the answer came down as if from the gods. The skin on her breast broke and as if having an orgasm itself, blood started to leak. As soon as a drop landed on his tongue, he knew he could have all the time in the world with her. He knew she would turn. He pushed her off him.

She stood and staggered back to the wall. His pause set confusion into her. But soon he was pulling at her pants. No clothing had come off him. With no bra, there was no need to wear any matching panties. Her shaven sex seemed to glow to his eyes. He pulled her back off the wall and laid her on her back. Her jeans were intertwined around her calves, trapped by the thigh high heels. He pushed her bound feet up and over his neck, leaning her legs over his shoulders. He swooped in fast, plunging his tongue to lap up her wetness.

She tried to reach out to him but found she could not move from the pleasure he gave. He turned his head and focused his fangs into her upper thigh biting hard into her. As his erection hardened within his pants, he released his venom within her veins. With the bite, he reached his right hand up to stroke her. She already pulsated, as he found her clit and pushed her over the first climax. He retracted his fingers and was ready to enter her when the outside world started to penetrate inward. There was a hard knock at the door.

****

Max slumped over in his desk; his body contorted in an odd fashion. He was gripping onto the edge of the desk as if hanging on the edge of a cliff. His claws dug into the wood. He fought this change with all his might.

He could feel the irritating itch burn at the back of his neck. He did not dare scratch it because his nails were already at full length. The change was very painful even although he had been living with this part of his race his entire life. It was worse when it was occurring like this, at an unexpected time. The full moon had no sway on him. His transitions seemed to be set to an alternate calendar.

The grey hairs on his back and scalp already started to grow out darker and thicker, at a quick speed. The wrinkles buried into the years of his face started to smooth out while his nose started to protrude. His chest burned and quaked. His ribs crackled as they grew and spread into a new form. His ears lengthened and Max already could hear that people were on their way to confine him. His back began arching and his left hind leg kicked back his old trustworthy chair. He attempted to remove himself from the desk. He tried to stand but failed. He dropped onto the floor and scurried to a dark corner.

Max's door swung open, and a raven-haired beauty stood entered his office. Her eyes scanned the room. Her olive skin blended with the shadows to give her an ethereal look. The flowing emerald Grecian gown she wore lent credence to this. All in all, she seemed out of place with her gentle features, but her presence in this dangerous domain spoke much of the strength within her. "Max, we both know it's time. Make this easy, ok?" She took another step forward. The light from the desk lamp breached past her eyes. However, there was no change of expression on her face. If anything, her bold red eyes shone brighter than any wildfire. She could hear a growl coming from the hidden shadows.

Max had shed himself of the trappings of humanity and embraced his heritage. He stood with pride on his hind legs. His furious gaze scrutinized the room and came upon Ruby. His eyes seemed to discern her, but he could not recognize her as a friend. Everyone was an enemy while he was in this form. He crouched down and backed into the corner. His sinewy muscles tensed as he prepared to bear down upon Ruby. However, she was ready for him. As he leapt towards her, fangs and claws extended, she whispered "*Ligo*" as she extended her right arm towards him with her hand clenched. When she opened her fist, a burst of blinding light came forth, striking Max, paralyzing him. Ruby kept her arm at the ready. She yelled to the figures that had been lying in wait behind her, "He's ready for transport. If my visions are correct, he should return to us in a fortnight."

Four men in armored suits carrying special equipment came into the office and bound Max in shackles before giving him an injection. Finally, his body went limp, and he collapsed to the floor. Ruby took Max's surrender as a cue to lower her arm. A gurney floated in, and two men lifted Max onto it. The other two men checked the hall for security's sake before Max was wheeled away, followed by the remaining men.

****

Khira came to on the floor of the bathroom. The floor was cold and smelled of dust and spilled margarita. She rose from the floor. Her legs felt shaky, and her head swam. Did she get up too fast or was it something else? She steadied herself on the sink and looked at around. She was dressed and alone. Her hair was tussled, but other than that it just seemed like she may have passed out in the bathroom. What the hell, she thought. She felt her clit pulsating as if just coming off an orgasm. The knocking got louder and more urgent. Someone was at the door. Could it be him to ravish her for real?

"Is anyone in there? A line is forming out here and I'm not afraid to call over management!" The voice on the other side of the door sounded like some young girl that probably was just a rich kid from the local prep school. Not Zachary, she thought.

Opening the bathroom door, Khira was not shocked to see what she was expecting. "About Goddamn time!" said the prissy chick, dressed in a simple overpriced black A-line dress and wearing patent Mary Jane shoes, as she shouldered her way past Khira.

Stepping to the side with her foot straying behind her, she tripped the young girl and sent her sprawling to the bathroom floor where Khira had just been moments earlier. "Oops," she responded as she pushed her way past the people in line and back to the dining room.

Khira returned to the dining table. It was empty. The bill had been paid up and Zachary had vanished. Before the frown could reach her lips, she saw that he had left a note for her.

Khira, call this number when the questions start. – Zachary

She realized then that she never told him her name. The questions were already starting, but she was not ready to call him. Not just yet.

Chapter Ten

Light silver clouds dressed and undressed a saffron crescent as if the moon was a burlesque dancer. The lamenting winds of the Texas hill country blew tickled the treated glass and echoed the distress of Lilian's occupied mind. She could not sleep. In truth, she had not had a full night's sleep in over 150 years. She had tossed and turned within the cocoon of white silk sheets upon her king size bed while Kitty slept on a pink velvet outstretched bench at the foot of the bed. The bench was the only touch of color displayed within the room. Lilian was prepared for the knock at her door as the distinctive footfalls outside the room proved as much an alarm system for her ears as any bell. A knock came to the door.

"Enter," commanded Lilian, as she gathered a nearby robe and sat at her vanity.

Awakened by the sound, Kitty stared at the door and tensed, waiting for some word from her mistress. Seeing Zachary enter the room relaxed her, but only a little. Zachary stepped into the room with his face devoid of emotion. Kitty stared at him, and Lilian could almost swear that she would hiss at the approaching man. The Mistress did not have time for such games.

"Come here, Kitty." The pet padded her way down from the bench to sit beside Lilian. Kitty tucked her legs beside her and rested her head on her Mistress' calves, all the while never taking her eyes off the man. Lilian pulled Kitty hard by the hair. "You have shown promise at keeping secrets. You are only here to be seen," her mistress scolded her while looking down at her. Kitty shot up a confused glance at her mistress. Lilian brushed Kitty's hair with her fingers to keep the pet at ease.

Lilian shifted her attention to Zachary. The air of her expression meant that the Lieutenant Governor would have to accept Lilian's choice to keep Kitty nearby during business. Lilian continued. "Now Zachary, explain your prolonged absence."

He walked over and knelt near Lilian, looking down but also away from Kitty's glares. He had not looked her in the eye since he had stepped past her threshold. "My Mistress, I met the required target," he said clearing his throat, "Circumstances..." Lilian reached out and pulled him towards her, grabbing a fistful of his shirt.

"No more excuses, boy. No more delays. I take it she is still alive. Do I need to send Reed to clean up your mess?" She removed her grasp of Zachary. Lilian had not raised her voice, but instead drew in the words as if whispers. "You let an Untouched delude you with intentions rather than actions. I thought you would have known better. I expected better from you."

Zachary could see her muscles tense and her eyes burn. He expected punishment. He was prepared for it. Lilian's eyes softened and her lips mocked a Mona Lisa smile. "Fortune is yours as you have found me on a forgiving day. I'll give you one more chance to kill her before she discovers our kind." Lilian pulled open a drawer from her vanity and reached for a lighter. Zachary saw this movement and handed her the tapered ivory candle from a nearby candlestick. She took the offering from his hand and brought the flicked the flame of the light to the wick. The candle's light danced within her violet eyes.

Zachary began to tense once more. His senses tingled and his breath began to pant. "Now give me your hand, darling." He obeyed. She took his hand and pulled away his sleeve leaving his flesh bare. Zachary began to sweat. With her long-manicured nail, she tore at the flesh of his arm and carved a line straight down the center. She then began to pour hot wax up and down his arm filling the bloody wound. Zachary hissed in painful delight.

Such delicious agony was not often afforded to him. He savored each second of pleasure as if it were his last. Then, Lilian took the candle away. Already his wound began to heal, and the pain receded. "You will only receive more of that treatment when you succeed. I know how much you enjoy that, so I hope that it will be incentive enough for you to carry out this simple task. Now go..."

Zachary attempted to catch his breath. His head still bowed, he struggled to rise and carry out his mission. He found his way to the door but could not find the desire to turn the knob. Zachary could not find it in himself to leave. Granted, a part of him wanted to take that last chance she had given him. However, if Lilian were to learn what happened and found that he did not tell her, then his life would be forfeited. He had to tell her. "Is there something else?" she asked, curious as to why he had not taken his leave.

He still faced the door, a civil war brewing within each thought. Finding no other option, he turned and confessed his error. "About that, my mistress...circumstances were delayed when I was in the process of feeding from her. I was unable to finish her off. Her blood has been *touched*." His eyes never met with hers; his head hanging down like a dog knowing he had been a disappointment.

Zachary braced himself for the strike that could end him. A possible thrown object piercing his skull came to mind. He was waiting to hear glass shatter at the very least. He had already succumbed to her ire enough times to know that her patience was at an end. He grit his teeth and waited, his fangs piercing his bottom lip. Moments passed and the only thing that hit him was silence...a terrible, ominous silence.

After a few more tense moments, Zachary raised his eyes and dared to look at her. She did not even return his gaze. Instead, it was as if Lilian was searching her mirror as if seeing something far away or perhaps far in the future. Lilian cleared her throat, yet still the words that left her were a mere whisper. "My darling, Kitty, please take leave. Check in with Eleanor. I must be alone with Zachary."

Kitty did not even look at Lilian as she crossed Zachary's path. She brushed against his bare arm on purpose, in hopes that her touch would bring a little bit of serenity. As the pet made her exodus, she planned to send a message out to Brânswood prior to her meeting with Eleanor.

As the door shut behind the pet, Lilian marched towards Zachary. Her violet eyes pierced through him. The anger was gone, but in its place was something else. Zachary could not say what it was, but he knew it was worse.

"You will bring her to me. Arrange to have the White Room ready for her. No one is to know for whom the chambers are prepared. If asked, claim it is for a special emissary to the court. See to it personally.

You will bring her here my routes. Once you have her, take her to the room and secure her there. Be sure to take the servant's entrance. No one is to see you either leave or return with my gift. This is your one chance at redemption, should I not decide to terminate you." Zachary gave a quick bow and went to track down Khira yet again.

****

Max was aware of his surroundings, and he was not happy. His body was still in the same state of transformation as before, but his mind was drifting back to human consciousness. His thought processes began to leave the feral beast behind and revert to his old self. If he were back at his desk sifting through papers, then maybe he could have had more control over his situation, he thought. However, as pleasant as the thought was, the reality was much, much worse. He was in his assigned cage, lying on a dusty brick floor. Manacles encircled his paws and neck as if steel jewelry. He was chained like a common dog, with enough leeway as to not feel "too controlled". He tried to sleep as much as he could to end his silent suffering, but the minutes crawled by.

His ears began to twitch. Slow and subtle, they moved a bit before they perked up. He could hear a voice. It was distant and hollow, like a whisper upon the wind. A woman sang a lullaby in the faintest timbre. Though his confinement was designed to limit his exposure to the outside world, his senses were still quite strong.

"Lorelai..."

He whispered the name under his breath, but it emerged more of a grunt rolling through his giant maw and teeth rather than how he imagined it in his head. It was her voice that taunted his wolf-like ears, singing to him with hope to tame him. This was one of her tricks from the early years. Even gone, it seems she still had control over his heart.

"The sky belongs to you, the sun and the moon too."

The words sung out in the stale air of the darkened cell. Max half expected a blue fairy to appear in the apparition of Lorelai. The lullaby continued, repeating, as he felt his eyes get heavy. It was time to see his love once more.

****

"She doesn't understand his desire to discern the secrets of their lineage and to cover up the tracks of their past lives," Max explained to Lorelai. Though his tone was spoken as a matter of fact, the expression on his face was anything but fact. "Is there any way you can get through to your sister that the 'gift' that was granted needs to be maintained through the years so as not to lose sight of the importance and power that it holds?"

The young Vampire sat at a desk across from Max. She was busy pouring through volume after volume of books questing for her own purpose. After a few more turns of the page, she spoke, "Max, Lilian is too busy gazing at Liam, fawning over his teachings, to care what he does. Truly, her heart has scrambled her brain. I am the much better pupil, so it will not matter in the long run. Although, even then, Liam is only finding the importance for his own ego rather than the Touched," Lorelai replied, without looking up from her books.

Max was not satisfied by her answer, but as usual there was not much he could do about it. He turned from her and gazed out the window to look upon the grounds. There were still some bare spots here and there, but the sanctuary's grounds were coming along. In time, it would be beautiful to behold. He turned from the window to reflect upon the construction of the chamber he now shared with Lorelai.

They were in the main study of the new instituted Brânswood building. Upon one wall, there was a massive bookshelf; constructed with beauty and was spacious enough to fill with many arcane tomes, although it was just a quarter full. On the wall behind Max was a depiction of a crude family tree. The names were faded, and its true origin lost, but it served as much a banner in their crusade as a reference to their work. Max moved over to sit at his new carved writing desk, while Lorelai twiddled away across the room at her station.

She had begun a new project. Max offered to help her; however, Lorelai played this project close to the chest, choosing to keep it very secretive; keeping it from everyone, from him and even her twin. She had been reading all religious texts that had been able to be acquired in their expanding sphere of influence. She read at a constant pace and almost never stopped, except to scratch notes within her journals. Every now and then, Max could not help but try and steal a glance from this beauty. Although she looked every bit the same as her sister Lilian, Lorelai had an angelic aura showcasing her own unique beauty, causing her to stand out above her sister.

He noticed every time she pushed the white strands of hair behind her ear and the way she pouted her plump, red lower lip when she was frustrated in her readings. He would smell the fragrance of ripe peaches emanating from her skin every time she was near. There was a sense of serenity within her presence that he found he could not be without. It was an eye to the inner storm that raged within him.

Max cared not for Liam, but he was thankful to the man for bringing Lorelai to him. Max had met Liam decades ago when he was still researching alone. In those days, he had little to call his own and his credentials were fair at best. Liam had picked up on Max being a werewolf almost from the start. Instead of fear or mistrust, Liam welcomed Max into the folds of his campaign. It was not what Max had expected. To be regarded and judged on his skills and merit was a refreshing change from how most people treated him; Touched, Untouched and all those in between.

Liam needed the lycanthrope for more than common tasks. Liam understood the uses of history and how it could help the present with the *forming of a new government within the Vampire culture. Max could help in the genealogy reports of squires and new incoming Touched, but also could keep up with the mundane issues of wills, land deeds, and name changes to help protect the identity of the hidden populace. There was also the fear of squiring someone that would release the Phoenix within the vampire. A Touched Phoenix could be the end of all existence. Tracking down potential born Touched Phoenix's was a necessary research within tracing lineage.*

It was through working with Lorelai that the nature of Brânswood also took on a new approach later in the development of the establishment. She had it in her to research the origins of the Vampires and the nature of the virus' strain itself that carried on through the generations. When Max would talk to Lorelai about her studies, he always detected a melancholy tone. He understood that she had no choice in what the gods had planned for her 16th birthday.

The werewolf culture, by comparison, was a heritage that one never escaped from. It was an inherited gene. One did not turn into a lycanthrope. One was born that way. It was because of this trait that Max was inspired to study genealogy. It was also the reason why Max swore at a young age never to breed. That decision was not made in haste, and until he had met Lorelai, he never thought to question it. He indulged in his reveries for a while longer before stealing glances of the young vampire hard at work reading up on a book of voodoo, biting her lower lip.

He finished up with his forgeries of land deeds and stood up from his desk. He stretched and then headed over to the object of his affection. "Do you think that we work too hard?" he asked her. He often used this question as a way of leading into an invitation to lunch. Today, it appeared as if she did not even hear him. Lorelai kept reading a few lines of text and then took notes down next to her. She wore a pastel blue blouse and white linen pants. Her hair was half tied back behind her but kept falling out of place. Lorelai began humming as she read. "I would take that response as a yes."

Lorelai looked up. "Did you say something, Max? I am sorry, but I cannot take a break right now. I feel like I am on the edge of the answer. I feel like..." she didn't finish her sentence. She brought up her thumb and forefinger to pinch the bridge of her nose. Max could sense that she was getting weaker by the day, as she did not always take to her "diet."

"I have told you before that you can drink in here. I understand that some needs must be maintained. Don't hurt yourself for the sake of appearances, Lorelai." He gave a half-hearted laugh to try and ease her discomfort of the subject.

"I will take a short break in a while, Max. It only hurts a little right now. I can concentrate through the pain, and it will go away."

"Nonsense, I'll send for a glass and that way you can continue with your work. The lab is just down the corridor. The drink will fix you up quicker than any aspirin."

Lorelai sighed, knowing that Max wanted to play the doting friend and that his intentions were honest, "Very well, you win this round, Max."

He smiled and returned to his desk. He pressed a button on the intercom. He could hear a crackle from the speaker, but no voice responded. The sun, adorned in front of his desk, shone with a bright glow. "May I have a glass of blood for Miss Lorelai?" Max did not bother waiting for a reply and the light of the sun faded out. Within moments, there was a knock at the door.

When Max opened the door, a young woman stood there with a glass filled three quarters of the way with a red liquid; the glass stood in the middle of a silver tray. "Thank you, Eleanor; that will be all." The young girl tucked the tray under her left arm, bowed, and turned away as Max headed back towards Lorelai. All of a sudden, his hand started to shake and the hairs on the back of his neck began to itch. "No...Not now," Max thought to himself as he watched the glass slip from his hand.

In an instant, Lorelai rushed to his side. With her Vampire reflexes, she reached out, caught the glass with precision and placed it on her nearby desk. She was also able to rescue Max as well. He fell to his knees. He shuddered at the thought of changing form in front of Lorelai. His nightmares contained his constant fear of losing control. He wondered now if perhaps he had been stuck in a horrible phantasm all this time. Praying it was but a dream, he tried to avoid looking at her.

He felt his fingernails grow, until they reached their full form. He began to shake and spasm. Lorelai held him and began to rock him, as if shushing a baby. He let out an anguished cry, while his hair grew out and his nose started to protrude. Lorelai held him and begun to sing a lullaby:

The sky belongs to you;
The sun and the moon too;
Nature of gods will hold you near.
Nature of Love will hold you dear,
Forever in their embrace.
Still your heart, still your mind.
The path of peace you shall find.
The favor of light will dim your fear.
The nurture of light will guide you here.
Forever be thy grace.

The fact that she was more sympathetic than nervous struck a chord in Max. While still feeling love for her, he also felt ashamed. He closed his eyes and wished for peace once more.

****

The lyrics faded, leaving a heavy oppressive silence in the cold prison cell. Max shuddered as if he could feel the cold for the first time. His eyes opened. Bitter tears blurred his vision as Max saw that he was in the small room alone, with just his memories. He was still in full lycanthrope form, but his mind started clearing, shifting between memories and his animal instincts. His mind returned to focus enough to realize that his heart felt betrayed that Lorelai was not there with him. He backed into the corner of his cage, as much as the chains allowed, and out of human desperation or perhaps animal instinct, he let out a long mournful howl.

Chapter Eleven

Khira sat upon an ivory stained hardwood flood. All the walls were white and there were no windows. She thought to herself that if the walls were padded, then she would be home. If Khira had not been sitting on the ground, she would have no bearing of up or down. This white room was bright, but something moving caught her eye, something that was not the same her as her surroundings. There was a good ring spinning on the floor. She could not help to stare at it.

The ring hypnotized her. Khira felt drawn to the spinning golden circle. She could not decide what she contemplated more: the physics of how the ring was in a constant rotation or whether what she was seeing was real. She felt trapped in the fantasy of the dream labyrinth from the movie Inception. Except she knew her vision did not display any time of reality, as the ring expanded larger a little bit at a time, growing on each twirl.

She did not move. She did notice that there was complete silence. There was no annoying buzzing sound from the overhead lights, no white noise. Even as the ring turned, no sound vibrations breached the air. The rotation moved in a consistent speed. As she looked at this now gigantic ring, she stopped to think maybe the ring had not gotten larger; maybe she had gotten smaller. Before she finished the thought, the ring fell towards her. She closed her eyes as the ring swallowed her.

She opened her eyes. The ivory floor was now red, and the walls of this room were now donned with stripes, alternating between the colors black, gold and gray. She placed her hands on the floor to stand up. However, once Khira touched the ground, she found she could not move her hands from the floor. In fact, they started to sink into the red liquid that seemed to coat the floor. She felt her entire body sink at a snail's pace into a floor made up of dark cherry red nail polish. Any movement towards an escape caused her to sink more. Her eyes looked up from her deteriorating cesspool and the last thing Khira saw was her own image laughing down at her, as if her double was Buffalo Bill and Khira was the woman down the well from Silence of the Lambs. "The lions have you now, little girl," her doppelganger shouted down and started to cackle as Khira disappeared into oblivion.

****

Khira's eyes opened, and she awoke to find her cousin inside her bedroom. Paige was standing next to one of the dressers and seemed to be arranging some of Khira's books. Khira had had her books arranged by genre and then by author. It appeared that Paige was arranging the books by the color of the spines. She failed to notice that Khira was awake. *Paige never comes into my room*, she thought. Maybe the rarity of it meant that this was just another dream?

Khira looked over to her nightstand and saw a glass of orange juice and some buttered toast waiting to be eaten. Looking at the food made her stomach churn. She felt acidic juices moving up into her chest, but she managed not to vomit. This was bad. With this being an unusual event with her cousin's visit plus her unwarranted hangover, a part of Khira wondered if she was still in her dream; she wondered if this was the other side of the white room she had fallen from. However, she did not remember feeling things in her dreams. She must be awake then. Damn!

As she tried to recall the dream, she could only remember the white room. With each attempt to recall more of the dream, she realized that she could not even think of the last time she had been awake. Everything had become so surreal that she could no longer tell the difference between the waking world and the dreaming one.

Paige caught the sight of her cousin shifting under the covers and approached the side of the bed. Khira sank back into her pillows and stared at her cousin through wide set eyes. Paige appeared to be moving in slow motion. Something about Khira's sight was different. If she stared hard enough, she could see dried tears upon Paige's face along with slight indentions caused by pillowcases. The details were minute. The visions themselves reminded Khira of a CSI drinking game.

She also felt as though her hearing were amplified. A loud, staggered cadence played in her head, courtesy of Paige's slow footsteps, accompanied by a heartbeat although Khira had trouble deciphering it between Paige's or her own. Then, Khira realized her heart was not beating hard enough for her to hear. In fact, as she touched her chest, she could not feel a heartbeat.

The drumming sound continued to echo without end, and it took all her effort just to screen it out. Once peace was restored to her mind, she thought she could still hear something else in the room. She tried to look for it; however, she saw nothing but a blur. By the time she was able to focus her eyes again, Paige sat beside her, bringing a wash-cloth to Khira's forehead.

"Hello, sleepyhead. How are you feeling? I was surprised to see you made it all the way up here on your own," Paige patted the cloth around her cousin's face and continued to play nurse.

"Wha..? How?" she croaked. Khira tried to form words, but her throat was dry. It took so much effort just to breathe. She felt so weak, and her chest was heavy. She paused and blinked. She thought she caught another glimpse of the blur in her room out of the corner of her eye, yet it vanished again. Putting that aside, she turned to her cousin and forced all her energy into the question. "What the hell are you doing in my room?"

"I was worried about you," Paige answered with apprehension. "Although, it sounds like you are finally getting back to your old self." Paige tried to continue the nurse act, but Khira kept pushing her hand away.

"It's not like I haven't come in late from a date before," she said as she remembered her prior engagement. She recalled going to a Mexican cantina. She also remembered the stranger. While she tried to grasp for more missing details, she yawned and looked at the clock. "It's only been a few hours."

"You sleep in like the best of them, Cuz. I hate to tell you this, but you haven't left your room for three days, sweetie! I kept checking for a stench just in case you died in here. You know...I could always use your room as a second 'office'." Paige tried to joke, but the worry was cemented in her voice. "I checked up on you and brought you food. You didn't touch anything, so I knew you were still asleep." An idea perked Paige's mood. "I know. I'll go get you some coffee to see if that will bring you around."

"Three days? Wow! I think that's a new record for me," Khira whispered. Khira took in her predicament as Paige headed for the door. She must be sick or something. Paige did not need to be up here trying to take care of her, but she was. How did she show her gratitude? By being her usual bitchy self. *Some family am I*, she thought. Paige reached for the doorknob. Before she turned to leave, Khira spoke. "I'm sorry, Paige, for snapping at you for being in my room. I know that I don't always say it, but I do appreciate having you here." Moments passed as Paige stared in shock and did her best not to faint. She began to say something in response but thought it better not to ruin the moment. She gave a simple nod and shut the door behind her. Paige continued downstairs to retrieve the coffee.

Khira laid back and closed her eyes. She could still hear every step Paige made going down the stairs heading into the kitchen, coinciding with her cousin's heartbeat quickening with each step. Somehow, even with her eyes closed, she could see these actions occurring. She felt a breeze brush past her. She opened her eyes. To her surprise, a short, overweight Mexican man sat in the chair near her vanity. He was looking through her things, checking out her makeup, and eyeballed some of the books Paige had rearranged. He wore an old suit jacket over a red shirt, the top button of his shirt was undone, and a loose blue tie hung around his neck. His hair was mussed and seemed a little out of date. "Who the hell are you?" she exclaimed. Turning to look at her, he appeared as surprised to see Khira as she was to see him.

They stared at each other for long moments, neither moving nor saying a word. The door swinging open broke the silence and stole Khira's attention. Paige had come in with a mug, cream, and *Splenda* all jumbled within her arms and held the coffee pot within one of her hands. "I've got a question for you," Paige stated as she stumbled her way back into Khira's bedroom. "Who's Zachary?"

Khira looked back at where she had seen the little Hispanic man, but he was gone. He must have been a hallucination of someone from the cantina, she thought. Turning to her cousin, she replied, "Who?" Her head still throbbed, and it took mountains of strength just to take in a breath. To be honest, her memory was not at its best now.

"Zachary," Paige asked again. "I saw the note from him stating that you needed to call him for questions or something like that. Was he the one you picked up at the bookstore?" continued Paige in her poor attempt at interrogation. When she mentioned the word "bookstore" Khira remembered bumping into someone there. The pieces of the puzzle were not falling into place as she still could not quite focus on much beyond the sound of Paige's heartbeat. Then a face appeared in her mind. First the dark blonde hair came into focus, then the steel blue eyes, and then full picture. For the first time, she recognized Zachary as the man from her dreams.

"Yes, he was. I mean he is. His name is Zachary Duvall. He owns The Historian's Hideaway apparently." Paige sat down on the bed and handed the mug to Khira and then poured in the coffee. She set down the pot and gave Khira the cream and *Splenda*. Khira moved her arm to take them, but again the movement seemed so slow. It was as if her body was learning how to move for the first time. Paige did not seem to notice any difference.

After fixing her coffee, she brought it up to her lips. It was still warm. She nestled the cup under her nose. She noticed that the pleasant eye-opening aroma was missing. She started to pour the elixir down her throat, but it felt like she was drinking acid. Instead of swallowing, she dribbled the coffee back into the cup. She put the cup off to the side of the bed and pulled herself up. She thought maybe the lack of smell was affecting her taste buds. However, she caught a slight hint of jasmine and vanilla from Paige's skin. A part of Khira yearned to taste Paige's arm, but she held back the desire.

The moments of silence did not exist even in the moments between Paige's heartbeats. The buzz of the lights, a slight whistle coming from the hallway, and the simple act of breathing were magnified to her ears. A fly's wings flapping would now be the equivalent to nails on the chalkboard.

Khira wanted to bring the coffee back up to her lips. She did not know if it was out of habit or because her throat felt so raw and dry. She tasted it again. She held it to her mouth and did her best to enjoy it. Forcing herself to swallow, the burning liquid slid down her throat, but not without causing her to let out a slight gag. Coughing, Khira replied smiling, "Went down the wrong way." Paige smiled at the sense that she was being helpful to her cousin, nursing her patient to wellness. However, Khira felt like the living dead. "Do you mind if I had some time to myself?" The smile left Paige's face. A frown of disappointment replaced it. Khira was familiar to seeing it. She was also used to being the cause of it. However, this was the first time that she cared about letting Paige down. "I'm just still not feeling up to par, Cuz. You understand, right?"

Paige got to her feet. "Sure, you must need a little more rest. Just know that I'll be here if you need anything. It's not like I'm going anywhere." She gave a small chuckle to try and hide the obvious hurt.

Khira reached out to take her cousin's hand before Paige had a chance to leave. "I know. And thank you for the offer." Khira gave the hand a little squeeze. The action in and of itself seemed to drain what little energy she had. She looked up at Paige and saw the smile return.

"Now I know you must be sick because you are never this nice!" Khira closed her eyes. With them closed, she could still somehow see. Beyond her sight, she saw Paige place some additional books on her dresser before heading out the door. This new ability scared her. What had Zachary done to her?

****

Kitty entered one of the pantries of the kitchen. The staff had not noticed when she came in, so she took a few minutes to herself before Lilian would expect her return. The small cupboard was perfect for her task of prayer and to get word to Brânswood. She pulled the door closed behind her and sat on the floor. The floor was dusty and would prove necessary for her mission.

Kitty took her finger and made a couple of intricate designs upon the floor. She pulled her knees to her bare chest and closed her eyes. She visualized herself on a beach at sunset. She could hear the roar of the ocean and the cries of the seabirds. The last rays of sunlight warmed her skin and the smell of the salty brine comforted her. The sky was a watercolor mixture of pinks, purples, and blues. The colors seemed to drip into the ocean along the horizon line. Kitty imagined an altar forming from rising sand before her with candles set upon it. She approached the shrine and taking each taper lighted them with her touch. She began to hum a chant very softly under her breath.

The waves of the sea began to crash and curl onto the shore. The water began to foam and swirl and there from beneath the waves, a beautiful woman emerged slowly from the sea. With each step towards the shore, the mane of the woman seemed to drag and pull the ocean's colors into her strands of hair. The colors roamed through the curls upon her head like they were still among the waves of the sea. Kitty began to speak.

"Kypris, I pray to you. Give me the strength to continue my task to let your love flow. This strength allows me to continue the mission I have accepted. Through the compassion you bring to others, I set more souls at ease." The spectral vision smiled and came closer to Kitty.

The glowing spirit rested her fingers onto Kitty's lips. A warm silky feeling washed over her as the Goddess Kypris kissed her forehead and let her grace sink into the young spy's heart and soul. Soon she felt Kypris herself fade into her own body while a blinding light engulfed her. Although the sun was now rested within the nest of the sea, the sky was still bright and blinding.

With her prayer through, Kitty could attend to the Sanctuary's business. She opened her eyes and found some scrap paper from a torn bag of flour. As Kitty took and touched her hand to the paper, and whispered, "Tòiseachadh a chòdadh teacsa." The paper began to glow. After taking a deep breath, she began her message:

Brânswood-

Khira has become Touched. Zachary turned her in a botched assassination attempt. Lilian has told him to bring her here, possibly to kill her herself. Please, Max, I need your guidance. Matthew does not know his connection to the family. I have seen Lilian's diaries and will attempt to get them to Khira when she is here. I am still in search of the labs. Reed doesn't know I'm using him, but he is smart and may find me out. I am scared but try to be diligent with the assignment Ruby granted me. –
Kitty

Kitty reviewed her note and once satisfied, stated "Cho-dhùin" before declaring "eadar-theangachadh." The words began to mutate into a different message that read:

Brânswood-

Alice has fallen down the hole. The White Knight had her for tea. The Queen of Hearts demands an audience with Alice, if not to complete her sentence. I beg for the Caterpillar to respond with advice. The Dormouse does not know that he is a pawn in on the board. I have seen the diaries of the Queen and plan to get them to Alice once she is here. I still look for wonderland. The Cheshire Cat does not know that I play him but I worry that his wit will discover my disguise. I am aware of how much is at stake and will try and fulfill the mission that the White Rabbit sent me on. -Dragonfly

Satisfied that she was refueled through prayer and her message was on task, Kitty gave one last demand to the note. The words began to leave the piece of paper. Once the paper retuned to a blank slate, the pet crumbled it and hid it behind some cans in the pantry. It was time to return to duty.

****

Zachary paced the floor of his bookstore office. The "mundane" workplace was one of his sanctums to retreat from the daily issues in the life of one of the Touched. But now the room seemed more like a prison. In here, he once pretended things were simple and could play the part of an average human who enjoyed books and the occasional stalking and killing of any one of his customers. But now, that life was encroached on by his duties to his Mistress. Outside these walls the looming threat of Lilian's rage hung over him like the Sword of Damocles itself. To make matters worse, the issue with Khira would not leave him. The memory of the restaurant repeated over again in his mind. He would pause and replayed the moment in his memory where his desire for Khira had overtaken him. It was a surprising moment, but if he had the chance to do it again, things would be different. He tried to replace the scene in his mind with one of him pressing razor-sharp knives against her skin. It was a fine notion and one that sent delicious shivers down his spine. However, the thoughts would fade and go back to him on the bathroom floor bringing her to climax. During the background recon he had done of her, torture was at the forefront of his desires towards her. Why could he now not savor those thoughts and act upon them? There was something about her.

He had never found himself so distracted before. While on the fast track to becoming Lilian's lieutenant, Zachary had always kept his focus on pleasing his mentor. Liam was already a ghost that Zachary would never meet, but whose presence remained strong in Lilian's soul. When she had told him stories of this great Sire, he felt closer to Lilian in a way that maybe no one had ever felt upon before. This sprang forth a confidence in him that maybe he would be able to fill the gaping footprints Liam had left behind and become Lilian's future Governor.

Today, however, any aspirations had become tainted with emotions he had never experienced before. His thoughts were not of how to become Governor or how to please his Mistress. No, they were of the girl. This Khira caused him to not only question Lilian's intentions, but his own.

Now because of his failure, she was becoming one of them. With his dark kiss, he had set forth another path of destiny. He began feeling emotions that had never touched his blackened heart. He felt a hunger for Khira, but it was not the hunger for prey. There was something within her bloodline, something about her soul.

He stopped his pacing and rested himself upon his desk. His hands sat amongst the papers and supplies and tokens of human life he had concealing the wooden surface. With a frustrated grunt, he swept all the materials off his desk and sent them crashing to the floor. The bare surface of the desk made him wish she were there, writhing under him. Ye gods, what was happening to him? He never wished for anything before.

He resumed his strides. Having time to ponder the issue, he was thankful the gods had intervened in his killing of Khira and he now knew why. He thought about calling her first in a rush to get to her and bring her back to the Manor. That would maintain his good graces with Lilian. However, he needed more time to make sure that was the step to take.

He had always strived for his goals but took it upon himself to make them happen. Zachary felt a deliberate difference towards his wanting for Khira. She was the key to his quest for power. Her fate was intertwined with his own. She was now a part of him and him of her. This was destiny to be sure and not to be questioned. He would continue his path to glory with Khira by his side, not as a pawn, but as his queen. Together they would rule, not just their own sect, but the entirety of the clans!

Chapter Twelve

Khira sat cross-legged onto of her comforter. Luckily, Paige had given her more time to rest in between the episodes of playing a doting nurse. Suddenly an image rushed Khira's mind of her cousin role-playing nurse for her Only Fans subscribers and other patrons. *Yuck.* Khira knew she should be thankful that Paige was willing to aid her with this illness, although having her cousin nearby seemed to be more harmful than good. Each of Paige's heartbeat was a percussive outcry, each breath, a gust of a hurricane's wind diving into her ear. Khira almost felt that her cousin's thoughts pounded against her own skull. She hoped whatever sickness this was would pass. Khira could only attempt to find some peace to achieve her next task.

The cell phone laid on the bed in front of her crossed legs next to the note that Zachary had left her at the restaurant. She had been practicing a conversation in her mind. After several attempts, all of

the imagined ways the dialogue could have played out, nothing satisfied her. She did not want to hear any explanations Zachary might
have. She did not want answer to which there were no real questions.
However, she knew she couldn't take a play out of Paige's handbook
to hide from the world the rest of her life.

Khira picked up the phone. She picked up the note. She laid both
back down, her legs still entwined. She unlaced her legs, got up from
the bed and began pacing, keeping distance from both the phone
and the note. She wanted to brace whichever emotion she was feeling
but one rammed into the next without settling on the confidence she
needed for this task.

She walked over to her vanity. She sat in the nearby chair and stared
at her stereo. She wanted to play music as loud as she could to block
out the chaos that collided within her room. Khira knew this could not
happen as she did not want to alert her cousin to impose once more.
She also did not know how the volume would affect her hearing since
she could hear her cousin from rooms away. She grabbed her a pair of
headphones and returned to her bed.

After placing the ear buds in their nest within her ears, she reached
and phone her phone. She pushed play on her music app and much
to her fear, the music blared through. She turned the volume down in
order to find some comfort. She skipped passed Brand New's "Jesus
Christ" once it got to the point of the singer asking what the Messiah
had done during the three days he was dead. The player jumped to
Phantogram's "You're Mine." Khira imagined Zachary commanded
her through song when the male vocalist chimed in. She did not want
to imagine him singing any more than she wanted to hear his voice on
the phone. Maybe the third time would be the charm.

The next song was Perfume Genius' "Don't let them in." Khira
lingered on the lyrics and had to stop the music. Music had been a

haven to her in the past, a way to lock out the outside door. However, today, the music seems to fail her much as her past had.

She stared at the phone. She imagined just throwing the cell across the room, hitting a wall and breaking into a million pieces. Instead, Khira typed out a message and read it over a few times. Before she could stop herself, she hit the send button to Zachary's number.

****

Lilian awoke to the pleasant sound of music. The introduction to Frédéric Chopin's Prelude, Opus 28, Number 15 was soft and melodious. It seemed to embrace her. For a moment, she had forgotten that she had a music player installed into her chambers some years ago. She had thought the music would soothe her to sleep, overcoming her often bouts of insomnia. Alas, it helped little. Kitty must have set it for her. *Such a considerate creature*, she thought.

Reaching over to her nightstand she saw from the clock that little time had passed since she went to bed, a little less than an hour in fact. She pressed a button upon a remote control situated on the nightstand. The music ended. By pressing another button, Lilian illuminated the room. All seemed as it should. Even her pet, Kitty, was sleeping curled up in a fetus position at the foot of her bed. Seeing the dozing form caused a stir in her memory as well as her loins. The little cat had talents. She had not been so pleased in a long time. It had been truly remarkable, enough to cause Lilian to slumber even if only for a short time. Still, for so little time having passed, Lilian was feeling quite rested, more so than she had felt in a long time. It was best to take advantage of it while she still had time to herself.

Stirring the little pet, Lilian proclaimed, "Awaken." Kitty's eyes fluttered open and after performing an exaggerated arched back stretch, the pet scooted up to her place at her Mistress' feet. "Leave me. I want to be alone with my thoughts. Please check with Eleanor on the status of the White Room and find Matthew for me." Kitty nodded without raising her eyes and quietly left the room.

Lilian sat down at her vanity and pulled out her hidden journal to release her thoughts. There was much that occupied her mind as of late, but there was something important that she felt she must transcribe. In between times of listening to Lorelai's ghost, Liam would tug at her heart. Dear, sweet Liam. How she missed him and his counsel. Thoughts of him would move her pen over paper this night.

I wonder how Liam would have dealt with Zachary's failures as of late. His absence reminds me that I still need him to run this sector, his house. I have never felt it to be mine. I often wonder why he gifted me the position of Mistress at the genesis of our organization. At times I am lost in the position I hold, cursed by the vacuum left by his death. I have my own failures that blind me brighter than the troubles Zachary brings forth, let alone Reed.

My "trusted" lieutenants are now by my side as to keep these enemies closer. This would be Liam's move, I trust. Now I must ready my strength for an audience with Khira in order to abide time and see what the gods have thrown at me. They take away the ones I love. Why do they bring misfortune and lay trouble upon my feet and weaken me? Do they bid it or do my own actions cause it, in leaving duties to those I know are so willing to betray me?

The blood had dried up in her inkwell. Lilian paused to consider if she should make any more confessions. Time felt to be moving so slowly; the sands so big and heavy, slow to drop within an hourglass. She decided her time would be served best by readying herself to face her adversary, Khira, should Zachary not fail to bring the newly Touched girl to her at posthaste.

****

Zachary sat in his matte black customized Lincoln Aviator in the back parking lot behind his bookstore. He could have gotten out and gone into the building, however, something stopped him, as if glued to the cushioned driver's seat. He thought that Khira would have contacted him by now. It had been several days since the encounter at the restaurant. His mind played over the punishment Lilian had given him when he had told her of his insubordination. A part of him was pleased that Khira had survived but also knew how much more complex this new bit of information would play in his already chaotic relationship with his Mistress.

He placed his hands at the two and nine of the leather covered steering wheel and gripped so tight that a normal steering wheel would have bent inward. Thus, the constant need for the Sector to have customized cars for the Touched higher-ups. He licked his chapped lips, remembering the sweet taste of Khira's blood. He needed more of her. He thought of showing up to her doorstep, he had known where she lived for a long time. However, he knew such action would leave him looking powerless.

A vibration from his center console broke his thoughts. A message from Khira came through. He was relieved, but also on guard with this news.

Since you already know my name, you most likely also know where I live. Come to meet me and explain yourself. Please know that this is not an invitation for anything more personal so please don't hold any expectations. Be thankful that I'm offering you this much. I will be anticipating you to arrive here around 2pm ~ Khira

This notice gave him about half an hour to meet her at her cousin's house. She only lived a few minutes from the bookstore. Due to Lilian's concern and demand of returning Khira to Thirlestane, he pulled his SUV from the parking lot and headed over to face fate.

****

David peeked through the blacked-out curtains in Paige's room to stare out the window onto the street outside. His security sensor told him that Zachary's vehicle was approaching. Within seconds of reaching the windowpane, David recognized the black luxury SUV take a slow left onto the street where the house sat. David closed his eyes as his reviewed the spell in his mind. His thoughts were broken when he heard a door open down the hall.

As Khira took the last footfall on the staircase, she was rushed by a breeze. She focused her eyes and saw the Hispanic man from before. He made no attempt to hide himself. He wore strawberry red silk gown with a shiny black pleather belt to show off a curvier figure. As David faced Khira, she could see that his brown almond eyes were adorned with fiery red eyeshadow with a golden cut crease. His false feathery lashes flapped up and down revealing his anxiety. He took a breath and with a wave of his hand, he stated with a deep masculine voice, "*A bhith na shuidhe.*" Khira was pushed back with a strong, invisible force into a leafy green microfiber sofa behind her. David cleared his throat and said in a high-toned breathier voice, "Please be a dear and just sit there a moment. Papi has work to do." He hovered over to peek through the peephole in the front door.

"What the fuck? Who the hell are you?" Khira demanded to know. However, he ignored her.

David clapped his hands together. When he began to spread his fingers outward, keeping his wrists, a small spark sizzled. He crossed his hands, having one middle finger touch the opposite thumb and then the next middle finger touching the other thumb forming an open rectangle. "*Sàmhach!*" His deep voice returned and penetrated throughout the house, causing a shake in its foundation. The force of his voice pushed the sofa Khira occupied back into the wall behind it.

She looked down and saw that there was a white chalked circle marked on the floor where the base of the chair now sat. She wiggled in an attempt to stand up, but found the back of her legs attached to the sofa as if they were pulled by a strong magent. She pouted. Khira began firing questions at him, but even with her mouth opened, the words remained silent.

David began to chant something while standing in front of the door. He clapped his hands once more. In a similar motion as before, he crossed his hands at the wrist, forming an "ell" shape before guiding it towards the door. "*Glaiste mach droch fhuil.*" He bowed his head. He repeated the motion of his hands and the strange incantation, two more times. A pale light seemed to emanate around the doorframe as if a halo before fading away. Seemingly satisfied, the man flipped a middle finger at the door. He continued to stare, as if he could still see outside. Khira attempted to speak again. While sound was beginning to return to her voice, the Hispanic man in drag shushed her into silence.

Moments passed while the two waited for something to happen. At first, the man seemed confident in his work, but now that it was all said and done, he appeared nervous. He stood at the door in silence. He turned to look at Khira, as if somehow she could do something to help. Before she tried to yell at the strange man, the house shook. The motion passed quickly and the man at the door, looking quite giddy at the action, declared, "Yes, it worked! Ha! That takes care of the douche pussy."

"What the hell was that?" Khira asked surprised that her voice returned to normalcy, "And who the hell are you?" *Douche Pussy? she thought?* Who could this strange man be referring to?

David floated to the couch and sat across from Khira. "Hello, Khira. My name is David. We have to talk."

****

Zachary parked a few houses away. He had stepped out the vehicle in a casual manner to hide his anxiety. He reached the sidewalk in front of Khira's house and made the slow walk up towards the door. He still did not know what he would say during this initial meeting since her transformation. His thoughts and feelings were a whirlwind of pandemonium, and it vexed him. He had defied his Mistress and mishandled what should have been the simple assassination of Khira. He had managed to get away from Lilian for the moment, but her wrath could not be brushed aside forever. He would need to explain himself before , but they returned to the manor. However he did not know if he would able to have any explanations since he could not rationalize his actions to himself.

"Damn that girl." he whispered as he came to the door. *All this trouble for one pretentious little human...Killing her indeed would have been easier*, he thought. Maybe they both would live to regret what happened today, but for now he needed to bring Khira back to Thirlestane Manor.

As he reached for the door, he noticed a shimmering haze lingering over the front of the house. It appeared like a curtain at the front of the abode. He quickly circled the structure and noticed it covered the whole house. He reached for the door and was quickly turned away by a spell. He reached out again with both hands and the shimmering haze flared within his sight. A protective barrier was erected around the house, thus forbidding entrance to Khira's home. He had seen this sort of trick before but had never anticipated he would see it here. Brânswood was involved; he was sure of it. They wanted Khira as well, or at least they wanted her out of Lilian's clutches. His information about Khira and her cousin showed no ties to Brânswood; he had never noticed any others who could be of their aid nearby. There must be something he missed, or there was an informant within Lilian's circle. There was no other way Brânswood would have known about Khira or that she would need protection at this moment.

"Very clever Khira, but you cannot hide forever. You eventually must come out, and I'll be here waiting."

Chapter Thirteen

Khira sat up and stared at David. After clearing her throat once more to make sure her voice had returned, she demanded "Who the hell *are* you?" David was offended for a second, but remembering his manners and the fact that she could not even see him prior to the *change* he decided to start again.

"My apologies, Chica. My name is David." He said while doing a southern debutante curtsy. Khira did not know what to think. Just when she was starting to make sense of everything around her, this happens.

She attempted to get out of the chair. Although her voice returned along with her attitude, Khira remained glued to the sofa. "You know, on second thought, I don't give a FUCK who you are. What are you doing in my house? How did you do that? Does Paige know you're here?" David became disappointed, sensing he was not being well received.

Granted he had been used to that, coming from a conservative family that opposed his flamboyant lifestyle; however, he thought Khira would be more welcoming for the news he planned to drop on her. The vital task at hand was to get her settled and relaxed before he revealed what she needed to know.

"I will explain everything in time. First, let me have a look at you." David hovered close to Khira, appraising and judging her every feature. She was about to open her mouth in protest, but sighed instead while David judged her. There was a stillness within this stranger. She was surprised that David did not produce the ear-piercing heart beats that Paige had when nursing her. "Well, you don't seem to be too much the worse for wear, except for this atrocious outfit you've got on," he said, wrinkling his brown pug nose.

"What do you know about it, shorty? Do you know what kind of hell I've been in for God knows how long?" Khira sank into the sofa. She wished she could return to her room. She wished she had never met Zachary. So many regrets filled her. Tears of blood escaped her eyes.

David abruptly became more solemn, his eyes sympathetic. "As a matter of fact I do, lovie, more or less anyways. You were seduced by a handsome stranger who poisoned you with his evil. Even now, he plans to take you against your will, if need be, and held off far away in a hidden place where you will be groomed into becoming one of...*them*. As simple as that might sound, darling, you are no longer in a Disney movie."

Khira's mind held onto one word that he had said. "Them?" she inquired.

David gestured one of his arms wide before bending it in a sharp motion at the elbow, making his arm parallel to the ground just below his chin. "Yes," David said in a cheesy Transylvanian accent. "A child of the night. A fampir...nosferatu...a Vampire, silly girl!"

****

Paige sat at her desk thumbing through one of the journals. She should be editing some of her most recent footage for publication on her website; yet she was drawn to the books by an overwhelming strange desire. She did not completely understand everything they contained. The last video she shot before the package had arrived played in the background. Sounds of pleasure emanated from the computer's speakers, adding a soundtrack to some of the passages.

She glanced up at the monitor, viewing herself straddling a Sybian, arms tucked behind as to show off her ample breasts. Her head tilted back for a moment before returning to the camera; her lips revealing a Mona Lisa smile, her mouth releasing a small moan. Seeing herself riding the saddle-like contraption in the video made her feel so powerful. She walked over to the computer and pressed pause. She returned to the bed. "Damn, I'm a sexy bitch," she joked aloud before her lips returned to the same smile that mimicked her face on the frozen screen.

Paige opened back the journal and continued to read a few more pages before shook by a quake from within the house. She glanced over at the clock to see what time it was. Double checking her watch, she saw that it was quite late. Her computer monitor had already gone into sleep mode. She had been so caught up with reading the journals that she had lost track of time. No matter, she thought, just another day in the asylum.

She returned to her computer set-up, rattling her vertical mouse to breathe life back into the electronics. She attempted to put some additional work into the editing of the video. She could not focus. Her attention kept going back to the stories of Lorelai, Lilian and Liam. Paige gave up on the footage. She could hear the genesis of loud voices booming from downstairs; sounded like Khira was on one of her rampages.

Then she heard David. What was going on down there? Before she could ponder it further, the room began to shake again. Objects began to fall all around her and the video cameras shook on their tripods. Rushing up to secure her belongings, she managed to keep everything from breaking long enough for the shaking to subside.

"What the fuck? Was that an earthquake?" she asked herself. Earthquakes had happened up in Oklahoma but never this far south before. She grabbed the journals, opened the door, and began to head downstairs to check in on the rest of her world. She heard the voices increasing in volume and hoped that everyone and everything was ok.

"Well, you don't seem to be too much the worse for wear, except for this atrocious outfit you've got on." That was David. And from the sound of it, he was just fine.

"What do you know about it, shorty? Do you know what kind of hell I've been in for God knows how long?" That would be Khira. *Sounds like she was back to her old self as well*, she thought. Paige was thankful that her friends were ok with whatever that quake was.

As she began to come down the staircase, she couldn't help but listen in on their conversation. She knew it was bad manners to eavesdrop, but she couldn't help herself. She sat down on a step and listened. A curiosity overcame her, as she couldn't remember a time when her two friends had conversed. She heard David give a recap of what must have been Khira's date although it sounded more like an episode of Real Housewifes. Khira seemed to be ok, but with her, one never knew what kind of trouble she would get herself caught up in.

Concerned for her cousin, Paige debated joining them in the living room, but felt best to hide out of sight as not to incur the wrath of old Khira.

"Them?" she heard Khira say.

"Yes." replied David. "A child of the night. A fampir...nosferatu...a Vampire, silly girl!"

That David is such a cheese ball, Paige thought. Always one for the dramatics, he never could take things too seriously. She swore that he was going to overdo it one of these days. Wait! Did he just say *Vampire*?!

****

The rumble of distant thunder mirrored Zachary's mood. A light pattering of rain came down, but did nothing to cool his anger. Zachary cursed himself a fool for allowing a woman to take advantage of him. Hell, she was nothing more than a young girl, which made his feelings hurt even more. "Damn you, Khira," he muttered, as he took shelter under some nearby trees.

He continued to pace about the grounds of Khira's home, keeping himself to the shadows. The lights to the house were on and he could hear raised voices from within. Zachary stared at the shadowy figures in the window. He wondered if Khira could be one of them. As he tried to discern what was occurring inside the house, he let his mind drift over to thoughts of Khira.

Memories washed over him of his time spent with her. He remembered all of those long weeks searching for her, finally finding her, and the long hours watching her from afar. Back then, she was just another assignment, another victim. Khira was not particularly attractive or powerful. The question was why Lilian wanted her taken out in the first place. It was such a mystery, yet not something that he given much thought to before.

An assignment was an assignment, and his devotion to his Mistress was unquestioned. However, over time, as he watched Khira dancing in the club or sketching in her book, he began to have doubts about what he was supposed to do. Capturing and killing Khira would have certainly been fun and a boon to his service of Lilian, but it was a waste of his talents. Simple kills were a job for the Independents, not his Sector. Thoughts such as those kept him from killing Khira outright, which in turn caused him to question his Mistress' motives. Doubt led him to confront Lilian about the mission at her court.

Anger mixed with an unknown emotion that dwelled within in. The question that lingered in his mind like a fog was wondering if he was upset at Khira because of the sex or because of the thoughts that plagued him after their encounter. Emotions flooded him, and he felt he just needed more time to deal with it, to suck it up and to figure out the best plan of action.

A breeze blew in from the north and carried a chill along with it. The wind stirred the boughs above him sending down the heavy drops of rain water that collected up there to splash on his head. The sensation was as invigorating as a baptism. If only Khira was there to share the experience with him. He thought about her huddling against him to fend off the cold. He envisioned himself taking her within his arms and comforting her against the storm, and beneath the trees he would take her, filling her with such pleasure and showing her how much she truly needed him.

It was a good fantasy, but that's all it was, a fantasy. He needed to be able to control her, dominate her and use her for his own means; to sup upon her supple flesh, ravage her body and devour her soul. He could not understand this necessity. Now, he waited for her. He felt the desire to see her that was for sure. The question was whether he needed her for Lilian...or for himself?

Zachary finished another patrol of the house and he still could see no possible way in. He wished he could figure out what was happening inside the house, but the vampiric shield kept him at bay. If that barrier was any indication, then she and hers were doing their best to protect themselves. The question was how?

Khira had no such power, though her skill as one of the Touched was impressive for one newly born. Her roommate was a reclusive shut-in who only experienced the outside world vicariously or through the Internet. So whom? *Brânswood*, he realized. There was no other explanation. The sanctuary must have gathered similar intel through their necromancing Phoenix to that which Lilian had obtained in her mission to eliminate Khira. He felt naive for becoming more of a pawn in the game of chess, a powerless tool. The Sector had only known of Brânswood's focus on the Touched. However, now Khira was a piece for both parties to win. "Very clever," he whispered to the night.

Now that the Watchers were active in the game, the rules could bend or break. Khira's home was essentially a fortress for the time being. She could stay there and avoid Lilian's wrath...and his affection. With help from Brânswood, she could have access to fresh blood plus any kind of magical protection they offered, such as the field surrounding the house. Yet that plan did not seem to align with Khira's nature. If he knew her as well as he thought he did, her rebellious, self-reliant personality would assert itself and force her to fend off her enemies on her own. If she was foolish to assume that Vampires slept during the day, then it stood to reason that she would most likely make that the time to make her escape.

The sky between the clouds showed that there were still a few hours until dawn, so he could afford to be patient. Not that the sunlight would produce much of an obstacle for him; an annoyance certainly and perhaps an inconvenience, but no more than that. "There is still much you need to learn about us, Khira," he muttered.

Chapter Fourteen

"What the fuck do you know about Vampires?" Khira inquired with a raised voice. David levitated from the floor a little higher than before and floated closer to his detainee. He hovered above her and stared down into Khira's gaze. He held his composure as her eyes reflected a righteous fury as forceful as a tidal wave.

"As a matter of fact, I know a great deal, my dear sweet lamb; more than you do at this point, but then again apparently you have *known* a vamp in the biblical sense," he replied adding a chuckle. David turned his back towards Khira and went back towards the winds, checking for representatives from the Southern Sector. Grunts coming from behind him tore his attention from a possible enemy and returned to his would-be student.

Khira struggled in her chair as David "tsk, tsk'd" at her disapprovingly. However, the more he thought of keeping Khira restrained could work against him, David decided to be more lenient, but by not too much. David brought his hands in a stop signal and then turned his palms towards him. He held his left hand in the air, palm down and waved his right hand over his left hand in a counterclockwise motion. He whispered "Lleddfu ei breichiau" five times as he continued to move his right hand.

The more David moved his hands, Khira began to feel her arms relax. Her fingers began to wiggle as a pins and needles sensation ran up her arm to her shoulders. After a few seconds, she bent her elbows and attempted to pull herself up from the chair, but her ass was still glued to the seat. After David had finished, he returned his attention to Khira. Her stare sent daggers since she remained stuck in her position. He wagged her fingers at her as if an angry nun annoyed by her student. His tone switched from playful to more poignant.

David attempted to collect his thoughts of what to say next. He looked around where Khira was sitting. He thought she would need some strength after her three-day coma. He whispered an incantation, which sounded like a garble of words to Khira. By the third time he repeated the phrase, she understood him to say something like "Cwpan gwaed yn ymddangos ger y Cyffwrdd." A wine glass with a red liquid appeared at a table near Khira.

"Why don't you have a drink? It will relax you." David stated in an attempted kind voice. His playfulness had left him knowing the task at hand. He gestured to the glass. For anyone else, it would have been assumed to be a Merlot. However, with David mentioning Vampires, Khira did not have to guess what it was.

"I don't want to relax. I want you to let me go!" she cried as she grabbed the arms of the chair.

David stared down at her sternly and replied, "You will stay in the chair and drink your blood until I am done enlightening you as to the peril we now find ourselves in. Believe me," he said with a voice that gave even Khira pause, "You have questions, and I can provide you the answers. You need it, especially if any of us have a hope of surviving."

Khira stopped struggling and just stared at David as he returned her glare. She did not know who he was or how he came to be in her home, but for some reason she felt she could trust him. No, not trust; she never afforded herself such faith, but she could at least believe him. Somehow, he seemed to know what he was talking about. She took the glass and drank it down in one swallow. "Ok. I'm listening," she muttered. David beamed at the response and pulled back to stand in the middle of the room.

"Now, where to begin. Ah, yes, *Bwrdd cyflwyno yn ymddangos,*" he said with a flourish. A swirl of light flowed through the room, and once it passed, it revealed a standard white board that one would see in a school or office setting, albeit a floating one. David coughed and straightened himself as if preparing to give a lecture. She didn't know it at the time, but in fact that's just what he was preparing to do.

"Excellent. Now class, pay attention. Today you will learn all about the wonderful world of *The Touched,* Vampyr Americana or what most people know as the American Vampire. Oooh..." he said accenting the words with spooky gestures that caused his words to spell themselves on the magic board. David was hoping for a little more of a response from Khira. However, Khira looked bored and a little frustrated. David knew he was going to have to get through to her the hard way. "Ok, Khira, all joking aside, it's time to learn what you need to know about what you're caught up in."

"Fine, enlighten me," replied Khira with a sneer. David smiled and prepared to let her know everything he knew about their situation. Once done, there would be no going back. Whatever happened from here on out would be with the knowledge that he had done what he could to make sure the girls were safe.

"First off, I need you to tell me what you think already know, given your transition, that way I can skip ahead to what's most important," David stated. Khira grunted in frustration. She wanted to get out of the chair she was stuck in and go back to her room. She supposed if she had to indulge the fat, floating, fairy-person, then she should do what she could to make things go quicker.

"Apparently, vampires are real. Although they don't appear to look like those crappy Twilight vamps," Just by stating the word, almost like accepting her new fate, she felt something strange in her mouth. Her front canines extended slightly. "Seriously?" she asked David while pointing to her mouth. He nodded and then gestured her to continue.

"You get turned by being bitten, though you didn't die afterwards. Not all people get that *gift*. Most people die. If you don't die, you just change." As far as she knew she felt like she "died" when she was stuck in her room after her date with Zachary, but apparently she was *gifted* instead.

David chuckled softly and replied. "Basically, the dying thing is something different than what you may have read about or seen in the movies. It's definitely not like my death was, where I just opened my eyes and wasn't in my gorgeous body anymore. It's actually a virus that changes you. The "Touched", as they called themselves, tend to have a bit of a god complex. Us sanctuary people just call them like we see them, vampires. The virus is not anything like a real death, although it may feel like it. Once the virus swims through the blood stream, some new vamps can feel a comatose death, like you did; while others convulse and look like they are auditioning for Linda Blair's role from *The Exorcist*. Others only experience what could be described as a bad hangover. Plus the Vampires that are born that way don't get to experience such goodness. If a person rejects the virus, then they simply die without any benefits."

David tilted his head and looked at Khira with an odd, sad expression. "I'm not sure whether to congratulate you or not, sweets." Khira grunted at the remark and glared angrily. David coughed nervously and continued. "Zachary is actually an underling. He works for a psycho who is the Queen Bee-atch in these parts by the name of Lilian. If Zachary turned you, it must have been by her design. However, more likely than not, she wanted you dead."

"Me? What the fuck for? What the hell did I do to her? I didn't even know Vampires really existed until about a week ago. Who the hell does she think she is?"

"Ah! For that, we need to go to the past in our time machine and learn the origin of the clans and of Brânswood," David retorted as if a college professor. Khira rolled her eyes and sighed. David ignored her, as he continued, "Well, the Sectors existed for many years lurking in the shadows of society. Back then, they were all disorganized rabble. Feudal, really. Whoever was most powerful would prey on those who were weaker. Some banded together for defense or to topple other clans or humans who were trying to drive them out. It wasn't until..."

"Yeah, none of this crap pertains to me. If I must submit myself to this 'lesson', can we get a little more to the here and now? I'd like to finish this up sometime this century," Khira interrupted. David huffed but switched his mental gears to comply.

"Fine, we'll move onto something more current. Now, Lilian. She pretty much holds the greatest power within the clans, or at least has gained the most respect amongst them. By that I don't just mean the local chapter, but almost all of the ones in this hemisphere."

"There's more? How many more?"

"Hundreds, maybe thousands; no one knows for sure. Brânswood has been trying to get an exact number for years, but has been unsuccessful as most of our informants end up dead before they can check in."

"Fuck me. Wait. Who's this Brânswood person? You work for him?" asked Khira. David smiled since he was finally getting to the good part.

"Brânswood is not a 'him', but rather a 'they'. Actually, it's more of an organization, really. It's what you would call the good guys or the white hats. See, back in the day when Lilian moved to town and started setting up shop, she was involved with another Vampire named Liam Wallace, although this is believed to be an alias named after William Wallace. Anyways, back then, he was the power behind the bitch. He was ambitious and sought to organize the *Touched* like no one had ever done before. He wanted to start a group that would help organize Vampires and integrate them to fit into society; help them hide in plain sight. He, along with some other clever muckety mucks, founded the Brânswood Institute to achieve this goal. Max played a major...."

Khira cut him off once more. "Hold it. You're saying that the good guys used to work for the bad guys? What the hell?"

"I was getting to that part, Miss Interrupt-a-lot. Now shush!" replied David. "Now where was I?" after a short pause, he continued. "Yes, Brânswood did indeed work for the Sectors at one time, but a schism developed between them after Lilian took over leadership. I'm not sure exactly what happened or why. All I know is that things turned darker, more decadent under her control and those leading the clans, being Max, Lorelai and..."

"Wait, did you say, *Lorelai*? Now, I think you are making up names or got all caught up on Gilmore Girls" said Khira who would have jumped out of her chair if she could have. David pinched the bridge of his nose in frustration. He could feel a headache coming on; a headache named Khira.

He waited for Khira to settle back down into her seat before continuing. "Yes, Khira, I did say Lorelai. You would have known the name, if Paige hadn't been such a pest and taken the books that Brânswood sent."

"What books?" Khira did not know of anything sent to her by whatever Brânswood was. "Who is Lorelai? Should I know her? Wait, I don't even want to know, do I?"

David looked confused. However, he knew what he had to tell her next. It was too important to hold onto anymore. He did not know how she would respond to the truth. He hoped the spell containing her would be strong enough.

"Lorelai is, er, *was* Lilian's twin sister. She had a falling out with her sister and inspired Brânswood to switch from being a place that helped Vampires into one that kept an eye on them to make sure they toed in line. I'm sorry to be the one to have to tell you this, Khira. I had hoped her journal would have explained this to you, but Lorelai was your mother." David winced and waited for the bomb to drop. He was thankful that Khira was secured into the chair; otherwise, she'd have most likely thrown it at him.

Khira just sat there staring at him with an unreadable expression on her face. After a minute of quiet tension, she replied with only one word, "Bullshit."

David sagged as the defense he was preparing lost all its momentum. "No, really, it's true, Khira. Lorelai was your mother, who makes Lilian your aunt. I'm really sorry, hon."

"No, my mother was Eve Chamberlain. She wasn't a Vampire. She was a homemaker and a teacher. Most of all, Eve Chamberlain didn't have fangs. She was human." A bloody tear peeked out from Khira's eye, but she stifled it before it fell.

"That is true, Khira," continued David, "but, she was once Lorelai, the Vampire. No one knows how she accomplished it, but she somehow managed to rid herself of her Vampire's body and turned into the woman who would eventually become your mother."

"She found a cure?" asked Khira incredulously. "There is a cure?"

David sighed and went to his board and started organizing the information for her. "Focus, Khira. We're not sure exactly, but we don't really view it as a 'cure'. Brânswood has been searching for one for many, many years and has had no luck so far. So, whatever it was that she did to become human again died with her. The only clues we have is that she must have put the secret down in one of her journals. Those journals are supposed to hold the key not only to Lorelai's state of mind, but also to the secret of how Lorelai was able to become your mom, Eve."

Khira sank back into her chair. It was hard to know what she was thinking. Was she thinking about how she never truly knew her mother as she thought she did? Yet, she never felt she really knew that woman anyway. Did the prospect of a cure for her newfound affliction give her hope to return to her former life? David couldn't be sure, but he wanted to give her a hug if it was only possible. Being dead really sucked sometimes, and not in the good way.

"So," started Khira, "if I'm related to this Lilian, then why does she want me dead? Are vamps not big on families? Plus, if Lilian is so dangerous, why did my mom stay within the same vicinity? Why would she put us at risk?"

"I don't know what your mother was thinking. We can only assume she wanted to hide in plain sight. While Brânswood knew Lorelai had become Eve, the only intel the sanctuary provided to the Sector was that Lorelai was no more. We still don't know how Lilian found out." David sighed. "As far as coming after you, maybe your existence reminds her of her unpleasant past losing her sister or maybe she thinks that you could become a threat to her and to her power. When the dust had settled, Lilian had your family killed," said David.

"So why track me down and attempt to kill me? Why all the bullshit? This is all too much." Khira was desperate to pull a Paige and hide from the world.

David wished he could give Khira a reprieve but knew he was arming her with information that could save her new life. "Vampire politics are extremely complicated and that's where Brânswood comes in. We've been hampering their efforts to find you, along with their other projects, whenever we got the opportunity. I was assigned to protect you and your cousin once we knew they were on your trail."

Khira became thoughtful and grew serious. "What about Zachary?"

"Again, Zachary," replied David. He gave a reflective pause to choose his words carefully. "Zachary is one of Lilian's lieutenants, her right-hand man, so to speak. He's a handsome charmer, who just happens to be a cold-blooded killer. He has stalked and killed more innocent victims than you would believe. It was when he was assigned to hunt you we knew they wouldn't make the same mistake twice."

"Mistake?" she asked. "What mistake? I never let anyone get close to me and keep to myself. How did he manage to find me?"

David pondered that and started drawing diagrams on his white board showing lines of progression and links between stick figures whom she assumed were supposed to represent all the people involved. "I don't know how he got put on your trail, but he managed to track you down through Paige."

"What? How?" The surprised of this revelation caused Khira to raise the volume of her voice.

"Shhh. Keep it down. I don't know. But it seems that they closed in on the family. One of the underlings had assumed that it was your aunt, not your mother, in the car with your father. He wasn't one of the bright ones to work for Lilian. Some bad intel made him think Paige was actually Lorelai's daughter."

Khira was dumbfounded and couldn't find her voice. She looked up to the ceiling, as if she could somehow see her cousin through the floor. She became sad as she took in the implications of everything that David was telling her. She continued.

"So, everything that happened to her, her accident, her mugging, all of that was them trying to get to me, but was pretty much a failure due to some idiot getting the who's who wrong?"

"Yes," confirmed David. "You have to understand, they had no idea what you looked like. It wasn't like they had your picture on file or that either one of you would look like Lorelai or Lilian, for that matter. All they had to go on was that they were looking for a girl your age and the Chamberlain name. When the hired help closed in on the family, he closed in on her by mistake. Her 'Day from Hell' was their attempt to kill her by thinking it was you. But once they got close enough to realize the truth, it was too late. The damage was done. After such a mistake, they pulled back and focused on verifying your identity before sending someone in to finish the job."

"Zachary," Khira stated in a flat tone.

"Zachary," confirmed David. "He did his best to find you, torture you, have his way with you, and kill you. Trust me; it may not have been necessarily in that order. Obviously, he failed. But considering what he did instead? Maybe he should have killed you. I'm sorry, Khira."

"But he didn't kill me. He could have, but he didn't. So why did he stop?"

"I don't know, Hon. But you might have made an impression upon him. Although, he's never really shown many emotions given he is a pure born. And yet, even now, he's outside waiting for you." Khira turned at the mention of that fact as if she could somehow see him through the walls. "Don't worry. The barrier I erected around the house will keep any and all Vampires from entering the house. So, you're safe for now."

"Safe? How the hell can you even say that word?" Paige demanded to know, as both her voice and presence broke into the conversation. With David's attention no longer on her, Khira was able to loosen her position on the couch. Paige came down from her perch with the notebooks in hand.

"Can you let me get up now?" asked Khira in a quiet, resigned voice. David nodded somberly before turning his attention back to Paige. He muttered something under his breath and waved goodbye.

She felt the pressure that was holding her down release, and she was able to get up from the chair to stretch. "Since my presence is no longer needed, I'm gonna let you two work this thing out for yourselves." Before she headed for the stairs, Paige solemnly handed the journals to the rightful owner.

David started to try and put words together for an explanation to Paige, but her anger preceded him. "WHAT...THE...FUCK!"

Paige waited in a huff. She paced back and forth trying to calm down. However, the more she attempted the angrier she felt. David hovered closer to her and began to form his plea, but she brought her hand up to stop him. She had difficulty forming words through the rage building within, aimed towards him at that moment. She was about to start on her tirade when the sound of thunder disrupted her thoughts.

Paige collected herself and wanted to calmly confront David. So much for the best of intentions, she thought. She sat in a chair near-by, to steady herself for the war of words that she needed to win.

"You knew that we could have been in danger this whole time. You knew that someone was after me. You used me in order to get to Khira. Who the HELL do you think you are? If you knew what was going to happen to me, why did you just let it happen and then go on to pretend to be my friend? But I was never really your friend, was I? We were just your assignment." She saw the glass that Khira had left on the table. She picked it up and threw the glass towards David. Instinctively, he moved although the glass would have gone straight through him. He approached her.

"How was I supposed to explain what was going on out in the real world, even during a time that you actually existed within?" he asked. Paige would not look at him. David tried once more to convince her that his actions had always been in her best interest. "I did not know that it would be you that cold bitch would attempt to kill. My death happened the same day as your 'lucky' day. Ruby had previously been the one keeping watch. She is my boss, and it was her that viewed my death and the events that happened to you as some sort of opportunity, as some sort of sign that I should be assigned to the house. For me, it has been a blessing. And Beeatch, you are my best friend whether you like it or not," he finished with a smile, still trying to win her back over.

"No." She spoke in a whisper now. Paige would not look up at David, because she did not want him to see the tears she was fighting. "You were never my friend." Her words fell solemnly from her lips. She stood up and walked over to the closed curtains, as if she could see through them. "If you had been my friend, you would have trusted me with the truth. If you had been my friend, you wouldn't have used me. If you had been my friend, you would never have put me or my family in danger. No, you were never my friend."

"Paige, if you would just listen to me, I could explain."

"Like you explained things to Khira? You played into it with jest at first and then dropped the truth of what you call the outside world as if performing for the Queen of England. The seriousness of what has transpired to both me and her surpasses any concept to you. Those events were homework to you and now you get to remind us that we are still not protected from harm VIA A FUCKING POWER POINT PRESENTATION? How dare you!" she scolded him in a voice that she had previously only used for her invisible clients. Yet this time, the tone of her voice left her with little power against the betrayal she felt.

"Paige, sweetie, I am your friend. I never had to make my presence known to you," he started his explanation, but she cut him short.

"Oh, thank you for doing that! Thank you for showing yourself. However, you kept who you really were at bay. You'd think that a person of your background would be tired of closeted secrets, but no, you maintained a backstabbing personality worthy of his own *Lifetime* movie. Get out," she demanded.

"Paige, if I leave..."

Once more, Paige cut him short, "*When* you leave, not *if* you leave. You *will* be gone by morning. You say that we are having problems with Vampires? Fine. I'll give you by dawn's early light to vanish. Until then, I do not want to see or hear you for the rest of the evening."

David wanted to try and heal this rift, but felt it was too late. Although his barrier would drop once he left, he knew dawn would not protect them. However, his words would not break through Paige's anger. He headed upstairs, leaving Paige standing stoic, staring out of a window. She did not even bother to see what was out there. Paige did not notice the handsome man, waiting for her cousin. She could not see past the pain drowning her essence. David had the answers for everything in her life. He could have eased her pain so long ago with the truth. Instead, he was just a guard to the prison she created for herself.

Chapter Fifteen

Paige's and David's voices intermingled in a complicated dance, travelling from the living room up the stairway. While Khira had concerns for her cousin, she knew Paige had to face this fresh wound on her own. Betrayal within the house was something Paige had worked so hard to avoid. Paige had been used to the harsh treatment from her cousin, but they were still family.

If she wanted to, Khira would be able to hear word for word of the argument with precision due to her new state of being. She opted for restraint instead and concentrated her strength to block the voices from downstairs. Khira hesitated before heading into her bedroom, fighting the urge to return to the living room to play mediator between the two. She knew better of it. Shutting the door behind her was like turning off the television from this Dancing with the Stars meets Real Housewives of Atlanta bad reality show.

Khira walked over to her window. She could see a black SUV nearby. There did not seem to be anyone within, but it was hard to tell with the windows tinted so dark. She brushed her hands down her body. *Is there still life in me?* she wondered. All the strength she had garnered to meet with Zachary had waned due to the interruption of the Discovery Channel lesson from David. Now, she had her own betrayal to deal with, her confidence.

She sat at her vanity attempting to find the character she would need to portray to face Zachary with whatever news he had for her. She did not want to let on that all these changes were terrifying to her. That was not her style. However, she really did not have a style to call her own.

She had adopted so many personas in the past, she believed she never developed one of her own. Her mother gave her the paranoid conspiracy theorist to try on, questioning everyone's motives. That could work towards Zachary, however, Khira did not own the strength at the moment; the power needed to be such a calculating personality.

While trying to figure out who to be, the rain of tears came down her face. Pink hued streams rolled down Khira's cheek, a mixture of blood with saline water. She wiped them away, however, they would not stop. Never had she felt so alone. Never had she wanted her mother here to tell her what to do next like she did in this exact moment. *What would Eve Do?* Khira thought.

To be technical, Eve ran away from Lilian. This fight was something her mother had attempted to guard her from. Yet, the harshness of the lessons that Eve had provided Khira also were to prepare for the possibility of being found by the Sector. It felt as if Eve knew Khira would not be able to escape this fate. Khira found the answer of who she should become for her confrontation with Zachary.

Khira reached for a cleansing balm and smeared the oily substance over her entire face, even her closed eyelids. She stretched out a hand to grab a make-up remover cloth and took off the makeup she had previously worn. She would need a different presentation for this persona. She laughed at the thought of using cosmetics as warpaint.

Before starting on her new look, Khira walked to her bed to where she had left her iPod. She turned the volume midway and kept it playing from there. She did not need the buds to hear the lyrics from Warpaint's "Disco//Very" came through, dripping of harmonized women's tongues, telling of a woman who would eat the listener alive. Khira grabbed her phone and returned to the vanity to complete her look.

She started to pick up a make-up brush, but before she could start her look, her mind took her off path. Khira thought of what warning to provide Zachary who was waiting for her downstairs. She inputted his number into her phone and started the text:

Give me a few to ditch these losers and then you may take me to your fearless bitch. Khira wanted to send this message to the vampire, however, thought better of it. Again, she thought of what her mother would send as a message instead.

I appreciate your patience for waiting for me and you shall be rewarded by my presence. I do have questions that I believe you could be the only one to provide the answers. I apologize for the delay and will be on my way out shortly. Satisfied with the cold tone of the powerful and calculating words she chose, Khira hit the send button.

After the stern tone of the text, Khira softened as concern for Paige's wellbeing washed over her. Khira listened for the war downstairs. She could not hear Paige or David's voices anymore. As if to reply to her thoughts, she heard the door of her cousin's bedroom slam shut.

She returned her attention to herself in the mirror. She still felt a little small and had a short Stuart Smalley moment. A light danced across her lavender eyes. Khira felt it may have been provided by her mother's spirit. Khira took a breath and began to apply her make up.

Khira was deciding which shade of liquid lipstick to apply when her phone buzzed a texted response. She grabbed it and saw it was from the number Zachary had provided her. *For you, I will wait. For you, I have your answers. For you, for you.* Khira gagged at the sentiment. However, it also gave her a clue that she may, indeed, have more power than expected.

She opted for fierce crimson matte shade. While her lips were dead on point, the shade remind Khira too much of blood. She picked up shimmering gold shade and dabbed a little bit in the middle of her lower lip. She pressed her lips together. She glanced back up to check her warpaint. The light came across her eyes once more before settling on a small box.

Khira picked up the small wooden hand carved jewelry box and opened the lid. Inside was a ring her mother had always worn. It was a simple white gold ring with small amethyst buds placed within. Khira slid the ring on the middle finger on her right hand. Khira felt strength passing from her mother to her through this token. Who else would have the power to help Khira tell these vampires to fuck off?

She grabbed her phone and a bag. Khira opened her bedroom door and peaked out a surveillance, attempting to decide which direction to start her escape. The hall was a ghost town. Downstairs was as quiet as a mausoleum. Khira made her way down the staircase, glancing over her shoulder with every step. Still there was no Paige and no David.

Khira stopped short of the front door. She readjusted the shoulder strap of her messenger bag and took another breath. *What would Eve do?* She reminded herself as if a rallying cry. Khira opened the front door of the house and stepped past the threshold into this new world waiting for her.

****

David had been demoted down in spirit to a mere shadow since his confidence dissipated after fighting with Paige. He felt all the spells within the house, fall apart as soon as Paige left him to be in the living room by himself. He had been fired from his protector role; a termination more daunting than any boardroom drama.

Ruby had likely witnessed the complete train wreck. If she had not already foreseen it or reviewed the highlight reel on her monitors, it would not be long before the Phoenix would summon him back to the sanctuary. He needed to ready himself to say goodbye to this life he had with Paige and Khira.

Growing up in a religious home, his life choices had always been judged. He was a gay man who wanted to be a queen. His parents never understood the need to perform as Cyn Latex. They did not see it as a role that God intended. However, his grandmother accepted him as she had married her faith with her scientific mind. By her idealogy, there was a difference between understanding and reality; however, at the same time, while the rules of science were concrete, ideas were evolving, much like humans. Death for most people had been thought as the extinguishing a light.

While his family religious upbringing believed in everlasting life through Christ, there was still an ending with death and a promise of everlasting life in Heaven. However, his Doña Maribel had thought of it as physical body no longer able to hold the energy or light within by scientific design not through saving grace. Either way there was no nirvana waiting to welcome David when he died.

His parents did not hold the customs for David as they had for every other family member. David had been thought of dead since he did not live a true Catholic life in their eyes. He had been judged more harshly by them than by any God. Still, he had a proper burial, paid for by his grandmother. Due to her beliefs, she did not believe he was no longer on this plane. She could only hope that she would still see him again. When David passed, Ruby had grabbed his soul and robbed him of that chance.

David learned that Maribel was more knowledgeable on death than his parents. He still existed by energy rather than a physical form. Somehow, Ruby had the capability to control this type of energy. Ruby liked to hold onto her secrets as tight as her powers. Max probably knew how Ruby became what she did, but the old man never gave into work gossip. The founding father never gave in to really treading outside the inner sanctum of his office. Whether through alternative astrophysical theories or something beyond, David did not need to understand how it worked. It just did.

The headache started to buzz first. Ruby was bringing him back into Brnswood. The pull would be more painful if he struggled against this action. Ruby would chose which domicile to transport him to from the house. He was a slave more than an employee. He accepted this as it may have been better than a true *death*. He had learned to close his mind and eyes so as not to be exposed to all dimensions at once. Within a single breath, he was no longer within the girls' home. Instead, he was in darkness.

David was surprised at first. He knew where he was somewhere within the Sanctuary without any indication of markings around him. He was in the void that Ruby had set aside as his room and board until his next mission, if there was one.

He failed Paige. He did not care that Ruby would eventually make time in her schedule to berate him. He still cared for his friend. He almost did not care if he remained through the end of time in this voided prison as long as Paige could forgive him.

Until he could see his friend again or Ruby gave him a new assignment, he would revert to his pure light energy, although he would still appear as a small speck within this darkness. He would keep memories of dancing to Todrick Hall while attempting to cheer Paige up after Khira had torn her down once more to keep some small hope that he could redeem himself.

While Khira had been the original goal of his assignment, David often wondered if he was meant to be there for Paige instead. She needed him much like he needed her. However, he had broken her heart. He would never need her to forgive him. That would be selfish to ask. He just needed her to heal. *My heart, I'm so sorry I betrayed you.* His light changed from white to a pale blue. A lavender line broke through the colors. David knew if he was physically capable, that purple line would be a stream of tears, mourning the loss of his friendship.

****

Eleanor stood before four pets with a to-do list in mind to make the White Room presentable for the stay of the mystery guest. Lilian had not informed the Lady of the Manor who would be the one to visit Thirlestane and Eleanor learned not to question her Mistress. Loyalty was in her blood; never having to go through pet training.

Victoria, Karina, Shaikha and Feliz formed a semi-circle. Victoria was small and plump in her physique. Her wavy long brown hair was up in a messy bun, showing off an undercut design of a lotus flower. Karina was slim and would at times attempt to shake her black curtain bangs that covered out of her bright green eyes as her head was lowered and keeping her hands where Eleanor had demanded. Shaika had bronze skin and silky black hair with soft brown highlights. Her mane went down to the middle of her back. Feliz could barely keep still, her golden chipmunk cheeks covering her brown eyes whenever she smiled.

Victoria, Karina, Shaikha hung their heads with white gloved hand out for Eleanor to inspect prior to beginning their chore. Feliz was more of a problematic pet, who was attempting to memorize all the details of the White Room, as if taking pictures, clicking with every blink of an eye. Eleanor cleared her throat, hoping that the sound would draw Feliz's attention towards her Lady. However, Feliz's ADHD had other ideas. Eleanor stepped closer to the absent-minded pet and clapped her hands. Eleanor's steel eyes caught the light grey eyes of the young girl. She looked towards the other pets and the word "oops" escaped her lips. She hung her head and held her hands out, palms up to match the other women.

Eleanor paced between the pets. The gloves themselves were the only items of clothing the pets wore for this task. Their bodies were hairless other than the locks that hung from their heads. She paused while collecting her thoughts, attempting to find the proper direction to give these pets to ensure the room would be immaculate, without the need for corrections.

Feliz's nose decided to break the silence with a big sneeze. As the pet had no attire, she attempted to get as much as she could within the crick of her arm. Eleanor walked over to Feliz and pulled out a white silk handkerchief. Feliz sensed the doom of having the Lady of the Manor pull so much attention to her, especially prior to the beginning of their assignment. As soon as she took the handkerchief from Eleanor, Feliz could not stop her tears from falling. She blew her nose and began to sob uncontrollably and attempted to return Eleanor's handkerchief.

"Go to the kitchen. I'm sure they could use your assistance as you are no help here." Eleanor scolded Feliz.

The pet shrunk her shoulders forward as she turned to leave. She glanced at the other three pets in hopes of some reprieve. The other pets did not move as not to face Eleanor's demeaning wrath that had been stirred by Feliz's behavior.

Kitty had been waiting outside of the White Room. She heard the commotion caused by the inexperienced pet and saw this as an opportunity to get information to Khira. As the door opened, Kitty thought a prayer to herself. She reached out to Feliz to grant the girl a little peace. Feliz returned Kitty's glance with a smile and headed towards the staircase, leading down to the kitchen. The tears vanished and a hop returned to Feliz's stride.

Kitty bent over to smooth her laced up thigh high soft leather boots, and to make sure the journal she had taken from Lilian's room had not moved too much. The boots were the only thing adorning the pet's body so she would not differ too much from the three other pets inside.

Kitty straightened herself and opened the door to the room. The other three pets had already started cleaning different posts within the room. Eleanor did not look happy that Lilian's pet had come in. Kitty did not know if the look of disdain was standard for the Lady or if it was due to her presence. Eleanor could have felt that Lilian did not trust her enough to prepare the room for such a secretive guest and needed supervision. Whatever the case, Eleanor changed her behavior and assigned Kitty to the closet and to the bed. Kitty felt relief as these were the two main areas she would need to visit anyways.

The other three were quick to make the room highly presentable. Eleanor gathered them while Kitty was still within the wardrobe. As

Victoria, Karina, and Shaikha exited the room, Eleanor approached Kitty.

"You are taking a bit of time longer than is required. However, the Mistress must have tasked her with additional objectives in mind. I trust that you will not bring Her name down."

Kitty bowed with respect. The pet respected the role Eleanor played just like the roles everyone else played at the Mistress' bequest. She just did not like how Eleanor ran things with such a tight fist. Kitty wondered if Eleanor had ever been broken like the other pets here. Kypris saved Kitty during her *training*. Kitty worried for the others that did not have such a helping hand in dealing with the pain. Eleanor gave a sigh and made her exit.

Once she heard the door close, Kitty reached into her boot in order to retrieve the journal. She walked over to the nightstand by the bed and laid it gently. She did not know what knowledge Khira would have prior to visiting the manor and hoped Lilian's journal could help. The words could strengthen Khira's fight, but something else would be warranted to help Khira if things turned physical.

Kitty returned to the closet. She went to the back and found the hidden safe that was found in most of the rooms for such honored guests. She had seen Reed use a master code before and entered the numbers on the keypad. Luckily a full bottle of blood was there as well as a clean empty champagne flute. Kitty took both before kicking the safe closed.

She placed the decanter and glass on the nightstand. Kitty opened the drawer of the nightstand, looking for any pieces of paper. There were none but there were at least a couple of pens. Kitty took one out and picked up the journal. She scanned to the back of the book and was able to find some blank pages. She tore one out. She folded the piece, with origami precision, into the shape of a cup. Kitty took the pen and wrote the words "Drink Me." The pet gave a little giggle as she placed the "cup" next to the bottle. She returned the pen and closed the drawer of the nightstand. Kitty left the room, returning to her Mistress.

****

Zachary spotted Khira as soon as she stepped outside her house. He took a parasol and approached her, shading her, and looking more like a chauffeur or a celebrity's bodyguard than a warden coming to take a prisoner away.

Khira paused at the scene. "Seriously? What century are we in?" she huffed.

"Trust me, please. It is better to be safe than sorry when it comes to the sun." While the day was slightly overcast, Khira was newly Touched and neither of the two knew how the sun would affect her. Zachary raced her to the SUV parked on the street. He opened the door for her. Khira halfway expected paparazzi to follow her since she was being treated like a Kardashian; famous without having done anything.

Once they were both inside, Zachary took a hard look at Khira. She looked past him, trying to mentally get him to stop staring and just start the car. He turned his head to focus on the road before him. "You have transitioned faster than expected."

"Hello to you, too, asshole." Khira snapped at him while folding her arms, looking as if she would throw a tantrum and leave the vehicle. He sped onto a major road, in hopes that she would not abort her trip.

Zachary thought best not to return the tone, but instead he attempted to defuse the situation as much as possible. Although Khira was coming willingly, it was not like the trip to the manor had been by choice. The two rode in silence for a time before Zachary decided on making a peace offering. He touched a few buttons on the steering wheel. The middle console opened. Two green tinted bourbon size glasses appeared. After a couple of more button pushing, a spout came over the side and started to pour a red liquid into both glasses.

Zachary took one of the glasses that sat closest to him. If she saw him drink it, maybe she would trust him enough to take a sip as well. The aroma tempted her. She had not been able to take anything without upsetting her entire body, other than the blood David had provided earlier. Her hunger was still adamant despite the short relief from the previous *snack*.

She took the glass and gave Zachary a judgmental glance. She held the cup to her nose. There was a copper smell coming off the glass with an earthy undertone. It was blood for sure. It smelled similar to what she had drunk back at the house. However, this batch seemed richer. She took a sip. The warm liquid slid down, bringing energy to her affect while also setting her mind at ease.

"I will only give you the answers to what I assume are the questions you would ask." He looked over to her. She returned his gaze with a cold stare. Zachary looked deep into her eyes and they seemed to change color for a moment. Her composure seemed to soften but, perhaps it was a trick of the light. Then without further ado, he proceeded.

"Vampire...Myth...No, that's true...You were targeted, but for death, not for this..." He paused as if to come up with whatever next question she would have, "Yes, I did enjoy it too." Khira wondered if reading minds would be a new trick for her to learn with her new forthcoming abilities. "A Touched cannot read minds," he continued but his voice seemed so far away.

Her head began to feel squeezed as if bits of asphalt being crushed between rubber grooves of the tires below. A darkness flashed within her, a deep depression and drowsiness overcame her. Something was wrong here, she thought. Everything was wrong! Khira felt like panic should wash over her. However, her body betrayed her and began to calm. She heard her breath quicken but everything else began to move at a slower pace. She felt her eyelids become heavy. She had to get away from him and from whatever he was planning. In her mind's eye, she saw herself pulled at the door handle but looking down, her hand remained in her lap. Her body felt like it weighed a ton. At first, she thought it was her sickness doing it, but it was different somehow. She looked back at him and seeing his smile, she turned her gaze down to her glass. He must have put something in her drink. She looked up at him confused and aggravated.

"Yes, I have drugged you. How else would I have gotten you to see Lilian?" Khira passed out.

Chapter Sixteen

Khira rolled her eyes open and examined the room she was in, soaking up the surroundings. She eased herself up to sit straight from the floor she had been using as a bed. She took in her environment but did not recognize anything. The room felt like it had to be someone's private library. The bookcases were structured by dark auburn stained oak. All the hardback books were so ornate. She guessed that the library was filled with nothing but first editions. The antheneum looked like something from the 19th century; this study was more ornate and more plush in comparison to The Historian's Hideaway.

She stepped up to look at the book bindings in hopes of getting a clue where she was. None of the books had titles or authors labeling any of the spines. She brought her index finger up to the books. The leather covers seemed to drip and bleed onto the floor, all of the books but the one she touched. Khira took the book from the shelf.

When she opened it, pages of ivory parchment paper were blank at first then, the book seemed to come alive with illustrations appearing before her eyes. Inside, the numerous pictures were all arranged in a certain way to tell a story. The pictures began to move and speak like a movie. The book became a talking photo album.

There were young, twin girls in the first photo. It was black and white; however, it looked like one of the sisters shed a tear of blood in dark crimson red. The other sister started to sing a lullaby, but Khira could not make out the words. The melody felt so familiar, and it soothed away her fears.

Khira turned the page. The next photo was that of a family. The twin sisters were now well into their teens. They were with their parents. The mother cradled a newborn child. Khira assumed the child was a boy, as the only thing not black and white in this photo was a blue blanket swaddling the baby. One of the sisters sang the same lullaby, but in a more calming voice than before. The other sister pouted and stared straight into the camera lens. Khira turned the page.

It was the same family. Instead of the baby boy, there was a gravestone with the name of James inscribed upon it. The parents looked older, tired, and worn. The girls looked the same as the previous picture, although they didn't stand together anymore. Another tear of blood dressed one of the girl's cheeks. The music stopped at this point. Khira looked over her shoulders to see if anyone was watching her. Satisfied She turned to the next page.

The two girls were picnicking in a cemetery. One of the sisters appeared happy, while the other simply lay down upon one of the graves. There was new music; it was not the soft voice of a lullaby. It felt more like a celebratory march rather than a reverie. Khira went to turn the next page, but as she tried she got a paper cut. The crimson drop ran down the page and then soon the whole album began to bleed. She dropped it to *the floor and the blood pooled all around it. The bookshelves disappeared behind a showering of blood. The floor also began to bleed.*

"I've missed you, Lorelai," whispered into her ears. She shut her eyes and tried to block out everything she had seen and heard. It was all so unbelievable. She collapsed on the floor as the pool of blood surrounded her. She could not move and found herself floating within a crimson sea. There was no more floor and no more walls, only darkness and blood. She managed to free one arm and shoot it past the blood, but the movement caused her to sink faster. She wanted to scream. Her new body betrayed her. Before the darkness claimed her, her only thoughts were of her poor cousin and of the man who had changed her life.

****

Zachary had no trouble roaming through the servant's quarters with his sacked up treasure over his shoulder. His heart, not to mention his loins, still demanded that he take Khira to his quarters or to the nearest bedroom, rip all her clothing off and have his way with her. His head, along with impending doom should he fail, kept him centered on the mission that Lilian dictated to him.

He adjusted Khira's limp body on his shoulder. Even unconscious she was hard to handle. His strength had no problem with her weight. However, he had not carried a body in this manner for some time. He missed it in a way. Times were better then.

Once he held her in a better position, Zachary had no problem racing up the back staircase. He reached the main hallway in record time. The pets roaming the hall had been trained well, as none seemed to pay heed to him, except for one. Lilian's new favorite, Kitty, passed him in the hall and upon doing so looked him straight in the eye in a very odd manner. Such behavior by a pet to any of the Touched merited a severe punishment. However, looking again he saw that she moved along lethargically, head bowed. Did he imagine seeing her stare? He shook his head and thought his plan must be causing him to be as paranoid as a werewolf. Zachary continued his way.

Finally, he found himself in front of the Emissary's quarters. He went inside and set Khira down upon the bed. He removed the sack. Almost instinctively, he adjusted her position so that she could sleep comfortably. He brushed her hair back behind her ear as to gaze on her face once more. Sighing, he took in the sight of her and smiled. She truly was a beauty. Her importance to him and his goals necessitated that he take action to help her. Zachary decided it was only fair that Khira regain her strength for the trials ahead. As such, he would give her a little gift to help her do so.

He was about to go into the safe hidden within the room's closet to retrieve some blood, when he noticed the filled canter on a nearby nightstand. There was a note that instructed "Drink Me". He added some text to the note. Someone had the same idea he had, knowing Khira would need something to at least bring her on a closer playing field to Lilian, but who, he wondered.

****

The tunnels underneath the mansion were dark and silent. Here and there the sound of dripping water or the scurrying of vermin could be heard throughout the passages. Dust and cobwebs decorated the halls, and one would not think that they had seen any usage since the construction of the mansion. The tunnels were as old as the house itself, dating back to sometime in the 19th century. Rumor had it the tunnels were used by bootleggers or smugglers to hide their ill-gotten gains or perhaps used to hide runaway slaves. Truth was, besides the wine cellar which had seen constant use and update over the years, the tunnels were forgotten remnants that were ignored by the servants and staff. However, the Touched were never ones to waste anything.

In a far-off passage, some distance from the mansion proper, stood a decaying brick wall. If someone were to encounter it while exploring the tunnels, it would mistakenly seem a dead end. A soft rumbling sound began to stir the stillness of the tunnel. Bits of dust and stone fell from the ceiling as the brick wall began to crack and open itself to reveal a hidden door. Eerie violet light emerged from the portal followed by a cascading mist, which settled down and spread itself like a creeping horror upon the floor. Reed emerged from the hidden lab as if he was somehow emerging from a distant world. He stepped away from the disinfecting spray that marked the outer airlock to the medical facility and stepped off to face one side of the split wall. Pressing a series of bricks in sequence, the walls of the laboratory began to close and seal themselves to resume its facade once again as an obstructing wall.

Dusting himself of any lingering material, Reed straightened his outfit and walked down the passage back to the mansion. Having to decontaminate himself each time he entered or exited the lab was an annoyance, but a necessary one. He could deal with the disinfectant spray, but shied away from the ultra-violet barriers that shielded certain parts of the lab. The light may be good at destroying any foreign material from contaminating the laboratory, but it also had the effect of harming the bodies of the Touched just as much as natural sunlight. The walk was a brisk one for most humans, but a short distance for a Vampire. In truth, Reed enjoyed stalking the dark forgotten corridors below the mansion. It gave him a certain sense of belonging as one would expect from a Vampire from Gothic times. In his mind, he made an imposing figure emerging from the dark crypts to plague the world of man once more.

Emerging back into the sanctum of the mansion, he focused his thoughts back to his duties and kept his wits about him as he presented himself to the members of his clan. One never knew who might be watching. As he made his way back towards his own room, his thoughts strayed. He hadn't been able to be alone with Kitty lately, which made him wonder if his little spy was beginning to wiggle out from his grasp. Perhaps he should find her and see what she has learned. It would also be good to impress upon her the fact that she was still his to control. That lesson was one that should never be forgotten.

He continued walking up the stairs into the main lobby. He wondered whether he should alter his plans to use Kitty as a scapegoat as well. It was good to have a Patsy in place to assume blame once trouble fell. On the other hand, it would not hurt to have her by his side in the end as well. No, it would be best to dispose of her once the time came, he thought. Pets and pawns are easily replaced.

He had already found himself in the forum of the main house and noticed that most of the staff was missing. Even on quiet days, there was a servant working or a pet moving about. However, silence hung everywhere. Either Lady Eleanor was slacking on her job, which was unlikely, or something else was going on. Curious, he decided to change directions and head towards the Parlor room. A visit with Mal would be a good way to kill time and make his presence known to the other Vampires.

Once he arrived at the Parlor gate, he noticed all the arrangements in the room had been cleaned and sorted. Where before there were only several Familiars bound for punishment, here he found the room loaded to capacity. Every cross, cage and harness were occupied by Familiars, some of them new. Each Familiar was dressed in elegant bonds of various makes, obviously displayed for inspection. There were no other Vampires about or any Keepers attending the room. If that was the case, then it meant that other arrangements were being tended to which usually meant a visitor had arrived, and the attention to detail indicated it was a very important visitor at that. His interest piqued, he decided to forego visiting Mal and head up to the higher corridors to see what he could learn about this special visitor.

****

Ruby sat at her desk, browsing some of the latest messages from her little *birds.* While Max had his past projects with tracing the Sectors, her research would bring forth the truths to the secrets of the Touched, thus elevating Brânswood. While she sifted through papers, Ruby caught a faint glow from the corner of her eye. Her sensor was quick to alert her of an incoming presence. The glow reached through the bottom of her door, seeping in and out like a neon mist. Ruby straightened her papers before piling them at the right-hand corner of her desk. "Enter," she commanded.

The door did not move. Instead, David phased through the door. He hovered toward's Ruby's desk, stopping a few feet shy of her workspace. He bowed and raised his head but would not look at her. He began to whisper, "Ms. Kanas..."

"Enough. Why are you not at your post? Oh yes, that's right, you have been dismissed," Ruby announced, embarrassing David by reminding him of his failure.

"Yes ma'am. I have come to ask my next assignment. I wish to return to the Archives, if I may," David requested, still not making eye contact with Ruby. He would rather spend the rest of his time at Brânswood not having to really interact with people. He pushed a memory of Paige out of his mind, realizing how similar they would now be as inmates in their personal prison cells.

"I do not have any new assignments to give out, yet. I just acquired some new projects, but I do not believe that you would be qualified for any of them. I have nothing within the sanctuary to offer you," Ruby commented as she retrieved a cyan jar from the bottom drawer of her desk. "I do, however, have some *space* for you here in my office though," Ruby told him with a smirk. The tone of her voice caused David to instinctively look up, knowing he made a grave mistake.

When he raised his eyes, he noticed that her arm was already stretched out towards him, palm open. The pulsating red ball from her hand grew brighter and brighter. David tried to turn around or even will himself to phase through the floor, but he was too stunned to attempt any endeavor. He felt his essence drawn to her as he began to glow a pink hue. He seemed to fade into the aura embracing him. His last thought was of Paige as his features vanished. He consciously knew he remained in the room although he was no more than a coral ball of light. He hovered one more second before flying straight into Ruby's hand.

She smiled as she closed her hand. She stood and walked over to a cabinet with several ceramic containers. She chose one and lifted the lid of the jar to deposited the soul inside. She quickly replaced the lid. "Selio," she commanded of the vessel. She then placed the jar back in the drawer of her desk. Her pat on the back was short-lived.

Her head started to throb. As she lifted her hand to her temple, she staggered back into her chair. She began to take slow deep breaths. She opened her eyes, as her inner eye began to open as well. A new scene appeared to her. It was fast but detailed with all six senses alert so she could feel the blood fall from her temple, smell the musk surround her, and hear the shallow breaths of the victim within her own ears. The vision was gone with a flash.

Ruby collected herself. Her eyes returned to their normal color. A smile crept onto her face. "Now, that should definitely make things interesting," she stated. She inhaled once more to regain composure and then she pulled forth the lab reports from their nest.

****

When Khira awoke, she was buried under mounds of white linens in a huge feather topped bed in a very large white room. If she had not known better, she would have imagined that a marshmallow had exploded. She sat up quickly and felt her head throb. She wondered what Zachary had slipped her. She began to look around. On the end table next to her was a glass that appeared to have cranberry juice in it. There was a note beside it reading:

Drink me, "Alice". Yes it will make you feel better. Trust me.

The note contained two different sets of handwriting. The words "Drink me" were in one. The other words matched Zachary's handwriting from the previous note he had left her.

"Not on your life," retorted Khira. How could Zachary even think she would trust him after recovering from being drugged. She moved out of bed but felt out of sorts. She could not find her balance. She looked back at the note and then took the glass. Khira imagined having the angel/devil debate on her shoulders. For a moment she wondered if she was still under the affects of the drugs or if this would be a new aspect of her life brought on by the chronic illness she must now live with. Khira tossed both the angel and devil out of her mind and decided either way, the drink would not kill her at least.

It was not cranberry juice, but some sweet and sour syrupy mixture. As she swallowed it did not seem like she had swallowed anything. She was surprised that the liquid was smooth, not having the same acidic affect that the coffee had. She felt that the thick red fluid just absorbed into her. A surge of energy filled her. Indeed, feeling better, she could now focus on the rest of the room.

She noticed a vanity across the room. Eerie familiarity came creeping back to her. Maybe she was back in her dream, and she would wake up back home listening to Paige doing what she does best. She closed her eyes and pinched herself so that she might wake up quicker.

Her eyes opened, but nothing had changed. Khira suddenly felt anger overwhelm her. She wanted to throw something at the mirror to shatter it and pick up the shards and tear away at this dream's facade should that be the only escape. The glass in her hand came to mind. She was about to hurl the tumbler into the mirror, when suddenly there was a knock at the door. It was the first time Khira even noticed the door. Without waiting for a reply, the door swung open.

A small red-headed girl poked her head around the doorway and after staring at Khira for a few moments, finally tip-toed inside. The young girl wore a tight white top and short black shorts causing Khira to think this girl was more lost in this place than she was. Upon further inspection, Khira realized that the clothes were actually painted onto the young woman's body so that she was actually not wearing anything at all! The girl was holding another glass of liquid and another note. She presented these items to Khira in such a grandiose manner that it was hard not to hold back a giggle.

This female had a power that made Khira's anger resolve into more of an aloofness. The girl seemed to wait for a response from Khira and nodded towards the note. Khira expected it to be another note from Zachary but was surprised to recognize the handwriting as being similar to the words "Drink Me." The elegant handwriting was not from Zachary. The note read:

You may call me Kitty. I am a gift from my Mistress to tend to any of your needs.

Puzzled, Khira looked at the young woman. *Who gives people as gifts?* She wondered. She figured the drink would be the same as the one she had before, so she went ahead and exchanged glasses with "Kitty". The young girl took the empty glass and went over to the table where the mirror had been set. Khira watched the girl move about fascinated at the odd spectacle in front of her. She looked back down at the new drink she held. She was still sated from the first glass, so she set it down on the nightstand and went back to watch Kitty work. Kitty had set down the empty glass on the vanity and from a drawer retrieved a golden compact, a wooden hairbrush, a golden comb and a little jar. She arranged the items neatly upon the table.

Once finished with those duties, Kitty returned to where Khira was and sat on the floor nearby, looking up at her. Khira did not know what to do in response to all these gestures. Looking down at the girl, Khira could only think of one thing to say. "Thank you. That is all I guess." Kitty smiled nodding then rose from her place on the floor and left the room, taking the empty glass with her. *Just call me Alice...*she thought to herself echoing Zachary's words.

Chapter Seventeen

Kitty took swift, gentle steps, leading away from the white room. Her new course took her away from the living quarters, heading down towards the parlor room. Her Mistress had instructed her to find Matthew after tending to Khira. The parlor would be the best place to start her mission. Kitty did not like dealing with Matthew, and she visited the parlor only when it was necessary. Too many memories stirred within her every time she stepped foot beyond those walls. However, orders were orders.

"Do you think a bold act could change the course of history, like a drop of water changing the direction of the sea?"

Ruby's words rang through Kitty's thoughts as she trekked towards her destination. They were repetitive, reminding her of her purpose. She could not help but remember why she was at Lilian's mansion and what Brânswood expected of her. Ruby and Flynn, her teacher, had convinced her to help in Brânswood's mission to find a cure for vampirism. They knew Lilian's entourage was up to something nefarious. Ruby wanted Kitty to go undercover within the local Vampire's organization to discover what it was. Flynn had arranged for Kitty to become one of the clan's new recruits by having her answer an advertisement in the local paper that Lilian's cohorts would place every few months.

Money was the biggest bait to lure in potential Familiars. To some, money was a bigger temptation than everlasting life. Money also served as a cover.   Fake medical trials would be advertised. The offer of free rooms, meals and generous pay looked too tempting to poor college dropouts, the homeless or other transients to pass up. There were obvious tests done first at a random warehouse, blood tests, drug tests, stamina tests, IQ tests, the works. The cover of the trials allowed the subject's blood to be tested up front. This permitted the coven to determine if the person in question would be able to withstand the training and conditions endured by their Familiars; to see how easily the person's will could be broken down and then molded back in the coven's favor; and to enable the coven to know up front who could be turned to a vampire and who would be lured into a false belief they were on that path to become Touched.

Kypris made Kitty a prime candidate for Brânswood. Through her priestess training, one lesson Kitty learned firsthand was how close the boundary is between pleasure and pain. Her faith allowed her to not only experience love through pleasure, but through pain as well, as it should be with all things. As such, she should have been immune to the psychological reconstruction employed by the Touched upon their servants. Kitty decided for herself to fake being mute. Being silent meant she would be regarded as harmless and that it would allow others to lower their defenses around her, thus enabling her to obtain vital information that she could use in her mission. Fate set into motion, as Ruby would have seen to it.

Focusing back to her task at hand, Kitty continued down the hall. She turned down towards the grand staircase and stopped for a few seconds. She looked back towards the hall where her Mistress remained, but soon, her thoughts turned to Reed. At first, she had been able to use an alliance with Reed to her advantage to get in as a pet to Lilian, but now his own ambition was becoming a liability to her cover. She had been able to sway him thus far with the blessings of Kypris and keep him from discovering her true intentions. Yet he was strong in both will and form. Although Reed had been through all the same familiar training as Kitty in his own time, Reed had will enough to move past his training in order to achieve his own goals; otherwise he would never have been able to reach the position of Lilian's Lieutenant. Kitty continued down the staircase.

Reed was someone Kitty had not counted on. Although she surrounded herself with the teachings of love, she couldn't afford herself to feel such emotions towards others. She did not feel love towards Reed. If anything, despite all her training, all her teachings, fear dove into her heart when he was around. Fear was a new emotion and it had initially excited her. Now fear only caused her to doubt how committed she was to her mission to Brânswood. She needed to deal with Reed soon. She must concentrate on her duty, but which one? She had a duty to the Sanctuary and a false one to the Sector. Did this also allow room to have a duty to Reed as well? The question was, how necessary was the relationship with Reed to achieving her goals.

Kitty paused at the entrance of the parlor room and shivered as a chill passed through her. She glanced across the room. Her eyes stopped at the empty cross where she had last seen Flynn, her teacher. Remembering his status during her last audience with him, she could only assume Kypris took pity on his suffering and carried him away to her loving embrace. Kitty found it difficult trying to find peace through a wave of mourning. Still, she would not risk blowing her cover over such a trite obligation. She took a deep breath to center herself. She proceeded into the room to look for Matthew.

Fortune shone on the pet as the young boy was still there, caring for his more recently trained charges. Matthew was taking a sponge to a blond, muscle-bound man. The Familiar was beginning to look as if he would cry out from pain. There were deep scratches all over his bare chest, which were just now starting to heal. His member was wilted, yet also red and swollen as there was something tied to it, weighing it down. Matthew exuded a quiet pride while sponging water over the Familiar's wounds.

Kitty walked up to Matthew and draped her shadow over him. Seeing the darkness pass over his work, he stopped and looked up at her. As a rule, her natural glow could turn those around her to her favor. However, Matthew could care less about this pet. He had witnessed how many pets Lilian went through. She was replaceable whereas he was a true favorite of the Mistress. Kitty could not be certain if he was immune to her charms or if it was merely something in his nature. She had to work harder to impress her endowed presence upon him. He stared at her for a few moments before looking back and attending the young man's wounds again. Kitty took a judgmental stance, crossing her arms, tapping her foot while looking down at him. With a cold stare at the back of his head, she cleared her throat.

"I take it the Mistress of the House has sent you to command my presence? How thoughtful," Matthew responded, without giving the pet a second glance. "Since I know her better than you, I'll continue my duties here and at the lab. *Then* report to the Mistress, as not to truly disappoint." Kitty stopped tapping her foot. She centered mass and dug her heals into the ground. Her toes began to spread. If he wanted to have a standoff, she was willing to win. Matthew looked back at the silent sentry. The young boy caved. "Fine, you can stay and help me finish up."

****

Max pounded away at Ruby's door. "Open at once. We have business to be dealt with now!" He screamed through the wood. Silence responded. He paused, grunted, and began to bang his fist fervently against the door again. The frame shook, but the door remained closed. "I know you are in there."

"Oh, you *know* I'm in there. Are you a Phoenix, now?" a female voice sauntered towards him from down the hall. Max's ears twitched. He did not turn towards Ruby as she approached the outside of her office door. She took a key out to unlock the door and swung it open.

Max waited as she stepped past the threshold. She snapped her fingers and lights and monitors flickered. Max entered. He glanced around the office. He noticed on one of the monitors what appeared as a screen saver. It was a demented artist's version of Madonna and Child. "Diffoddwch." Ruby commanded. The monitors switched off. "What can I help you with today, Max?"

"I'm tired of the games, Ruby. I know that you have someone at the Southern Sector. Flynn has been missing and I'm getting messages that make no sense." Max spoke around Ruby. He couldn't remember the last time he actually was in her office. Something smelled off. His nostrils enlarged and soaked in the odor. Max looked back at Ruby. She was up to something, and the stench was her.

"You are correct. I put Kitty at the sector. I just," Ruby wanted to choose her words with care, as not to set the lycanthrope off, "*forgot* to tell you. I did not know that Flynn would follow her. My visions did not lead me to believe either party was in danger. My understanding though is unfortunately, we have a new position available and we will need to check to see if Flynn had any next of kin. I did not sanction his activities." Ruby took refuge behind her desk. She waved her hand, signaling Max to take a seat to get to business in a semi-professional manner. However, Max was not up for it.

He barged towards her desk, placing both hands down in an aggressive manner. The maneuver did not intimidate Ruby. She kept her resting bitch face mask at full. "I smell bullshit from your pores. I understand that some decisions must be made at the quick, but you are playing dangerously close to recklessness. The Sector business is not a part of our initiative. Our goal was to see to Khira. Did you know what would happen? Why do I think you move the pieces yourself rather than foresee anything, you manipulative bitch?"

"Feel better now that you got that off your chest?" Ruby inquired. "When I came to the Sanctuary about a decade ago, I did not even understand the gifts bestowed upon me. I had always been curious with the dead but never with events, my own actions or whatnot. I'm thankful for everything Brânswood has provided me and have even more gratitude that I have been able to help out. However, my *visions* for lack of a better term are just intended consequences. They do not always come true. You know this. I have to process my gifts before bringing them before anyone." Ruby took a breath.

Most of what she said was true. She had no control of whether her visions were a beacon of truth or threads of fate. In the beginning, the visions came at random times and intermingled with her approach to her necromancer spells. She remembered seeing Max prior to meeting him. She saw him in his full werewolf form before he had even graced her doorstep. Her visions did not tell her what choices to make. Once, she figured that her apparitions were not stones in a fated path but more like skipping rocks in a timeline pond, she started to manipulate things to benefit herself. Max never had seen that side to her until now.

"When you came to me, you taught me, you molded me, and I wanted to do anything to pay you back. I could see how I could help. I feel like you have been a little distracted or overwhelmed of late. I only wanted to be of assistance." Ruby could feel an itch behind her eyes. The monitors called to her, but she had to attempt to be civil with her boss. She could not afford to lose her position of power.

"I understand your willingness to aid the Sanctuary, Ruby." Max sighed. He had been feeling overwhelmed with memories of Lorelai while attempting to keep Khira protected. "However, you have to keep me informed of your alternative projects, especially when it comes to the Southern Sector. The Sanctuary's involvement should not tip any scales. The Sectors acknowledge our existence as we play on our side. Should the balance shift then the Senate could get involved. Better we have the enemy we know. Now, is there anything else you are hiding?" Max inquired.

As if on cue, one of the clay containers up on a shelf to Ruby's right vibrated. Ruby ignored David's attempt for attention. "No sir. While you are here, I can provide you the reports I've put together." Ruby pulled open a drawer in her desk. After perusing through some of the intel she had been keeping from Max, she pulled out a couple of colored folders. While she had multiple folders with information on Khira and even Paige, she pulled out lighter folders that had less information. She had to offer a branch of good faith to remain in Max's graces. She included a folder with the background on Kitty. "To let you know, David is no longer at the Chamberlin/Montgomery residence. Paige did not like his deception of why he befriended her. I will let you look over these reports and will stand by your next decision."

"Have you had any premonitions regarding Khira lately? Anything you haven't shared during our meetings?" Max inquired while taking the folders from Ruby.

"I'm sorry that our protection did not keep her from turning. Every vision I had had involving Khira, always had her being part of the Touched. Rest assure, she is strong. Plus, this result is better than the death Lilian had desired." Ruby stated in a plain tone. She could not feign the appropriate affect that Max would expect. Max was too close to this case due to his history with both Lorelai and Lilian.

Max stood up and walked towards the door. He steadied himself at the wooden frame. He brought up the folders in one hand and patted them with the other. He spoke without looking back at his associate, "I appreciate you admitting as much. I will review these and provide you the next move of the plan shortly." He cleared his throat and left Ruby's office to return to his own.

"Trowch," Ruby commanded. The door closed behind Max. She turned her chair back towards her monitors. "Chwaraewch." The monitors flickered back on. "Back to work."

****

Kitty's heart began to beat a little faster as she followed Matthew down a corridor leading away from the main house. She could not believe that what she was sent to discover here at Lilian's domain may be revealed so soon. Yet, something inside her also saddened her mood. She had cemented a good place within Lilian's walls. She had come to feel like wouitld be better for her to do good work at Thirlestane than back at Brânswood. It was her duty to retrieve any information she could and take it back, but what would become of her after she had done so? Once completed, could she ever come back to the mansion?

Kitty and Matthew had moved away from the house proper and now traveled within a damp and dark hallway. Kitty was surprised that she was not overwhelmed with an aroma of mold and decay. A part of her knew that this hall's decor probably functioned more as a disguise than actual neglect. Kitty thought of how the coven was a disguise within itself.

The Vampires had strength, but they did not feed on people. They did not even feed directly off the blood from the bins left by the Familiars. Lilian's coven seemed to use a more traditional method of gaining the respect and fear of the local community. Having spent the money to build up the sanctuary of the town, Lilian was able to hide her coven in plain sight. Bodies did not show up with fang marks. Lilian could show her face in daylight, although she would take the persona of some long-lost niece or cousin in order to keep the pretense of the timeline. It was so easy for the populace of Thirlestane to keep a blind eye to the evil behind the mansion's walls. That evil was a mere façade of what Lilian had once been capable of.

A knocking sound bore into Kitty's wandering thoughts. Matthew kept kicking against a wall. It appeared as if they had reached a dead end in the hallway. Before the young boy could get agitated, a step slid out of the wall. Matthew dropped the plastic bag he had been carrying and jumped up on to the rocky step. He began to punch a sequence into cobbled stones that decorated the wall. He hopped down and kicked the step back into the wall. A hiss trumpeted the grand entrance of cascading mist escaping from the wall, much like the fog of dry ice. The dim light brightened as Matthew pulled the body into the next room. Kitty tried to contain her excitement. "Are you coming?" inquired Matthew.

Kitty stepped into the chamber. The light reminded her of the warm embrace of Kypris or maybe it was truly her Goddess comforting her nerves. As she pushed the cart further into the room, the door behind them closed. A series of beeps sounded, startling Kitty.

Matthew looked back at Kitty and rolled his eyes, as if she should not have expected anything new in this chamber. Suddenly a hard spray began to move from one end of the room to the other. Before Kitty could compose herself, another hard spray began from the floor of the room, moving towards the ceiling. As the second spray stopped, the young pet wondered what was next. She took mental notes on how meticulous the entrance was, as compared to the laboratory at Brânswood. Another door began to open. Once fully expanded, two people in white hazmat suits stood at each side of the doorway, standing guard.

Matthew stood there awaiting some movement from the guards but became quickly agitated when neither of them moved. "Someone take this body now. The Mistress is awaiting me and you are keeping me on the clock." Still neither guard moved. Instead, a different person suddenly appeared and began to drag the corpse away. "Follow the body with the cart. I'll let the guards know to give you the exit code when you are finished. I'll go see what the Mistress wants. Don't screw anything up." With that, the young boy made a quick exit back through the previous chamber.

Kitty watched the boy leave and by the time she turned back, the body was already dragged halfway down the aisle. There were shiny silver lab tables set up on either side of the aisle. She began to push the cart on the intended path. Her stride was long but slow, as she tried to take in the whole set up. It varied from Brânswood's labs, but that was understandable considering the capital that Lilian had maintained over the years.

One section of the lab seemed to just be purifying the blood through an interesting sort of contraption. A white lab-coat clad assistant stood on a ladder and poured the contents from what looked to be an aluminum metal bin, much like those upon Kitty's cart, into a golden machine. It almost looked like an automatic ice cream machine with a clear front showing that the blood was getting turned and stirred. Dark blood flowed from the machine through some kind of tubing where it reached a chamber then passed through some sort of filter. The blood appeared lighter in color and moved to a new machine. A spout on the side of the machine showed where blood poured out into something that looked like a wine bottle. They must filter what they drink, kind of like water, Kitty thought.

Another table had one of the metal bins on one side, while three people took samples from it. When they were done, they scattered to different workstations. One of the lab technicians took a drop from their sample and prepared a slide. He slid it under a microscope then turned on a monitor nearby which autofocused and showed the different red blood cells. Another lab tech took her sample and drew out some of the blood into a big needle. She took the needle and stuck it into a sealed test tube, then another and another. She stuck the three tubes onto a rack. Then she turned to a small refrigerator behind her and pulled three small beakers from it.

The tech took a sample from the first beaker into a needle and plunged it into her first test tube. She took another sample from each of the remaining beakers and repeated the process of entering the mystery fluid into the remaining two test tubes. She replaced the beakers back into the fridge behind her. She placed the tubes into a centrifuge. The last tech had taken the most miniscule sample. He took a needle and extracted some blood before placing small drops on something that was on top of his table. He turned a timer and then proceeded to write down something on a legal pad.

Kitty took more mental notes as she turned back to the one, she was supposed to be following. Again, the assistant dragging the body had gained a big distance but seemed to have stopped. The assistant had lifted the corpse onto a table and appeared to be waiting on Kitty.

Kitty started her strides once more. Something caught her eye that caused her to pause. She recognized Flynn on one of the table slabs. He had multiple tubes connected to him. It appeared as if any remaining blood was being flushed from his body. A shudder came over her. She fought the urge to break down and cry, but she knew she must continue to stay at the mansion and be worth the death of her teacher.

She continued, only to be in for more of a shock when she saw what would eventually happen to Flynn's body. At the next table, body parts had already started to be sawed off of other corpses. A large woodchipper stood menacing behind the table. Another assistant took a severed leg from off the table and climbed up a ladder. With a drop, a grinding sound protruded from the machine and bits were packaged at the side of the machine as if mulch. Kitty turned her head in disgust. She tried to re-center herself, focusing on Kypris, as she finally made her way to the end of her path.

The assistant waiting for her began to take bins off the cart and place them on a conveyor belt. One bin after another was guided to the tables that Kitty had already passed. A stack of papers was on the end of the table. It was a checklist of how the blood and bodies were processed. She carefully took a copy when the assistant was looking away and began to fold it in a very intricate pattern, forming it into an origami ring that she slid onto the middle finger of her right hand. Just as she finished the assistant turned to her and said, "You can take the cart back to the parlor room. You are not authorized for an exit code just yet, so let one of the guards know that they will have to remove you themselves." Kitty tilted her head. She wondered if all of the excitement and sorrow that she had experienced through her exposure to the lab extracted all of the strength and power she gleaned from Kypris. She took a step closer to the tech to measure if she had any influence. A small blush graced the cheeks of the assistant. Kitty sighed with relief. She took the cart and made towards the exit. She did not want to waste too much time gathering any more information and could only hope that this would not be her last visit.

Chapter Eighteen

Matthew knocked on Lilian's door. While he waited for permission to enter, he reviewed in his head what he could remember from the lab reports. The technicians were diligent in their work, so abnormalities were few and far between. "You may enter." His Mistress's voice broke his thoughts. He turned the knob with one hand and pushed open the door with the other.

He walked into the room with a silence hanging over him. Lilian laid in bed. As he was figuring out where to start, Lilian removed herself from under the covers and sat on the side edge facing him. Lilian spoke first. "How are you getting along with my new pet?" Lilian had sensed a jealousy steaming from Matthew. Most of the time, the young vampire had not given Lilian's pets notice. There was something about this new one that seemed to rub him the wrong way.

"She was not too much in the way. If she makes you," Matthew caught a cough in his throat, as if the words did not want to leave him, "If she makes you happy, my Mistress, she makes me, urm." He let the sentence trail off.

As if the pet's ears were burning, the door opened, and Kitty entered and closed the door behind her. She sat on the floor near the bed's edge. Matthew sneered at the pet. He understood the decorum of needing to wait for permission before entering. One of the lesser creatures of the manor should know better than to have the gall to make themselves at home.

"As you were saying my dear boy," Lilian spoke with a slight glee.

Matthew decided to change the subject. "I read over the reports and the technicians either made an error or there is something to be concerned with." Matthew paused, attempting to remember all of the verbiage on the report of the strange blood sample.

"Go on." Lilian demanded.

"Yes. One of the blood samples that remained after the crucible was tested and there was an abnormality found within. The white blood cells seemed to turn a blackish color and began to destroy all other blood cells before becoming destructive itself. Nothing had been added to the sample and the remaining portion has been refrigerated to help preserve it for further testing." Matthew tried to think if there was anything else to add before deciding that was enough information for the time being.

"Did the technicians know from whom the sample came from?" Lilian inquired. For all her time being one of the Touched, she had never heard of the abnormality. Granted, her Sector had only started studying and purifying blood within the last couple of decades. The HIV strain introduced did not affect the Touched but Lilian took the virus as a sign that the vampires needed to start being more careful with what they ingested.

"No, my Mistress. They had just recently begun to test the samples left from the party." Matthew responded. He got a horrible feeling. Lilian's reaction to the news seemed more off-putting than she normally behaves.

"Return to the lab and stay there while they rerun the sample. If there is enough blood available, they should test it multiple times. They also need to see if there is any trace that will help determine the origin. Also have them run a DNA comparison to what we have on file to make sure it is no one from this Sector. We need to know who the sample came from before proceeding with action."

"Yes, Mistress. Is there any more direction you would like me to relay while I'm there?" Matthew wanted to cover his bases while covering his ass for any bad news to follow.

"That is all. You may leave." With that command given, Matthew took a bow. When he rose, he gave Kitty another sneer before leaving the room.

"Come my pet, I have a treat for you before an errand you must make." Lilian walked to her vanity. She motioned for Kitty to sit in front of her. The Mistress picked up a silver handled brush and drew the bristles through the pet's tresses.

"I have a confession to make, my dear. My niece is here and I have been delaying the inevitable.

Things would have been so much easier had she died like the original plan, but fate has intervened, and Lorelai has played the protective mother once again." Lilian paused mid-stroke of brushing through Kitty's hair. The pet took the time to give her Mistress a slight puzzled look before nuzzling against Lilian's leg.

Lilian sighed and then continued brushing Kitty's hair. "I fear that Khira could bring the downfall of the Sector. If she is anything like her mother, she will not easily comply with the ways of being one of the Touched. Yet, if she is Lorelai's daughter, shall I not welcome her openly? Or do I take out the frustration of my sister's abandonment out on Khira?" The Mistress lost control of emotions. She felt so weak. As blood tears flowed from her lilac eyes, she opened a door within her vanity to pull out a bottle of the crimson power she needed.

Lilian put the brush down and twisted the bottle's cap open. She took a swig of blood in order to try and maintain her anxiety. Then a reminder hit her like a slap to the face. "And my dear Matthew. Khira and Matthew must not meet. Khira can never know..." Lilian trailed off.

Kitty was so close to getting the secret out of her Mistress. The pet lowered her head and her inner voice prayed to her Kypris. As she worshipped her goddess, Kitty rubbed her hand against Lilian's calves, hoping to put Lilian at enough ease to release the rest of the secret. The pet wondered what was so important that Matthew and Khira should never know each other.

"I cannot delay this any longer," Lilian spoke. "I will set up in the library. Please fetch Zachary and Khira to meet me there. This confrontation should take place as soon as possible. I must rip the scab to help with the healing. Oh Lorelai, what have we done?" The Mistress stood and left her pet behind.

Kitty took a moment to search the vanity drawers to see if there was anything more about Matthew but came up empty. She went to the door and opened it. To her surprise, Reed was in the doorway. He pulled her from the room and pushed her close to the wall. Her task of retrieving both Khira and Zachary would have to wait while she conspired to throw Reed off track. She knew she much end this alliance sooner than later.

****

Reed felt satisfied after completing some training to the Mal/Thor familiar. He had strapped him to an oak table face down. There had been a hole for the face to go. Reed had taken a speculum to the familiar's buttocks and stretched a little at a time. Reed had also taken clamps to Mal's feet that hung off the table. In between the stretching of the backside, Reed to alternate squeeze the clamps tighter.

At one point, Reed stopped both devices and simply tugged on the blond tresses of the familiar, pulling them back and raising Mal's head. The familiar let out a small gurgle and Reed let go of the hair. Reed returned to alternating the pressure between the butt cheeks and the pressure against the soles of the feet. Once the familiar stopped moaning and could only breath softly, Reed undid the devices and returned the familiar to his cross. Blood and urine ran down Mal's leg. The vampire was quite pleased with his work.

Reed decided to go and see what the fuss upstairs was about. He overheard three female pets as they passed him on the stairwell. One girl stated "I've never seen Zachary pace like that before. The Mistress must have punished him for something."

"No, I think the guest is more likely having some effect on the Lieutenant. It's her door he's pacing back and forth behind." Another one spoke.

Reed could still hear the conversation as he made his way to the top of the stairs. "I heard from Rose that Zachary has not played with any pets for the past four days. Neither female nor male pet at that." The first girl responded. "So, you may be correct in assuming that the guest has been occupying Zachary more than usual."

Reed's curiosity spun out of control. It was quite unusual for any of the Touched to not play with a pet between that many of days. Even the newly turned Touched are indoctrinated to use the pets at their musings. Reed turned the corner of the hallway. He could see his Mistress leaving her room and heading towards the library. He wondered why she had not called for his assistance with the guest and why Zachary was more important than he was. He was fortunate that Lilian had not come upon of any of Reed's plans to eventually usurp her. Zachary was still in the way.

After Lilian left her room, the door to Lilian's room opened moments later. Reed rushed to the entryway and found Kitty. She closed the door, and he scooped her up before pushing her against the wall. He turned and saw Zachary pacing back and forth down the hall, just outside of the White Room. Reed covered Kitty's mouth via instinct, forgetting for a quick moment that she was mute. Reed removed his hand, remembering Kitty would not say a word.

"You have information for me, my pet, yes?" Reed inquired. Kitty shrugged. Reed pushed her against the wall once more, this time with more aggression behind the action. "Do not dare lie to me. Regardless of the fact you have become my Mistress's favorite pet, remember who put you there. I can remove you from here, from existence. Understand me now?" Kitty bowed her head and gave a small nod.

"Have you seen this special guest?" Kitty raised her head with some resentment for the treatment she had just received. Then, she nodded once more. "Do you know why Lilian has been so secretitive with the person in the White Room?" Kitty attempted to pray internally but Reed's steely stare stopped her. Still, she knew what her response must be. The pet shook her head no, knowing that she had lied to him.

Their attention turned as Zachary had stopped pacing down the hall. He opened the door and let himself in. Reed turned back to Kitty, turning her head forcibly towards him. She did not speak while among the Touched and pets but that did not mean she was deaf. While she knew the life of a pet usually contained use, abuse and harassment, Reed was downright cruel most times. "Apparently Zachary knows our guest. Is this true?" Kitty nodded her head.

This time Reed asked himself more than he requested from the pet. "What bothered him so much?" With instinct however, Kitty pointed towards the White Room. She then held out the palm of her left hand. With her right pointer finger, she wrote the letter L, then the letter Z before pointing to the room down the hall. "Lilian had Zachary bring the guest here?" Reed interpreted. Kitty pointed her right finger on her nose to assure Reed he understood what she was attempting to let him know.

"Do you know where Lilian is now?" Kitty did not feel there was any harm of letting him in on the meeting location. Zachary would never let Reed in, as Zachary had seemed protective of Khira. She pointed back to the door before miming the opening and closing of a book. "I see. So..." Reed was interrupted but the sound of breaking glass from down the hall, coming from the White Room. Kitty released herself from his grip and headed towards the White Room, while Reed headed towards the library.

The double doors were just slightly open, enough to let light through. Reed knew Lilian well enough to know she would be sitting in the throne in the middle of the room. He had had his own excursions in this room so he knew where the best hiding place would be. He creeped into the room and took his spot, waiting for the action.

****

Zachary entered the White Room and found Khira sitting on the bed, her back facing towards him. She must have heard someone enter as her senses should have improved with the change. He cleared his throat to attempt to get her attention.

"Have you come to poison me yet again?" Khira inquired, still not looking towards her kidnapper.

"Honestly, would you have come otherwise?" Zachary responded. He wanted to rush to her and hold her. He wanted to kiss her so deep to leave her breathless. Words were beyond compared to all the emotions overcoming him. He wanted to speak and explain everything to Khira but she replied first.

"I'm sure you were only doing what you were told to do. I mean, you are Lilian's whipping boy, correct?" There was so much disdain and coldness radiating from Khira's words.

Zachary attempted to hide his surprise at Khira's mention of his Mistress. The mention of Lilian's name could only confirm that Brânswood had been protecting the house and that the Sanctuary had given Khira some information. Yet, he did not know what all she had been told.

"Lilian is the Mistress of this sector. I am one of her Lieutenants. Once you had turned, she decided that it was best to talk to you here at Thirlestane." Zachary stated in a flat tone.

"Once you turned me, you mean." Khira turned to face Zachary. "But that wasn't the objective, was it. Lilian wanted my dead body and yet you failed her." Her words hissed at him.

"Fate decided you should live."

"Live? This is life? No, this is a goddamn curse, you mean. You and Lilian both have made me into a monster." Khira's anger fumed. She stood up from the bed but kept her distance from Zachary.

"Let me explain," he begged of her. He wanted to ease this tension between them. He wanted to wash away the anger with kisses and embraces.

"There is nothing to explain," Khira's voice rose. "You were told to put me down as if I was a fucking dog. I was supposed to be dead. I was supposed to be protected. There were so many other things I was supposed to be before you two fucked up my life. I'll show you and Lilian what a bitch I can be." With that, she picked up the glass from the nightstand and threw it towards Zachary. His reflexes instinctively moved him out of the path, and the glass broke against the door. "There is nothing you can tell me that will make things better. You should just leave." Khira's voice whispered.

Silence stood as a sentinel between them. The door opened behind Zachary. The redheaded pet from before entered. She knelt and picked up the broken glass shards. She took them over to the nearest trash can by the vanity. She then attended to Khira. She brushed Khira's tresses behind the vampire's ear. Kitty took Khira's hands, and Khira felt at peace for a moment. Kitty nodded her head assuring Khira that all would be ok.

The pet then turned her attention to Zachary. She approached him and showed him a card. He read it. "Are you ready to confront Lilian? She has requested our presence in the library." Zachary told Khira. Kitty went back to Khira and took her hand, pulling her towards Zachary. While still holding Khira's hand, Kitty also took one of Zachary's hand. *This is not the one,* Kitty thought. She gave both of them a slight puzzled look and then pulled them towards to the door.

Khira pulled her hand from the pet. Zachary mimicked Khira. Kitty shrugged. Khira walked out of the room first. She proceeded down the hall but realized she did not know where the library was in the estate. *Hell,* she thought, *there could be multiple libraries in a place this big.* She slowed her huff and waited for Zachary and Kitty to catch up.

Zachary attempted to brush against Khira's hand to show a sign of support. He hated to be thought of as the enemy in Khira's violet eyes. Before he got close enough to her, Khira folded her arms as she continued to walk down the corridor.

Kitty hurried her pace to get in front of them both. She knew Zachary would see fit for Khira to meet with Lilian, rather than attempt to flee the premises. She had felt strong emotions from the Lieutenant, but Khira did not return those feelings. Something inside her, maybe it was Kypris speaking to her heart, told Kitty that these two were not destined to be with each other. Her priestess had never steered her wrong before, however, she did not know whether to trust that instinct.

The pet looked behind her to check on her companions. Zachary walked with his head hung down, turning to look at Khira every now and again. Khira held her head high with confidence or anger. Kitty could not tell the difference within Khira. Maybe it was a little of both. She had hoped the confrontation could be civil but expected would go poorly. Then her thoughts strayed back to Matthew. She frowned as she thought of the little twerp. She wondered why Lilian was so paranoid of Khira meeting Matthew. She would let Brânswood know of Lilian's concerns in her next communication.

As Khira followed the red-headed pet, she could not help but remember her dream. *The lions will eat you*, rang through her head. She felt danger with each step, but fury fueled her further. She needed to confront her aunt. She needed to show that she was not a weakling. Afterall, she was a changed woman.

Kitty stopped in front of the double doors that led to the library. She sighed as Khira and Zachary both stood behind her. As Zachary passed the pet and opened one of the doors, Kitty took Khira by the hands. *You are strong. You are a survivor*, Kitty thought as she clutched Khira's hands. Kitty then stood behind Khira as the vampire went to confront Lilian. Kitty followed, closing the door behind her in order to keep any intruders out of this intimate meeting.

Chapter Nineteen

When Khira broke the threshold of this new room, she felt an overwhelming breeze come to the back of her neck. The hairs on her arm stood on end as if warning her of her doom. If she had any Spidey senses from having been turned into a vampire, they were telling her that she was trespassing into danger. Khira reminded herself that if Lilian had truly wanted her dead, the Mistress would not have requested her presence at the manor nor have gifted a guest room and a pet, unless her aunt was hoping to kill Khira with her bare hands, since Zachary had failed at that mission. She paused, took a deep breath, held it for a beat to center herself and then she exhaled. Feeling more determined, she took a few more steps further into the library.

Aromas of dark cherry oak and musty pages calmed her nerves. The walls were covered with over-packed bookshelves. The spines of the books looked old, and Khira wondered how many first editions were held within. She could see three free standing bookcases deeper inside the chamber and leather sofas laid about here and there. The room was large so Khira imagined there must be even more bookcases behind these front ones. This library almost reminded her of Zachary's bookstore, but with less charm. Kitty seemed to disappear behind the bookcases, so Khira focused her attention elsewhere. She was not in a hurry to meet any demise that Lilian might have in mind for her.

There were three tables just strides away from the entrance: two were cedar in color and circular in nature; each table displayed a bust. One bust was of a young handsome man, chiseled out of ivory marble. While stark in nature, the man's face featured a predominant a dimple in each cheek complimenting a sly smile. Even if it had been a portrait, Khira felt that the man's eyes would display the same coldness the bust mirrored. The other bust was a lion's head made of glass. *The Lions will eat you,* called once more to Khira. *Maybe they already had,* she thought to herself. Each circular table flanked the third table which was long and rectangular in nature; it was made of glass with gold adornments. It was the type of display table that a young girl may fantasize that Snow White had slept in. She walked over to peek to see what treasure may be hidden beyond the glass.

Within the case appeared to be an old family tree tapestry. The canvas was faded and light tan in color. Pastel threads of lavender, pinks, and powder blue connected one family vein to another. Khira counted 7 main "familiar lineages." She imagined the tapestry had been darker at an early space of time; both the canvas being a deep copper, once displaying vibrant strands of deep purple, blood red, and royal blue leading to different houses.

At the top of the family tree was a coat of arms shield within a red circular top banner. A white dragon stood as the left shield supporter of the red border while a black dog stood to the right, both creatures were on their hind legs. The Shield layout was split into four charges. The left upper charge displayed a white lion on a red background. The upper right charge showed an open book on a black background. A raven caught in midflight hung upon a white background in the lower left-hand corner of the shield. A white full circle, perhaps the moon, shown from a red background on the final charge. A shiny glint catching the soft light of the room caught Khira's attention.

The tapestry seemed to wrap around a sword. All the features of the weapon were coated in silver; the pommel was stamped with a lion that was similar in nature to the glass bust. The grooves in the grip were part of the same metal. The guard loop was built of three gold and silver intertwined braids. Most of the weapon was hidden within the folds of the tapestry. She placed her hands on top of the glass. She did not care that her fingerprints probably smudged the pristine display. The articles inside drew her in. She leaned over the case when she heard a clicking sound.

Her concentration to the tapestry was broken by light streaming from the back of the room. Kitty returned to her side and took her hand to lead her to the Mistress. As she was led to her destiny, Khira looked back towards the door, wondering if she could still escape this fate. Kitty squeezed Khira's hand. A warmth came over the vampire, allowing Khira to find some inner strength. As she exhaled, she readied herself for a fight against Lilian.

Kitty led Khira past the bookcases to a sofa in the back of the room. She saw a woman with white hair sitting in a lush Queen Anne chair, red velvet peeking through the ivory tresses. Kitty waved Khira to sit on the sofa. As she sat on the cold brown leather, Khira noticed Kitty take a place on the floor at Lilian's feet. Khira took a look into Lilian's lavender eyes and could see a glimpse of her mother in there. Zachary sat in a smaller chair on the other side of Lilian. He held his head down in shame. *I guess he has shame for not killing me off,* she wondered.

"So you must be..." Khira started but Lilian held up a hand in a gesture to hold her tongue.

"My dear Khira, to be perfectly honest, I had wished you dead. However, I am not a mistress of fate and the powers that be have vetoed that request." Khira was taken aback by the honesty but still wished her body would leave the chair. However, it was as if she was shackled to the chair by invisible manacles. She could not move. "The ancient gods before us have fated this day and they have fated your destiny to be Touched like us. Well, not exactly like us because we too are as glorious as snowflakes, but not all as fragile. We are, as modern gothic miscreants have dubbed us, 'Vampires'." The woman paused dramatically.

Khira was unsure what Lilian had expected her response to be. Was she supposed to be surprised? David had already given Khira the information to attack Lilian. "Well, auntie...." Khira started before pausing, "Or since we live in Texas, would you prefer the term Tia?" If Lilian was surprised, she did not show it. However, Zachary finally looked up at his Mistress with a puzzled look. Khira took in his expression and then checked Kitty to see if she would mirror the shock that Zachary had displayed. Kitty just sat contently next to her Mistress, serving her purpose.

"Auntie will suit me just fine. I can only assume the Sanctuary has reached out to you, since you know our relationship." Lilian paused, hoping that Brânswood was at least still in the dark in regards to Matthew. "You at least might wonder why I had Zachary bring you here. I am confident that the spies did not reveal that."

"Well, Auntie, since you were honest with me regarding my death sentence, Auntie, I'll be honest with you. I don't give one single fuck why you brought me here, Auntie. I'm sure that my mother had hoped this day would never come. She must have truly hated you, Auntie." The repeated staccato rhythm of Khira's use of the term "Auntie" whistled through the air as if daggers thrown at an assailant.

Lilian looked wounded at the mention of her sister. Things would have been easier if Lorelai had embraced the Touched way of life. The Mistress felt her pet rub against her leg. This act allowed Lilian to regain her composure. "I do apologize that our introduction is not the typical family reunion. And while I had first hoped you would be killed after my sister's mistake of bringing you into the world, I have since had a change of heart."

"Heart?" Khira inquired. "From my understanding, you are a cold, heartless bitch."

"Now Khira, please know that you can have..." Lilian responded without flinching at Khira's obscenities.

"Have? I don't want a fucking thing you could offer me. In fact, I just wanted you to know that your niece is dead. You have created a monster who despises you and I don't want to know you any more than that. Keep your hands and your playthings away from me. I want nothing to do with you." Khira stood up and left the library, slamming the doors behind her.

Lilian looked at her Lieutenant. "Well, go after her. Make sure she doesn't leave the premises, yet. I'm not done with her." Zachary stood and bowed towards his Mistress. He took his leave. Lilian then looked at her pet. "My darling, I am terribly sorry you witnessed that, but as you know, this life we lead is a dark one most of the times. I must get some solitude while I decide what to do next with my niece. Please fetch Reed. I'm most certain he is probably teaching the familiars. Bring him to my room after you have found him." Lilian walked to the double doors of the library and paused. Khira had gotten to her by using Lorelai against her nature. A tear escaped her eye and blood ran down her cheek. As she wiped it away, *never again* Lilian thought.

Chapter Twenty

Kitty found herself alone in the library and thought it was perfect timing to get a message to the Sanctuary, updating them regarding the meeting between Lilian and Khira. She stood behind the chair that Lilian had occupied and closed her eyes. "Gweledigaeth feline" fell from her lips in a whisper. She opened her eyes and her vision sharpened. She examined the back bookcase. She found a discrepancy in one of the book spines compared to the others. She walked over and pulled at the spine. A secret door opened from the bookcase revealing piles of Lilian's journals. She chose to pull the ones dated around the time that Lorelai had become human to see if Lilian had any insight on Lorelai's plan to leave The Touched behind her.

After pulling a few journals, she closed the door, concealing the vault of journals once more. Kitty crouched behind a potted Mountain Laurel tree and prepared to enact the spell that allowed her to communicate with Brânswood. She glanced around nervously. Hope-fully, the collection of books would keep her hidden should someone enter the room.

Kitty slid the paper ring off her finger and unfolded it. She waved her hand over the list and whispered, *"Rwy'n cyflawni'r gorchymyn i gyfathrebu."* A few seconds passed, and nothing changed. She slowed her breathing and concentrated harder. Better centered, she tried the spell once more, a little louder this time. A voice responded.

"Pass-code, please."

"Dragonfly," Kitty responded.

"Proceed."

Once the piece of paper radiated a hue of soft blue, she spoke. "I was able to enter the lab. Attached is a list used there for testing. I hope that this will help in our mission." Kitty paused and considered her words carefully before she proceeded. "Lilian and Khira met today. It seems that David had provided Khira with the information regarding her lineage. Lilian wants to keep her here for the time being. I want to aid in her escape. I feel she would be better served...." She heard movement to her left. "I think she would be better...." Kitty started to repeat when she recognized a voice coming from behind one of the bookcases.

Reed stepped out to spy on the female speaking in the room. He knew that his Mistress had already departed and he had assumed the manor's guest had left first. *What was her name again,* he thought, *Was it Kennedy or Khira? Doesn't matter when the Mistress is done with her.* "You?" Reed sputtered the words out with great disgust.

Kitty knew immediately that she needed to get this message out before Reed did any damage to it or to her. *"Cyfieithu."* Kitty guided her hand over the page while the information disappeared.

Reed knew his little spy was multifaceted but was surprised she worked for the enemy. "Aren't you full of surprises" muttered Reed, his voice deep and full of ire.

Kitty shrank back and assumed a submissive stance. He walked slowly up to her. Every stride was determined and sure, like a stalking panther. He towered over her and the cold darkness of his shadow did more than merely envelop her.

"So, it was *your* voice that I heard? To think the sound that pricked my ears belonged to the quiet little cat. You certainly are full of surprises, Kitty." he said finally, his gaze piercing deep into her. "I had thought to find a means of tracking down Zachary and getting in Lilian's good graces. But instead I find you here consorting with Brânswood?" He snatched the paper from her hand and examined it but, by that time, the information was sent, and the page was left blank. He crumpled the page within his hand and tossed it aside, elongating his fangs afterwards.

"I knew that someone here was a spy for Brânswood, but I had assumed that the old Familiar Zachary had uncovered was the plant, but instead it is really *you*...so much the better," he said with a predatory smile. "Your betrayal ends now. If you value your life, swear true loyalty to me. You are an insignificant pet, but you could be of service to me by spying on your Mistress. If not, I turn you in to Lilian, thereby regaining her trust. With Zachary's deeds in question, I become Lilian's favorite and I regain my control here. Either way, I win."

Kitty shook her head vigorously as she was backed into the corner. Reed had the drop on her and she knew she could not escape him. She could only hope now that her final message got through to the Sanctuary.

****

Max walked around his office, delicately touching a book or examining a pile of papers to see that everything was as it should be. He still felt a little itchy, but whether that was due to his tweed suit or some hairy remnant of his transformation, he could not say. Although things appeared to be in order, something still felt off to him.

He examined his desk. Many messages had come in that he had not noticed before. The most recent missive nested at the top of a stack of papers. It appeared to be from Dragonfly. Max examined the message. It seemed distorted and had not been encrypted.

"Hrmmm," he grunted in concern. He focused his eyes, and words became clearer. The message was cut off; however, from what Max could make from it, the letter seemed to contain a record of procedures for extraction and examination of human blood. Finally, a look into Lilian's dealings, he thought. The information would be useful in figuring out exactly what the Vampires were up to in their hidden labs. The girl must have just discovered the information to relay it back to Brânswood. He did not remember if he assigned Dragonfly at Thirlestane or if this was one of Ruby's manuevers. Any assignments her mentor Flynn had provided Kitty before caused Max to think these previous tasks had been much more mundane. Something was amiss.

Max looked down again at the note and read about Khira being at Thirlestane. He also noticed there was a break in the message. Something was wrong, but he needed to be sure. While he knew Ruby could discover what had transpired at the mansion, he come to mistrust the Phoenix. Anger fueled him; he was angry with Ruby but more importantly, he was angry with himself for failing both Lorelai and Khira.

With a swipe of his hands, he sent everything to the floor, leaving his desk bare for the first time in many years. He grasped the ornate wood of the desk under his hands and tried to stifle the feelings that welled up inside him. Fury, fear, resentment, humiliation...he could not sort through them as he once could his manuscripts.   He fought against the tears and pulled himself from his desk. He could see the gouges left by his nails. Just another thing ruined. As the scurries attempted to "clean" his desk, he noticed the scratches he made had remained. They were smoother and almost polished, but still there, nonetheless. *Good,* he thought, *something to remember me by.* He slumped back in his chair, exhausted.

He took his head between his hands and began to sob. The soft whimpers of pain were halfway between human moans and wolf-like howls. After a few minutes he stopped, exhausted from the hurt. He stared at something hidden among the debris littering the floor. Something shiny and silver peeked out from beneath his papers. He reached down to retrieve it, shooing away the tidying critters now moving his things. It was the silver frame of a photograph. The photograph was old and had faded with time, but through the sepia tones of age showed the face of Lorelai. He had taken it many years ago, during their time at the mansion. It was the first thing he permanently kept on his desk after she had gone. His eyes welled with tears as the heartache washed over him again. His thoughts were of her and what she would think of him now. Would she be ashamed of him, at what he had become? He could not bear the thought.

Despite what Ruby thought, he was not useless. He had done more for Brânswood in the years before she was born than she ever would in her time here. He would show her. He would show everyone how "useless" he was. He still knew a thing or two and would prove to everyone, especially himself, of what he was still able to accomplish.

He rummaged through his desk picking up this thing and that, anything that could be of use to him, and placed it all in a satchel he had held over from his field days. The effort renewed his strength, and the determination focused his mind. He knew what he had to do and would do it alone. Max felt the newfound determination strengthening him. He was girding his loins in preparation of his task. Once he was satisfied that he had all the tools and items he needed, he walked towards the door.

Opening the door, he looked back at his office, his home, perhaps for the last time. Something stirred inside him. He was forgetting something, he was sure. He made a mental checklist of everything he took when he stopped and noticed the photograph. *Lorelai.* She was always there to watch over him and since she had gone, he believed that she still did in a way. He reached for the photo and took it from its frame, sticking it in his jacket next to his heart. "I will never leave you behind, Lorelai," he whispered reverently through the tears welling up from his eyes. "I will make up for my mistakes and prove myself to you. Since I couldn't save you, I will go out and save your daughter." Composing himself quickly, he exited the room and with a grim smile of determination, sealed the office and started off on his mission.

****

Reed grabbed Kitty by her collar and pulled her backwards up towards him. "Heed me, Kypris," Kitty said weakly as she pointed the fingers of her left hand. She turned and struck out hitting Reed hard in the throat. His gasp lasted only a moment, but it was enough for him to release her. She slid down and ducked between his legs, stepping up behind him. She kicked hard and pushed him back from behind. Off balance, he tripped and landed on the potted tree breaking the ceramic planter. Snarling in rage, he turned around and leapt for her. She dodged quickly around a nearby sofa, narrowly missing his strike.

"You cannot run, little one. There is nowhere for you to go!" growled Reed. Kitty leapt up from the floor to take hold of one of the free-standing bookcases. She tried to leverage herself using the shelves and escape his grasp; however, she was not fast enough. Within the blink of an eye, he was able to cross the room and grab her leg with the intention of pulling her down. She squeaked in alarm and kicked out hard with her other leg to catch him full in the face. She kicked several times and used every ounce of energy to get him off her, but his strength was obviously greater. She could feel his grip tightening around her leg. She winced from the pain and struggled to break free. She held on for dear life as Reed pulled her away from the shelf. As her grip began to fail, the shelf began to tilt and began its descent to the floor.

Seeing the heavy shelf descending upon him, Reed released Kitty to brace himself for the collapsing blow. She scrambled to climb over the shelf as it fell and leapt off it, barely managing not to be caught underneath it as Reed was. The heavy wood of the shelving and the large books within crashed down on Reed scattering wood, paper, and debris all over that side of the room. Kitty knew that the collapsed pile would not hold him long. Already, she could see the debris shift around him and his arms groping for control on the floor.

Reed shifted his weight under the heavy shelf to bring his legs up underneath him. With a quick push from his legs, he exploded out from underneath his literary prison and searched for Kitty. He saw that she had scurried under one of the circular tables closer to the door. Reed's attention was briefly reflected by a gleam of light that sparkled from within the display case He had to credit Lilian's ceremonial side for having displayed Liam's sword there in the library. While the Touched were allergic to silver, Liam had purposely made his weapon out of the element that would harm his enemies the most. Kitty was not one of the Touched so while the weapon could damage the pet, Reed had other plans of torture.

Kitty attempted to curl under the table, but she ended up kicking one of the legs by accident, causing the table to tumble over. The glass Lion's head that had decorated the top of the table smashed against the floor, scattering several pieces across the floor. Seeing Kitty failing at concealing herself, Reed pulled her right leg from the ground and lifted it to the same height as his shoulder.

As he had lifted her leg, her body had picked up some of the broken pieces of glass on the floor. Kitty winced in pain and twisted her body in hopes of easing herself from Reed's grip. He held a tighter grip on her right ankle. She took a breath and found the courage to kick Reed in the chest with her left foot. With Reed taken by surprise, he loosened his grip long enough for Kitty to escape. She headed back toward Lilian's chair to take the time to catch her breath. She could not take too much time as she felt Reed ready to hunt her down.

"Here, Kitty, Kitty, Kitty!" Reed taunted as he stalked his prey. Kitty cringed at the thought of him toying with her. She made to move to a new hiding spot at the other free-standing bookcase when, with lightning speed, Reed crossed the room to appear instantly before Kitty. Shrieking in alarm, she backed away and ran in the opposite direction. Within seconds he stood before her, obstructing her again. No matter where she turned, there he was.

"There's nowhere to go. You're trapped," said Reed with delight. "Accept your fate. You know you want to. I can give you everything you desire. Or I can give you death." Reed lunged at her, but Kitty was prepared. Dropping into a split, she arched herself down as low as she could go with the intention of having Reed rush past her, crashing into a massive bookcase. However, his senses could not help him avoid the case, and inertia compelled him into the wall.

Kitty panted hard as she gathered herself and backed into another corner opposite from the doors out. She thought hard on what to do.

She could try and escape the room. Once out into the mansion proper, there was little Reed could do to catch her before she could find a place to hide or a way outside. However, if she escaped, then Reed would reveal what he knew about her and all her work infiltrating the coven would be lost. All the blood, sweat and tears she had endured would have been in vain and her precious teacher would have given his life over for nothing. The alternative was almost too much to bear. It was not in her nature to inflict pain unjustly and to take a life; even one as evil as Reed's, was a transgression of the teachings of Kypris. She would have to count on the forgiveness of the Goddess and hope that there were exceptions made. More pain and death would follow if she did not find a way to disable Reed and make her escape before anyone came to investigate the commotion. Kypris forgive her; she knew what she had to do.

Kitty looked around the room to find something to use to her advantage, then maneuvered to set herself in position. Reed had recovered by this time and with a feral growl moved to ambush her. Kitty could see that he was beyond reasoning at this point. The beast had overcome him. He would kill her and feast upon her blood, should she let him catch her. There was no going back now.

Crouching low, she prepared for his strike. With furious speed, Reed lunged. He was almost too fast to see; luckily her instinct told her when to strike. As he came upon her, she lowered her head into his stomach, allowing him to lift her up. She managed to slide her body down and twist it. She maneuvered her legs to cross around his neck. She pushed herself away from his body only to swing back, using the momentum and the power of her legs to toss him over. His confusion of what took place gave Kitty enough time to ready her next move. She waited for him to stand. She ran towards him, leaping up to kick him in his chest, knocking him back into the glass display table.

The glass caved in and almost welcomed Reed into a warm embrace. One of the shards dug into his neck and slid down, severing his jugular. He flailed about bleeding from numerous other wounds. He reached to pull himself up by reaching out to anything that could be of assistance, but the strength gifted to him before was quickly fading. The aging parchment, detailing Lilian's family tree, now lay streaked with blood. Reed rolled over to face Kitty and smiled through his bloody lips.

Kitty waited to see if Reed was really incapacitated or was laying a trap for her. Sensing his pain, she got up and walked over to him. She spied the sword within the table lying under Reed's head and moved to take it. Reed laughed through the blood on his lips seeing her intent. Kitty paid him no heed as she gripped the handle tightly and slid it out from under Reed. With a prayer to her Goddess Kitty asked for forgiveness of the sin she would commit. Careful not to cut herself the broken glass, she placed her feet on both of Reed's feet, hoping to keep him connected to the table.

"Excellent...I knew you had...potential." he gasped.

"So did you," she whispered pushing him back to impale him further upon the shattered display. With what remained of her strength, she plunged the sword deep into Reed. The sword bit deeply and inflicted its damage upon Reed's already broken flesh. He groaned in agony as the flesh about the wound swelled and enflamed. Kitty stepped back in awe of the effect she was seeing. She realized then that the sword was special. The blade, coated in silver, had been used to kill Vampires. Reed struggled to remove the sword, but that only did himself further harm. After a few grueling moments, Reed's body ceased to struggle and lay bleeding on the library floor.

Kitty struggled to catch her breath. She wiped down the handle of the sword with a piece of Reed's shirt and cleansed herself as best she could. She had to get away and put as much distance between Reed and herself before reporting back to Lilian. "Goddess, forgive me," she pleaded. She went back to retrieve the journals that she had removed from Lilian's vault before making her escape from the library.

Chapter Twenty-One

Khira made her way back to the White Room, determined to steal as much as she could from her aunt. The previous failed death sentence made Khira feel like she was due these items. Much like her mother, Khira felt vampires were cursed.

Khira went into the closet looking for a bag to stow away her swag. She heard the door open. She figured Lilian must have sent a pet to check in on Thirlestane's latest prisoner. However, Khira took a small whiff and recognized a musky sent. She was not going to allow Zachary to detain her against her will. An ache resided in her heart. Paige flashed into her mind. It felt like the fight between Paige and that little Jiminy Cricket wannabe. When Khira had left, the house remained silent. She worried that her cousin was left alone. Khira worried what Paige could do to herself amidst being alone and depressed. Khira found a large purple tote bag and stuff as much clothing as she could. She left the closet, not even glancing up to see that Zachary took up residence on the white bed.

"I wanted to check on you." Zachary sat upright and scooted down the bed, taking some of the comforter with him.

"And I want you to leave. I guess we both won't get what we want." Khira retorted as she dragged the tote bag over to the nightstand. She rummaged through the drawers as Zachary stood up from the bed and started to go towards Khira. She left the bag at the nightstand and turned to go towards the vanity. Zachary reached out for her arm in hopes of stopping her. She pulled back her arm. She would not be deterred from leaving the sector. Khira went towards the vanity once more. Again, Zachary stood before her, blocking her path. He reached out for an arm so that he could pull her in and embrace her. Khira was not having it. Although Zachary had not touched her again, she pulled her hand back. She made a fist with right hand, her thumb out, and went to punch Zachary. He had the strength and power to stop her, but he allowed Khira to contact his cheek. She surprised herself that the anger had not subside itself with the one punch. Her hand should have hurt but unlike her heart, the hand did not throb in pain.

Khira did not want to let Zachary deter her exodus. She turned to make her way back to the vanity. Zachary strode towards her, grabbing the back of her right arm. Khira turned and slapped him with her open left hand. He stared at her. Desire fueling his instincts; anger combusting behind her eyes. He drew her into him and kissed her. She took a step back to slap him again, only for him to hold her by her wrist. He pulled her towards him and kissed her again. She moved her head away for a moment, before returning her lips to his.

As he picked her up, Khira wrapped her legs around him. He took her to the right side of the bed and placed her down gently. He took in the sight of her. Khira appeared so angelic against the white background. She reached up to him to pull him down onto the bed with her. She wanted to regain control of her life and her sexuality. She thought of this as another one-night stand to release her desire. The difference between having sex with Zachary as compared to a night club fuckboy was that she did not have to put on a persona. She was being herself in the moment.

They both tore away their clothing as they were rushing to embrace each other. This would not be interrupted like in the Mexican Cantina. Still Zachary did not want to take his time. He had been longing for this moment since turning her. Fully nude, Khira scooted back on the white comforter before arching her back and bringing her knees up. Zachary slid his pants down, stepping on the legs to get them quickly off his body. With force, he entered her, and she gasped. She was so warm inside that Zachary could barely contain himself. The two bodies combined and moved with grace. With each push from Zachary, Khira contorted her body closer to the middle of the bed. Zachary turned her over and re-entered her with a mighty thrust. Khira wanted control and not only turned over but switched to be on top of Zachary. While hovering above, her hair floated down around his head. He pulled her tresses hard. She slapped him to remind him she wanted dominance. She bent down and bit at his neck, tasting his blood before the wound healed itself. Khira went back into her riding position, alternating thrusts to keep Zachary off track. She planted her hands on the headboard for a bit more leverage. She began to pump faster and faster, hearing his almost inaudible groans of delight.

She had to act now while he was distracted. With her right hand she slapped him a couple of times before punching him. The violence excited him more as he came inside her. As Khira felt his penis throb inside her, she grabbed the decanter from the nightstand and crashed it down on Zachary's head. He gave her a puzzled look as his eyes started to droop. She returned her mouth to the other side of Zachary's neck and began to drain blood and energy from him. He would not keep her from leaving the premises.

****

When Ruby had begun her path at Brânswood, Max became the father figure missing in her life. Now, he was more of a nuisance. If this was a normal life in a normal society, she would have played the role of doting daughter entrusting the care of her father figure to a nursing home. Although, she felt that maybe she was more of the trust fund baby keeping the dying patriarch alive to sign the checks. Ruby had to babysit Max to keep up appearances at Brânswood. Otherwise, Lilian could find the crack in the foundation and bring down her opposing force. Ruby knew the importance of balance and thus Max must remain at the Sanctuary, at least for now.

After the whim of nostalgia left her, Ruby sat back into her large leather chair. She slid her hands down the arms of the chair and began to take slow deep breaths. Her deep red eyes began to cloud over with a creamy milky liquid. She could go back to work now.

She swung her chair around to face the back wall. Most of the visible screens had gone blue; while the four she had turned off now appeared as a shimmered glamour over the wall. "Resume 2, 5, 6, & 8 and replay 3." The screens flittered with a glittery blue hue before other colors slowly came into focus one by one, creating the scenes that had been visible before. "Focus on 6." The picture covered all 8 screens. The view was completely black. Prior to Max's interruption, the scene had been of Kitty and Reed. "Rewind." she commanded. Lines blurred over the wall as colors began to flicker and Reed's death played in reverse.

"Stop," she said to the display.

The psychic-type television paused on a view of Kitty crouched in a corner with a paper glowing in her hand. "Continue." Kitty continued relaying her message until distracted. Ruby had to watch. She had to check and see that what happened played as it had in her vision. She did not predict the future; instead, she predicted what people intended to do. In her original vision, Kitty was tortured and raped at Reed's hand before dying from her wounds. The Brânswood mole never had it in her to turn on the Vampires. Her lovely *Kypris* taught her to be a lover, not a fighter.

That was not the reason why Ruby sent her there. If anything, Kitty served as a surveillance camera for Ruby. Through the pet's intentions to help Brânswood, she would be able to maneuver throughout Lilian's coven and allow the sanctuary insight on their enemy's grounds. The young girl was led to believe that she could do well by retrieving information, but she was a mere vessel.

Ruby focused on waiting for the fight scene about to transpire. Previously she had seen Reed retrieving Liam's sword. In her vision, Reed had stealthily taken the weapon from the case, keeping it wrapped in the tapestry since the silver would have damaged him. While Kitty was finishing her message to Max, he rushed her and pinned her leg down by thrusting the sword through her thigh. She had foreseen what pleasure he took in raping her before she died by his bite, as she was one who would not turn to become one of The Touched.

However, Ruby noticed a change. Reed did not go straight to the display case but instead confronted the pet. Kitty furiously fought to stay alive. There is something to say about a woman scorned, and it seemed that Kitty would feel condemned to revenge Flynn's death. The teacher's visit to Lilian's coven had been unplanned, but at the time, Ruby could only guess the gods fated out something beyond her vision. Either way, Flynn's death was collateral damage. This was not a war to annihilate evil, but a war to maintain balance. Ruby guessed that the death of the mentor is what sprung Kitty into action rather than the simple fact of the need for survival.

Ruby assumed that foreseeing Kitty's death was a part of keeping balance, since the seer really had no foothold to have sent a mole into the coven to begin with. She watched as it appeared that Reed had the upper hand, but she had already sensed a turn in the tide. With the thought passing through her mind, Ruby saw as Kitty flip Reed before kicking the vampire into the display towards the front of the room. Kitty surprised her once again by staying to make sure he was dead. The kid had learned much while being within Lilian's embrace.

"Enhance," Ruby commanded from the screen and then called to the screen to pause. Ruby was able to glance at what had been displayed within the case. It had not only been Lilian's family tree done in tapestry but clues that Ruby had heard about. "Capture," Ruby commanded once again. A flash went across the screen. A smaller paused picture of the scene flew up to the upper right hand of the screen and stayed there. "Move to file case number 478395 and date stamp." Within a second, the smaller picture disappeared. "Resume."

Kitty continued to wipe her fingerprints off the hilt of the sword by using some of Reed's clothing. Once the mole would leave the room, the room should go black until Ruby would ask the camera to follow where Kitty could currently be. Yet the room did not go dark until about 5 seconds after Kitty left. *What could this be? Have the gods given me more to retrieve from this tragedy?* Ruby asked herself. "Rewind 10 seconds and playback." The screen did as commanded. Once Kitty made her exodus for the second time, Ruby made one more command, "Pause."

Ruby scanned the scene with her eyes. Since she had not predicted this outcome, Ruby had to focus more on what she needed to catch, what the gods wanted her to catch. Then a small red flicker caught her eye. While the scene had been paused, there was still movement. Ruby extended her right arm towards the screen and opened her fist. A ball of red light hovered next to her hand. "Retrieve," Ruby told the screen. The small red flicker that had previously alerted Ruby's eyes from the scene of Lilian's library pulled from the wall towards the ball near Ruby's hand as if she pulled taffy. After a few seconds, Ruby's ball of light turned from red to green, and the seer closed her fist. She opened a desk drawer with her left hand and pulled an open jar from the bottom. Her right hand began to shake as if sensing a prison sentence was imminent.

Ruby placed the jar on top of her desk. She pulled her right hand towards her mouth. "Would you prefer to face the judgment of your gods? You longed to be so close to immortality I thought I could offer this gift to you instead. Take it or be gone." Her hand stopped vibrating as if accepting Ruby's judgment instead. Ruby rested the back of her right hand against the table before bringing the jar's open mouth on top of her closed fist. She loosened her grip, allowing the green spirit to leave her ball and sprint up towards the jar. Ruby covered the mouth with a now open hand. The ball of light returned to a red light while playing guard to the spirit in the jar. Her left hand turned the jar back onto the desk. "Seal," Ruby commanded, and the jar obeyed. She sat back into her chair. "Yes, it seems like the gods have smiled on us both."

****

Max emerged from a sewer pipe, shrouded in his wolf form. The sewers would be the quickest way to the outskirts of town, based on the map in his memory. He allowed his instincts to lead him towards his fated destination. Although he would just have seemed like an oversized dog wearing a satchel if he had gone through the town, this just seemed easier. He had not been out in years but the modern day, the modern ways, would not have surprised him. He kept in touch with today's pulse by watching marathons of *Grey's Anatomy, Supernatural,* and *CSI* on his days off. One of the benefits of having seers on board at Brânswood meant that he had seasons of the shows that had yet to been written. Still, he was not about to interact with the outside world. It did not have what he wanted. Nothing did. He lost all of that years ago.

He shook moisture off his fur and shed his bag. It would take a few minutes to get back to human form. Luckily, with turning by choice, there was less psychological transference. He had taken on his lycanthrope form to travel faster. He was close enough that changing back to human would benefit him more. The time to change back would still take its physical toll. He took some deep breaths while his fur began to slowly drop away from his body. His paws thinned out to mold back into fingers as his hind legs straightened.

After returning to his old, overweight human shape, Max removed some army green pants and a large oversized cream-colored tunic. He quickly got dressed. He thought about putting his shoes back on, but the rough skin and old calluses protected the bottom of his feet as if they were leather. His footprints would also be easier to disguise within the wildlife outside than modern shoes. In fact, should he have the need to change form while out and about, it was cheaper to go barefoot than ruin another pair of shoes.

Once he got dressed, he doubled checked his satchel to make sure all the items he had taken from the sanctuary were still there. He had gotten so used to the scurries cleaning and moving things beyond his control that he would not be surprised to find one or two within his bag, tidying up. Luckily, no purple nuisances were found inside. He looked up at the mid-morning sky and got his bearings. He took a scent from the air, although it was unnecessary. It had been years since he had travelled there; his instincts would continue to guide him beyond his senses.

He allowed this walk to serve as a kind of sabbatical. He tried to meditate and push memories of Lorelai out. If he would serve her best, it would be without distractions. He needed to focus on getting to Khira. He must protect her now from both Lilian and Ruby. He never imagined that Ruby would become the cunt she demonstrated that she truly is. He knew that if he brought Khira back to the sanctuary, he would regain some power. However, his heart worried that he should not think such things of using Lorelai's daughter to squeeze himself back to proper standing.

His ears shifted as he heard crows nearby. Crow's End was such a better name for the town, and he should have figured that the change of the name of the providence would change the course of history. You can put a pig in a fancy dress, but it was still a pig and to call it any other name served no purpose.

Max found the main trail and shifted his path to lie further east of it. He would still follow the same route but would use the camouflage protection of the trees to aid him. The mud felt good, cool against the balls of his feet as he picked up speed. At first glance, anyone could underestimate the strength Max still possessed. He liked it that way. He just had to remember that Ruby underestimated him as well.

He knew he was getting closer to the mansion. The trees started to thin out a little by landscaping design. His ears perked up. He heard a vehicle approaching, so he ducked behind some foliage. The dark SUV had personalized Alaskan license plates. They read "NDP WAR4." He could only assume that Lilian had ordered the Independent Sector to finish Khira off. He had made the right decision in coming here. Now, all he had to do was protect Lorelai's daughter. Nothing too daunting, just normal heroics. Another mess for the Sanctuary to solve.

****

Kitty left the library and was in luck to find the hall empty. She took the journals and covered her breasts by embracing the books. She tried to look calm and attempted to put the memory of Reed's death behind her. She had to remember her mission to the Sanctuary and provide as much information to Khira as she could, as if the journals could arm her with weapons against the Touched.

Kitty knew her days at the manor were over after killing a Lieutenant. Even if no security cameras were in the library, she was confident that Matthew would point the finger her way just out of spite. She decided there would be one last mission and then she would leave the Sector behind her.

She came upon the door to the White Room. She put her right palm on the door while still clutching the journals against her chest. She whispered a prayer to Kypris. Through the door she felt a mixture of passion and anger. It was a common combination on the spectrum of lust. Then wrath conquered desire and Kitty felt a determination. She took her hand off the door and bent down. She slid one journal under the door and then the other.

With her final task for the Sanctuary completed, she took a breath to find the strength to leave the home she had been in the last couple of months. Kitty would miss Lilian because although the Mistress could be vicious, the pet knew her actions had come from a broken heart. Lilian had never gotten over Lorelai leaving the Touched behind her. In Lilian's mindset, she had gone through the ultimate betrayal of her better half, her twin.

Kitty knew her exit should be easy. A representative from the Independent Sector was coming to assassinate a political familiar that had no longer become effective for the Touched. From what the pet had learned of the Independents, they tended to bring a team, even if the Wolf, their most notable assassin, was assigned the task. There would be the executioner and then a cleaner's team plus a PR team. The Independent sector had made killing an art form. Kitty had been lucky that the Sanctuary had not sent her there instead of the Southern Sector. No number of prayers would have prepared her for that assignment.

She would miss the mansion, not because of all the decadence it provided but because Kitty knew that she could have made a significant change to the training of pets. She believed the volunteers needed to be broken to want to serve the Touched. Alas, she needed to make sure her actions of eliminating Reed would remain a secret as she left this life behind.

****

Khira looked at Zachary's unconscious body. She felt a twang of guilt but knew from what transpired between them, he would try and stop her. She still was planning on leaving the manor. Thoughts of her mother came to mind as Khira contemplated her exit. She felt she owed her mother to give Lilian some parting words.

She went into the closet and pulled some items down from hangers. She did not look to see if they would coordinate with each other. The clothes kept in this wardrobe were far from her style. It did not have the ingredients to help her put on a role to say goodbye to her aunt. She would simply have to be herself.

Khira pulled on a lilac pleated skirt and zipped it up. She strolled out of the closet with a black short sleeved buttoned up blouse. She walked over to the bed and checked on Zachary to make sure he was still out cold. She had drained a lot of blood from him. His slowed breathing let her know he was still among the living, but she did not know how long he would be in this state. There was much for her to learn about the Touched and she hoped that the Sanctuary would take her in after her exodus of the mansion.

She placed the blouse on the bed and bent down to pick up her underwear and bra. She sat on the edge as she slid her legs through the holes of the underwear. A snorting sound came from Zachary's direction. She looked down at him while she pulled her panties all the way up under the skirt and then she brushed down the pleats to make sure none of the skirt had gotten trapped in the underwear. She put on an ivory bra and started buttoning the obsidian blouse when Zachary turned to his side. She paused mid-button and when it seemed like Zachary could be mistaken for some of her past frat boys sleeping off a bender, Khira continued to get dressed.

After completing the ensemble, she returned to the closet to check if there were any pairs of shoes that one wears to a civil confrontation. She found some black ballet slippers that were the perfect size. *I may be Khira tonight, but I might as well be Cinderella too* Khira thought to herself with a giggle. As she left the closet, she heard something by the door. Maybe her aunt decided to make another strike or maybe Lilian sent her pet, Khiria was unsure. The door itself did not open. The knob did not turn. Instead, two journals slid underneath the door.

Khira took both journals and stuffed in the bag she had been preparing when Zachary had made his visit to the White Room. *Maybe the Sactuary has spies here.* Obviously, Lilian did not know about anyone sent to help Khira as they would most likely be executed, or at least that is how David made it out to be like. However, if Brânswood had a spy at her house, it would make sense that they would try to have someone at the Manor as well. Khira grabbed the bag and walked back to Zachary one last time. She brushed away his hair from his forehead and gave him a slight kiss. One last stop and she could close the chapter on this recent nightmare.

Chapter Twenty-Two

Khira stalked the hallway, using her hearing to attempt to find Lilian's bedroom. Her aunt's voice beckoned her. She did not know if the voice was real or inside her head. However, the voice changed and became louder. She saw Kitty and a Victorian dressed woman leave a room. That room had to belong to Lilian.

While the library went a little unplanned, Khira felt more prepared for this confrontation. For a brief moment, she had hoped that Zachary would have been able to share her family time with Lilian having him be a buffer. However, she was now sure she could take care of things herself. This made her smile a little, although she was still somewhat unsure if he would come to her rescue or not.

Khira clutched the handle of her bag that she wore across her body as she opened the door and attempted to enter the room like a ninja. She wanted to catch her aunt by surprise. She thought of what she would do or say first yet Khira's musings were interrupted by Lilian. The Mistress rose from a chair at her vanity and took aggressive strides towards her. Instinctively, her foot stepped back to move away but steeling herself against the fear, she stood firm and confronted Lilian. "You think you are so clever, don't you, little girl?" growled the older woman as she stood over Khira's slender frame. "You thought you could catch me off guard, but I have played this game so much longer than you. Lorelai had plans other than what the gods fated for her. Look where she ended up. I believe that truly makes you your mother's daughter."

Khira looked at her aunt and could not picture her kind mother looking anything like this cold cunt. "I don't know who this 'Lorelai' person is you are referring to," replied Khira, "but *Eve*, my mother, was a remarkable woman and sacrificed her life so that I would become someone special. When she died, along with the rest of my family, I was left alone to find my way in the world. I don't know if she would approve of my life before, but I know she would most definitely not approve of it now." She stared hard into Lilian's eyes, almost challenging her to correct her statement.

Lilian did stare back, but instead of correcting Khira's claim, she instead attempted a different approach. She tried reaching out with her senses to see if it was guile that fueled Khira's words or if it was truth. For some reason, she could not sense the girl's intentions. In any case, the look in her eyes told her all she needed to know. There were still some secrets hidden from the girl. That would prove most useful, she thought.

Lilian stepped away from Khira and dropped her confrontational manner. She looked back to Khira with a softer, almost sympathetic expression. This had the desired effect of catching Khira off guard. She was sure the last thing the girl expected was to see a soft smile upon Lilian's face.

"I am sorry, Khira." said Lilian with false compassion, "I forget sometimes that the woman who bore you became a different person once she had gone from the clan. I am...was...very protective of my sister. She was more than my twin. She was the other half of my soul. We were inseparable and more alike than you'd believe sisters could be. I believed that all I had left of her were my memories. That is until I learned of your existence. I thought that maybe something of my sister was left in you, but it seems that is not the case."

Khira shifted uncomfortably under the touchy feely look in Lilian's eyes. She knew Lilian lied through the broken truth of her words. Nevertheless, the thoughts she presented reflected Khira's own when she thought about the person, she believed her mother was and the reality.

"Yeah, well I got some news for you, Auntie. She never, ever mentioned you. Not even once. Nothing was ever said about 'Vampires' or the mansion or anything of her old life. I don't think you knew your sister as well as you thought, or even knew her at all. From what I do know of my mom, I know that she was nothing like you. Maybe 'Lorelai' never really existed for either of us."

Lilian turned away from Khira's words as much as she did the girl herself. She fumed at the thought of such lies. Lorelai was her sister true as any could be. No one knew her sister better than she did. She would never believe that she could be such a fool as to not know the heart of her own true blood. However, Lilian was unable to understand why Lorelai longed to be human again.

Khira could see the anguish in Lilian's eyes and the trembling rage building in her body. Her senses could not quite discern what Lilian was truly feeling. She probably did not know herself. *Would she kill me now*, Khira thought. If there was ever a time where she could strike Khira down without any witnesses, this would be a good time. Still, she had plenty of time and opportunities to kill her before now. If she was going to do it, she would have done so by now. Still, maybe it was best not to press her luck by provoking her. Then again, maybe Khira could use that to her advantage.

Lilian began to pace around the bedroom circling Khira. She shot the girl a look of irritation that Khira had seen from others before. She grabbed the bag handle tighter as if it was armor to protect her from her aunt. Khira knew that she was really getting under Lilian's skin.

"Lorelai's restlessness seems to still huddle within your eyes, my dear." said Lillian, a sneer upon her lips. "She couldn't accept the grand destiny that was given to us by the gods. She left, but discovered that no one really leaves me unless by my command. As fate would have it, you were born to replace her. Accept your destiny and join the clan at my side."

Khira moved away from Lilian and walked about the room contrary to Lilian, always keeping a step ahead of her. "Let me tell you something about your little clan. I got a good look at things while I have been here and let me tell you, you can keep this place and shove it up your ass. I would prefer to see what Brânswood has to offer me." Lilian's eyes widened at hearing Khira's words. No one had the audacity to say such things to her before let alone have the audacity to bring up the Touched's enemy. Seeing the effect, Khira continued, "Don't get me wrong, the Playboy mansion look is great, but come on. You have some real issues here. All the naked boys and girls running around fucking everyone and everything like it's just another Saturday night. How fucked up is that? And don't get me started on giving people out as pets. Really, is that the only way you can get people to worship you is to threaten them with death if they fail you? If so, then you must not be doing such a good job, because those vamps out there hate your guts, FYI."

It took everything she could not to react to Khira and her caustic taunting. She knew it was only a pathetic game to get her to react. Lilian was better than that. She was stronger than that. She was the Mistress of the clan and no words from a spoiled child would ever get her to lose her restraint.

"If this is what it means to be a Vampire, then it's no wonder your sister left you." Khira barely had time to react as the words left her mouth. Lilian appeared almost out of nowhere and slashed at her, clipping her across the shoulder that did not carry the bag. Lilian's nails were like talons and if Khira had been a second slower, her arm would have been torn from her torso as easily as if she were made of paper. Luckily, Lilian was off her game and Khira moved away with only deep scratches, which healed at a quick pace. The blood that she had drained from Zachary must have strengthen her.

"Insolent little slut! How dare you question me and my sister? I was ruling this land long before you were ever born. Everyone here lives and dies in service to me!" spat Lilian. Khira maneuvered around some furniture and grabbed her bag tighter. Even though the wound had healed it also began to itch.

"Oooh, did I touch nerve there, Auntie Lil? I'm sorry. I thought maybe you knew how much of a bitch everyone thought you were. All the little vamps whispering out there in the halls think so. I bet all your Pets do too." Lilian growled as she rushed towards Khira again. Khira felt her strength rise as if she were a succubus feeding on Lilian's paranoia.

As she danced about the room, swiftly moving from one place to another, Khira punched hard and caught Lilian square in the face. Lilian stumbled back, trying to maintain her balance, but fell and lay splayed upon the floor, hissing in anger, blood dripping from her nose. She stared daggers at Khira, eyes burning and fangs extended. No one had ever laid a hand upon her in such a way before. She continued to stare, trying to collect her strength while Khira sat upon her throne and looked down at her supposed "Mistress".

"Hmm...not bad," said Khira. "You know, you look good down there on your knees. I guess you have a lot of practice. Maybe I'll stick around and keep you that way. This throne would probably suit me better than you." Khira rushed off before Lilian could reach her. Lilian's strike split the door of her closet into kindling, but missed Khira entirely. Khira spied a large window off to the side of the room that, if she was lucky, she could use to remove the White Bitch from the room and give her a chance to escape. Positioning herself before the window, she took a casual stance and began to laugh.

Lilian looked bad. She had never been challenged this way before in her life. Her clothes were torn, her hair out of place and her position compromised. She had hoped for a different future, but it seemed fate had destined Khira to die after all. She should have torn the little tart limb from limb, yet her body seemed to betray her just as everyone else had. If it took the last of her strength, she would use it to make Khira pay.

"You look tired, Miss Queen," laughed Khira. "Is something wrong? I thought the 'Queen of the Touched' would put up more of a challenge. Guess, you aren't really supposed to be the queen after all. Guess that was supposed to go to my mother." Khira was certain her plan would work. Everything leading up to that point told her it would. However, she underestimated Lilian. Instead of rushing head-long into the window like she planned, Lilian instead placed herself right in the path where Khira was going to be. Lilian's hand caught Khira's throat in a vice-like grip and lifted her from the ground. Her bloody, vampiric features sent a chill down Khira's spine. Gone was the smug, self-indulgent queen and in her place stood a stone-cold killer.

"You may have been able to fool me once, child, but not again," snarled Lilian as she applied pressure to Khira's neck. Lillian carried her niece's body towards the window. Khira kicked at Lilian, never managing to connect. She brought up her hands, trying to use every bit of strength she had to keep from choking under Lilian's crushing grasp. If she was to survive, she would have to rely on desperation.

"I'm...s..s..sorry...I..never meant...to..hurt you. Forgive...me..." gasped Khira, struggling to speak. Lilian did not seem to hear her. Rage and anguish clouded her eyes and the beast within had risen to the surface and threatened to consume her. Before Khira could pass from this world, she whispered one last word to Lilian. "...sister."

Somehow, the word penetrated the fog clouding Lilian's mind. Where once she saw the spoiled, impertinent girl who vexed her, she now saw her beloved twin sister choking under her grasp. Shocked, she released Khira and trembled, unable to comprehend what was happening. It was then that Khira bent down.

In her mind, she conjured a scene where she flipped Lilian over her shoulder. Yet, she was drained from any remaining Touched gracefulness and lost her balance. She reached out, grabbing Lilian and fell through the nearby window. The weight of both women quickly crumbled any railing nearby.

As Khira felt Lilian fall away from her, she only gazed into the sky. She saw her bag flying towards her. Then, she thought she saw Zachary looking down at her, reaching out to save her. Her thoughts turned to her dreams and of the warnings she was given. She never felt the blow as she hit the ground hard. Light exploded in her vision and blood swirled in her eyes.

Darkness rushed in to claim her but before she succumbed to the fall, she spied Lilian unmoving upon the ground next to her. Approaching them from the darkness was an old man cloaked in shadow. *If it was death*, Khira thought, *he needed a better tailor.* The little light available nearby started to fade as Khira's eyes closed.

****

Max kept his stance at his post at the back of the house. The hairs on the back of his neck perked up. At first, he thought maybe a cold front was about to blow through. He tried to shake it off, but then a sound alerted him.

Kitty stepped out of a doorway into the night air. Max caught scent of the young mole and looked around for any sentries he may have missed since finding his hiding spot. When he assured himself that the two would be safe, he quickly left his position and swept Kitty across the doorway in a swift, graceful motion. He led her behind some foliage nearby to screen their conversation.

Max set Kitty down. He shook his head while keeping watch and taking a scent from the air. The small redheaded thing of a girl lost her balance after such surprise and fell back upon her butt. She became ashamed of how must look to the Master of Brânswood. Once Max's paranoia receded, he reached out his giant paw of a hand for the petite Kitty to take. She got her bearings and took a breath. Finally, she decided to start her report. "Master, there is not too much more to report except that I think I heard Khira enter Lilian's room. I was with Lady Eleanor and could not blow my cover. I apologize if my presence here has compromised too much against the integrity of Brânswood. My intentions…"

"Relax, little one. It's all right now. It is I who should be apologizing. I should have supervised more over what your objectives should have been while at this post," Max said with a small white lie. He did not want the brave mole to know that her position inside the clan had been little more than to humor Ruby. "You don't have to give your report all at once. That's not why I'm here."

"Yes. I hate to question you, but why are you here, Sir? Is this about Khira? I can look after her. I'm sure I could help her escape the mansion. Although I may need escaping myself. I was caught by Reed...."

"Again child, relax."

"Yes, sir." she replied. Kittty bowed her head to continue her show of respect. She was about to speak again and report of Reed's death when she felt a pain in her side. It subsided quickly. When she looked up, she thought maybe Max had felt the same sense as the expression on his face turned dire. He felt the scream through the veins on the back of his neck before the glass even broke.

The two bodies fell quickly from the window above. Little crystal shards rained down on Kitty and Max. He shielded the girl from the falling glass, shaking them off quickly. "Leave now, so that your cover is not blown. The sanctuary does not want you punished for being where you are unwarranted, but also please try and delay anyone who follows out. I will investigate. When you are able, send word to Ruby, but you need not tell her of our meeting. I can express that to her. Now go, quickly," he instructed Kitty. She nodded and slipped off into the night.

He brought his cloak up around his head and quickly proceeded to where the bodies had fallen. He first set eyes upon Lilian. Max shuddered, trying to keep memories of Lorelai from flooding back into his mind. He reminded himself that this was not his love returned in the flesh. He examined her body. She did not flinch and seemed to be in deep sleep. The fall could have easily killed an Untouched, but for Lilian it was a different matter. He only had a quick second to decide of action. He briefly went to Khira. Her eyes were open, but soon closed. Her body too would need some time for repairs. Max knew that she could get the proper treatment at the manor yet decided that was not the best place for her.

Max took some deep breaths, reaching for some strength within him. He lifted both women and treaded some distance from the manor. Guilt took residence in his heart, but he reminded himself that he was not using Khira as a pawn by taking her back to Brânswood. He was merely giving her a chance to heal in the Sanctuary rather than within the purgatory of Lilian's coven.

****

Zachary woke up in a daze in the White Room. He did not know how long he had been there. He got dressed and decided to look for Khira. If she had been smart, she would have just left. However, from his past observances, Zachary knew that Khira would want to have the last word with Lilian.

He walked to Lilian's room and heard a commotion outside the door. As he opened the door, he could see the two women fall out the window. He rushed to the balcony. Zachary's shocked expression would not leave his face as he looked down from the edge and saw the two bodies there. For a second, he debated on jumping straight down, but remembered he had not had any nourishment since having sex with Khira. The fall could sentence him to the same fate as his Mistress and new ally.

He wanted nothing more than to race down the stairs and nurse both women back to unlife. However, duty called and he had to put forth the good of the coven before his own feelings. He was still a ranking member of the Southern Sector and a Lieutenant within the clan. Appearances had to be kept to maintain the integrity of the clan. He vaguely remembered the Southern Sector had been expecting representatives from the Independent Sector to take care of a local political problem. Eleanor and the pets would be keeping them entertained. They may not have even gotten distracted by the falling women, knowing the reputation they kept.

He would soon need to be the leader he was trained to be. Still, he wanted to be by her side, next to Khira. He decided that he must travel through the maze inside the mansion quickly but keep a nonchalant air to him. Zachary thought ahead and conjured up excuses he should need in case he was stopped by Matthew, Eleanor or one of the members of the Independent Sector. So many reasons came to his mind, but his heart pushed most of the logical ones down deep into his soul, tucking it away behind his true goal. He was lost in those thoughts when a hurried young girl bumped into him.

"Sorry, sir" said the red-headed pet as she paused for a brief moment before him. She raised her head so that her eyes met his and then scampered off. Zachary almost did not recognize Kitty. Suddenly, he realized what had just transpired. The mute pet spoke! He looked back towards the direction in which she had fled, but only saw a sea of wannabes. He wondered what the hell was going on under this roof.

His stomach quickly turned. Zachary wasted no more time to try and reach Khira. He made his way out of the back doors. A gust of wind knocked into him and he heard leaves bristle near-by. The whole scene felt wrong and staged from some horror flick. However, in this movie, Zachary was both the good and bad guy. He stood beneath the window. He saw blood and glass, but no women. Lilian and Khira were both gone.

He perked his ears and glared out into the woods, but to no avail. Zachary had no choice but to return inside and prepare the excuses he had for the audience remaining inside. Afterwards, he would try and track down Kitty to see how she fit in the scheme of things. Zachary found himself in the position of power that he thought he wanted but had no queen to be by his side. Responsibility first and then he vowed that finding Khira took precedence over the coven. Power or not, it meant nothing without her. Zachary straightened his attire and greeted Lilian's guests. Eleanor approached him and steered him away from a PR rep from the Independent Sector.

Eleanor took Zachary aside. "Have you seen the Mistress? I have some disturbing news for her." Zachary did not have the strength or the integrity to tell the Lady the truth of the disappearance of Lilian nor of Khira.

"You can report to me for now," the Lieutenant stated, attempting to sound confident enough not to betray any secrets.

She took a pause, trying to find the proper words. "Zachary, it is about Reed, sir." She took in a quick breath to steady herself. "He's dead, sir."

****

When he felt safely separated from any remaining sentries on the premises, Max set down the bodies. He rummaged through his sack to find something that would help secure them to his body while he travelled back to Brânswood. Neither woman stirred from their slumber. Hopefully he had made the right decision by not only saving Snow White, but the Evil Queen as well. He wondered if Ruby had a hand causing this disaster. Yes, Max despised Lilian, but he understood his standing. One does not question the gods, but instead learns to balance on the wave they send. He thought everyone at Brânswood had learned these during their studies. Max knew how difficult it was sitting on the sidelines, watching the chess match, knowing a better move to make, yet sit back and let the game commence the way it was meant to. Liam's and Lorelai's death reminded him of this. One life taken for the other, he thought. Max might forgive himself some day.

He glanced over at the bodies. Lilian should have been able to at least make some noise of life. Yet, her slumber erased the evil in her cold demeanor. Her porcelain skin blended with memories of Lorelai. Then, Max's eyes strayed over to Khira. She was his unintended pawn of this game. He despised the move but knew it would be the best way to protect Khira while she was in this state. Max looked out into the woods once more and then glanced up towards the sky. He must move quickly. Dawn would break soon. The women would continue to sleep in the daylight, but Max knew it could delay their healing. Hollowness resided in him while he wondered what their dreams could be.

The old man tied the women loosely together to serve as a way to balance them on each shoulder. His strength from his wolf form surged through him slightly, fighting against the true age of his muscles. This was a daunting task the gods had trusted to him. Time was not something on his side though. His strength would be enough to quickly clear the sewers and then breach the underground of the sanctuary. For a moment, he wondered what Ruby's expression would be once he showed up at Brânswood with the key and the enemy. "Ah yes, checkmate," he whispered under his breath. He headed back home with his new treasures.

Epilogue

Khira sat on a light grey washed wooden bench on the grounds behind what was once Lilian's mansion. She did not remember how much time had passed since the fall from the window. Hours, days, months since healing...she had stopped counting time all together. Clocks seemed to have lost meaning here at the manor. Her broken bones and the scratches on her skin were quick to heal after the incident, but she could not say the same for her state of mind. It felt like a lifetime ago that she was ignorant of vampires and all the misdeeds that Lilian had planned for her. She sat, knowing that she should be thankful to be alive; thankful to be able to feel the cool breeze brush against her cheek, to smell the fresh cut green grass that tickled the bottom of her bare feet, and to see the purple haze drift over the cotton candy pink sunset. Yet, she could not find it within her soul to feel much emotion about everything that had transpired. She never mourned for her aunt. She never felt pride for *killing someone so evil. She wondered if she had truly exacted her revenge for her family's death by pushing Lillian out the window. For a moment, she even wondered what her mother would have thought about all the events that had happened.*

Khira realized that although Lilian was gone, she would never be able to erase any of the damage that her aunt had perpetrated throughout her lifetime. Maybe that was never a job for Khira. There was still plenty of time to repair what was left of her own life or perhaps "afterlife", depending on how she could look at it.

"May I sit down next to you?" Zachary's voice penetrated Khira's thoughts. Khira turned to looked up into his soft grey-blue eyes, extracting as much strength from them as she could; the same eyes she had found comfort in time and time again in her dreams. Zachary had played such an important part to her recovery. Kitty had conveyed that the Lieutenant never left her bedside while she was in a short coma. He had assured her that he corresponded with Paige to ease any worry that Khira's cousin may have had about her. He had mended relations with the other sectors and allowed Khira to take Lilian's throne. With the changing of the guards, Khira had also released pets within the Southern Sector, although Kitty had decided to stay behind at the manor.

"Of course, sit." Khira scooted over to the other side of the bench creating room for Zachary. As he sat, he took her hand in his without saying a word. She noticed, but it felt like such a natural thing these days. They sat there in comfortable silence for quite a bit of time before he broke the ice once more.

"You don't have to stay here if you don't want to. You have a home, and you should no longer be in any danger. If anything, with Lilian gone, you have garnered respect throughout the Sectors. I have appreciated the leadership you have shown, but you did not need to feel like you

must step in. It may not feel like it, but you should live the life you want. In other words, you are free." Zachary told her.

"Am I? I don't feel free." she replied. "I don't feel trapped anymore, but I do not feel free either. To tell you the truth, I don't feel shit." Zachary smiled at her brutal honesty. She continued, "Go ahead, smile at my situation. Mock my pain." She leaned into him in a playful manner. Both Khira and Zachary looked at each other as if some confession of love would escape and betray them; however, silence ruled over them instead.

Finally, Zachary spoke, "I don't want you to think that I want you to go." Khira was caught off guard by his comment. It was true that their relationship, if it could be called that, was not of the normal variety. She still held great contempt for him for turning her, but she finally understood the hold that Lilian had on Zachary. Not waiting for a response, he continued. "Yet, I don't want to be the reason for you to feel like you must stay. I just want you to know that I deeply care for you. As much as I brought you a new life, you also did the same for me."

Khira stared into Zachary's eyes to see if she could discern the meaning of his words. As much time as Zachary had spent by her bedside helping her during her recovery, Khira still had trouble believing his confession. If the little time she spent with Lilian had taught her anything, it was that she must hold onto her defenses to maintain her survival. Maybe the voice in the head was still of her mother's telling her to always be on guard. Her mother taught her to trust no one. She had new gifts with her Vampire form, but no experience behind them. She felt like a brand-new bat mobile without the owner's manual. Every moment she stayed at the Southern Sector, she questioned whether she could learn more about her illness there or if she would be just better off on her own. She remembered David mentioning Brânswood and wondered what help they could afford her.

Finally, she replied to Zachary. "And in many ways, you don't know what to do with your new life than I know what to do with mine. While you have been a big help during these past months, I don't know you. You don't know me. Hell, I don't even know myself. I never have and that is why I kept losing myself inside different personas." Zachary nodded in response to her statement and could not help but remember the night he watched Khira dance in the night club. He smiled. Khira saw the smile and thought it still seemed a little hollow from the man she had been spending so much time with.

"Then stay," he replied. "I want you to stay." Zachary tried to bring Khira's hand up to his lips to softly kiss her fingertips, but this time her instinct told her to pull her hands back. She stood up and walked a distance away from Zachary.

She pushed some stray hairs behind her ear. Without turning back to look at him, she stated, "It's good to want." Khira gave a half-hearted chuckle. She remained looking forward, not needing him to see the pain in her eyes. The problem was that she did not know what she wanted. She was afraid of feeling too comfortable within the coven to the point where she felt she would never be able to leave, much like she had married into the Soprano family. "Let's just continue our lives for another day. For now, this is good enough, isn't it?"

Zachary stood up from the bench and strolled up behind her. He put his hands on her arms and pulled her back into him. He just held her, as he didn't know what else to do to fix the situation. The gods had such a sick sense of humor to bring them both to this point of the story.

"I won't make you any promises. I know they are easily broken, and I have yet to earn your trust. You say I don't know you, but what I do know is that during the time the gods have given us, I care for you so much. In fact, if this is what it feels like, I love you. However, I don't feel like you

truly belong here. I want you to stay, but I feel selfish for asking it of you. Sooner or later, you are going to have to wake up. Wake up, Khira."

****

It was dark, but not silent within the void. She could hear people walking around her vicinity as if stampeding horses. The scribbling of pens to paper scratched at her ears. She was overwhelmed by the mixture of aromas around her; cheap cologne clinging to sweat, polished leather from a pair of shoes, burnt coffee lingering in the air. The most dominant scent, however, was the coppery smell of blood. While her nose focused on its surroundings, Khira's skin began to itch. Her brain told her fingers to scratch, yet they did not move. After the itch became stronger, Khira began to feel each muscle slowly contract and buzz with a sore tingling sensation. Her muscles burned and ached as if they hadn't moved in months. She tried to open her eyes, but the lids felt like they were glued shut.

All the sudden, a new sensation hit her skin. She felt as if she were in a warm bath as liquid crashed into her in small waves. Her heart felt like it had begun to race, and the itch returned. It felt like each hit of water pushed needles into every pore of her body. Again, she tried to force her eyes to open; however, they only fluttered a bit.

Her ears perked again when she heard a familiar male voice say her name. She could not remember who it was. Suddenly, she remembered Zachary telling her to wake up, but she did not know if that happened or not. Khira did not know if she hoped that it was Zachary now calling her name. A piercing hum entered her ear, making the reoccurring sound of her name sound far away.

Hands began to massage her muscles and more musky scents came closer as she suddenly felt surrounded, but still she could not open her eyes to see who may be there. Khira felt her heart surging between stress and anxiety of whatever had happened to her. *What is this nightmare*, she thought although she would have preferred being able to yell it out to anyone who could hear her. She then tried to speak, tried to get whoever was handling her to stop, but again she was paralyzed.

The humming started to subside as the sounds became clearer. The voice from before was intermingled with other murmurs swimming in her ear. She thought she heard the word "vitals" and "pressure" but could not be sure. Khira tried to search past the dream and remember the last tangible event. In a flash, she saw Lilian's violet eyes steep into her soul. She heard a female voice overcoming the other voices. Khira then felt hands grasp the side of her hand. A pulse went through her body and the hands released their hold. "It will be very soon. Prepare a room for her. He will re-introduce her. I must take my leave for now, but contact me if there are any more complications," the woman's voice commanded. Khira felt the female presence leave her side.

The liquid that had surrounded her subsided. As it left her skin, she felt bumps breach her skin. Even without visual confirmation, she knew she was naked. A new wet slimy liquid dropped onto her chest. It felt cold at first but quickly warmed her up. Suddenly, her eyes began to flutter and ache. "Goody, she's coming to," the male voice from before spoke. It was not Zachary's voice, but it seemed somewhat familiar.

Finally, Khira was able to open her eyes. A bright haze faded around her. A shadow came into view, looking over her, judging her. Details started to scramble into place. Dark wavy hair was meticulously set near pasty white skin. Devilish eyes stared down at her. It took a little bit, but she soon recognized her new companion from Lilian's coven.

"Glad to see you back among us undead, Khira" Reed responded to his patient. He added a sinister chuckle that stabbed at Khira. Screaming would be good, she thought, but no sound left her. "We'll take good care of you." Khira could only hope that this was a nightmare.